MW00659296

The Twelve Saints of Christmas

Karen Baugh MENUHIN

Copyright © May 2024
by Karen Baugh Menuhin

Published by Little Dog Publishing Ltd

All rights reserved. No part of this book may be reproduced or used in any manner without written permission of the copyright owner except for the use of quotations in a book review.

This is a work of fiction. Names, places and incidents either are the product of the author's imagination or are used fictitiously. Any resemblance to actual persons, living or dead, events, or locales is entirely coincidental.

NO AI TRAINING: Without in any way limiting the author's [and publisher's] exclusive rights under copyright, any use of this publication to "train" generative artificial intelligence (AI) technologies to generate text is expressly prohibited. The author reserves all rights to license uses of this work for generative AI training and development of machine learning language models.

ISBN: 978-1-7393323-3-4

First paperback and ebook edition.

Heather and Gareth,
for all your kindness and care

CHAPTER 1

December 1923

'But how did he die?' Swift repeated the question as there hadn't been an intelligible answer.

'Well, now, that is indeed a conundrum,' the elderly gentleman seated opposite us replied. 'I do wish I could be of assistance.'

'You saw the body, you just told us you did.' Swift was talking slowly and patiently. 'Surely there must have been something to indicate the cause of death?'

'He was smiling. I'd never seen him smile before.' Lord Balthazar Cholmondeley reached a hand to stroke the fur on my dog's head. Foggy, my little golden spaniel, was sitting watching proceedings. Proceedings which included tea and biscuits, and he was particularly fond of biscuits.

'Could you please describe to us what you found on the day?' I asked politely but pointedly, because it hadn't taken long to realise Balthazar Cholmondeley's attention was inclined to wander off.

He blinked below a thicket of white brows; an affable

chap, plump with a rather fuddled look to his rosy-cheeked face. He was togged for a cosy afternoon indoors: a blue velvet smoking jacket straining across his tummy, a matching cap with gold braid over curly white hair, black trews and embroidered carpet slippers.

'I could, yes, yes.' He picked up a bone china cup from the lacquered tray at his elbow and cradled it between soft hands. He reminded me of my uncle Melrose; easing into his dotage, oblivious to the frenetic world beyond the walls.

'Right, and...' Swift tried encouragement.

Balthazar blinked again. 'Ah, now, Jasper was in his room sitting before his hearth, much as we are now.' He nodded to the fire blazing with dancing yellow flames in the grate, warding off the late afternoon chill. 'Although it was his bedroom, and this is, erm...' He paused, apparently in confusion.

'The library,' Swift reminded him, although the crowded bookcases surrounding us on every available wall made it pretty obvious.

'The library, indeed, indeed. Such a marvellous place. We have all the philosophers, you know. And the Greeks and Romans – anyone who could write, really.' Balthazar Cholmondeley smiled genially, then took a sip of earl grey tea before carefully replacing the cup on its saucer. "Cholmondeley" was pronounced "Chumley" in the archaic manner, an anachronism entirely befitting the old fellow.

I reached for another delicious orange shortbread. The Temple House cook was obviously adept—the biscuits were baked to perfection. Barely a crumb had fallen to mar the fine brocade of the dark green chair I was occupying, nor the wine-red carpet beneath.

'Jasper appeared perfectly comfortable,' Balthazar continued. 'He was in his grey suit and waistcoat, rather worn, but he was very careful with ah…*ahem*…money,' he whispered the word, then continued. 'Well, he had a book open on his lap. It was Dickens' *A Christmas Carol.* He rarely read a book of any sort, but I thought it rather appropriate in the circumstances…' He leaned forward and dropped his voice again. 'Misers, and ghosts from the past, you know, forewarning his retribution.' He nodded for emphasis, then looked carefully about as if to check no spirits were listening.

'What do you mean by that?' Swift was quick to ask.

'Oh, nothing at all.' Balthazar's blue eyes widened. 'Merely that his miserly ways may have caught up with him. Well, perhaps he wasn't truly miserly, he wouldn't be here if he were, would he?' He lapsed into contemplation again, or I assumed that's what it was.

I gave Foggy the last of my biscuit, then snaffled another as there were plenty left.

'You said he was "sitting", so you found him in his chair?' Swift clarified.

'Not I.' Balthazar straightened up. 'It was old Jiggens who found him—he's the butler. I expect you've met him…oh, haha, of course you have, he fetched our tea, didn't he?' He indicated the lacquered tray bearing a silver teapot, biscuits and the usual whatnots. 'Old Jiggens had taken up Jasper's afternoon refreshment of hot milk and brandy. The servants are very rigorous about routine.' He suddenly raised his arms as though in alarm and spoke in a squeaky voice. 'Sir Jasper? Are you indisposed, sir?' He lowered his arms again, a smile on his lips. 'Jasper didn't answer, well he couldn't! And he was positioned in a most ungainly manner. Doubled over in his chair — so much so, that his nose was almost touching the page. It was quite unlike him, he was an upright fellow most of the time — stiff and thin. Rather broom-like, I have always thought.'

'He was dead?' Swift asked with determined patience. I knew he was itching to take notes, but there was something about Temple House – the cosseted grandeur, the atmosphere of scholarly contemplation — that evoked deferential reticence.

'Oh, yes, quite dead. Poor Jiggens was confounded. I was the first he alerted, it was... erm...upstairs, I believe. I was proceeding along the corridor and Jiggens came from the room and approached me. "M'Lord, m'lord!" he exclaimed, "It's Sir Jasper. Would you please come and observe?"' He shook his head. 'I did indeed observe, and we agreed that Sir Jasper had passed away and had done so some time earlier.' Balthazar sighed loudly then picked up a biscuit and bit into it.

The fire crackled in the grate as we waited for him to expand, but he just nibbled the orange shortbread, his eyes glazing over.

'Was there any sign of injury, or blood?' Swift prompted.

Balthazar frowned at his biscuit. 'Blood?'

'How did Sir Jasper die?' I asked. 'Knife in the back? Strangled with a shoelace?'

I'd been trying to bite back increasing irritation, although it wasn't aimed at the doddery old fellow. Chief Inspector Billings of Scotland Yard had telephoned my home in Ashton Steeple last evening and ordered Swift and I to attend Temple House near Bath. It had meant changing all of our plans and I'd raised numerous objections. Swift was keen to go, of course, and first thing this morning we'd set off from the Cotswolds in my Bentley along with my dog, my cat, and butler, Greggs, through the falling snow.

It was a freezing journey, battling drifts and ice, and we'd entered Bath to find it hosting a merry Christmas fair. I'd inadvertently driven through the middle of it thanks to inadequate navigation advice from Swift and then negotiated a long, steeply rising lane to discover a large Tudor mansion surrounded by stone walls and extensive grounds on a high hilltop.

Lord Balthazar Cholmondeley had opened the door and shown Swift and me into the library for reasons none of us understood, then rung for refreshments.

Balthazar's lips opened and closed, struggling to form a reply. 'No, no blood. Not a mark on him. Merely dead, as though he'd drifted off and then continued onward to the distant heavens…' He paused, biscuit between fingers. 'Although one could not be certain it would be heavenwards. At least not in Jasper's case.'

Swift pricked his ears up at that and leaned forward to ask another question.

He was interrupted by the opening of the door. The elderly butler, Jiggens, stooped and tottering, entered carrying an elaborate silver tray.

'M'lord Cholmondeley,' the butler proclaimed in a thin voice. 'There is a missive from the upper chamber.' He held out the tray, which bore a single folded page.

'Ohhh, the Regent.' Nerves momentarily shook Balthazar's voice. He unfolded the note slowly and proceeded to read in silence. His brows twitched, then he bent to throw the paper onto the fire. 'Gentlemen, you are summoned.'

The butler bowed stiffly in our direction. 'If you please, sirs.'

'Are you escorting us?' I asked as I stood up.

'I believe my grandson, young Jiggens must do so, sirs,' he quavered. 'The stairs are rather a trial these days.' He barely reached my elbow, shrunken by age; he was thin and frail with wispy hair and faded grey eyes. His tailcoat was rather too long at the back and the cuffs fell over his wrists.

'I will entertain your dog, Major Lennox,' Balthazar Cholmondeley offered, holding out a morsel of shortbread to Foggy. The dog took it gently in his soft mouth then crunched it in a single bite. Balthazar chortled. 'Clever doggie.'

'May I lead you to young Jiggens, sirs?' The butler peered up at Swift and me, trembling hands still clasping the tray.

'Please do,' Swift agreed. He sported a grey city suit, which looked out of place in the ancient mansion. I'd worn my best winter tweeds, tie, and favourite waistcoat. We'd brought a change of togs in our carpet bags with us, but they'd been left with Greggs in the hall, along with our snow-spattered coats, mufflers, hats and whatnots a mere half hour earlier.

'This way, sirs.' The butler led us through to a wide passage, the walls panelled in dark polished oak, floors covered in wine red carpeting. He wobbled along until we reached a spacious hall set in the centre of the house, where he stopped. A young man waited by the threshold.

'Young Jiggens, sirs,' the old butler said, then shuffled away when the lad stepped smartly forward.

'Hello, sirs, I'm here to help you. We Jiggens have been servants to the Saints for nearly two hundred years.' A slim lad with a friendly grin on a pale face, sandy hair and bright blue eyes; he wore a smart livery in green with red piping— which was perfectly cut to fit his lanky figure.

'Really? Do you have a portrait in the attic?' I said lightly as we crossed the broad expanse of the hall.

He laughed. '*The Picture of Dorian Gray* by Mr Oscar Wilde. No, sir, the position's been passed from father to son. Back at the start, the first Jiggens was a lowly boot-boy and he fell in love with a scullery maid. The Saints gave them dispensation to marry and in thanks, they pledged a lifetime of service. We carried on the tradition. We've not let them down and they haven't let us down either.'

Swift kept a stern policeman's face although I could see bemusement in his dark eyes.

'Right, jolly good,' I said. 'Haven't seen my butler, have you?'

'Mr Greggs is downstairs in our parlour, sir, with Cook and my auntie Essie,' Jiggens replied. 'Auntie Essie is housekeeper. Getting on like a house on fire, they are. Even opened the sherry and it's barely dusk.'

That didn't surprise me. Greggs held a particular penchant for liquor and ladies at any hour.

Jiggens guided us past a huge Christmas tree positioned some distance from the crackling fire in the wide stone hearth. The tree was decked with pretty baubles, candles, porcelain snowmen, angels and myriad little brass bells.

Holly, ivy and branches of pine had been formed in swags and tied with red ribbons along the top of the panelled walls. It smelled and looked the very epitome of Christmas.

We gained the broad oak staircase to climb the carpeted steps, young Jiggens chattering all the way up. 'You've been allocated rooms in the men's quarter, sirs, that's on the first floor where all the bedrooms are. The Regent says it's snowing too heavily for you to carry on, but don't you fret, we'll make sure you're warm n' comfortable. There's no better place than Temple House to make yourself at home.'

'We've been sent to investigate a suspicious death, not move in,' Swift said drily.

'I know that, sir.' Jiggens dropped his voice. 'But Sir Jasper dying unexpected like that has upset the house and the Regent says it's best not to cause alarm. Most of the Saints don't even realise the death might be suspicious, and no-one's keen on explaining it to them, neither.'

CHAPTER 2

We arrived on the wide first-floor landing where passages led off. The same red carpet covered the floorboards, the walls were painted a delicate buttercream yellow and crowded with dark portraits of sombre men and women, mostly in Victorian dress.

'Did you attend Sir Jasper the day he died?' I asked, thinking I might as well act the detective.

'Yes, I did, sir,' Jiggens replied earnestly as he turned toward a long corridor. 'I took up his mid-morning tea and ginger snaps. He was just as usual, but a bit more grumpy and complaining about the snow. Don't know why, because he hardly ever went out. Then he didn't come down for lunch. We thought he must have dozed off, which he did sometimes, and we knew better than to bother him because he shouted if we did.'

Dark oak doors were set at regular intervals along the passage; between them were more portraits: regency beaus, women in powdered wigs, bearded men with starched white ruffs, Elizabethan ladies in pearls and silk. As we continued, the portraits became smaller: a handful of dull puritan types, then plump abbots in richly embroidered robes and a few stilted mediaeval chaps from the long-ago past.

'Did you see the body?' Swift asked as Jiggens strode along.

Jiggens nodded, his grin fading. 'Grandpa called for me to come. He only goes upstairs one time a day, it's as much as he can do now. I'm usually running up and down, but the provisions arrive from the City at four o'clock. That's the same time as the Saints take high tea in the drawing room. I lay it out before I go and meet the carrier out back. Any of the Saints who don't come down gets a tray, which Grandpa takes up. He knocked at Sir Jasper's door, 'cos he must have been peckish by that time, seeing as he'd missed his lunch.' He let out a sigh. 'Well, that's when he found him. Lord Balthazar was there too and he went in, then Grandpa came down, calling for me.' We'd been walking briskly, but his steps began to slow and he finally stopped and lowered his voice. 'Y'see, most of them are pretty old, it shouldn't be a shock when they go, but Sir Jasper had seemed fit enough. When I saw him he was just sitting in his chair bent over a book, not a mark on him. I was sure he was dead though, he was white as a ghost. I guessed his heart must have given out — that's assuming he had one.' He gave another lopsided grin, then sobered. 'I shouldn't speak ill of the dead, but as you're detectives, I doubt you'll be mealy-mouthed about them that's gone.'

He had a mature head on his shoulders, despite his youth.

'What made you think it was suspicious?' Swift asked.

'It wasn't me as thought it was suspicious,' Jiggens replied. 'The Regent will have to tell you what he knows, that's if he's of a mind to do it. He keeps things tight to his chest, suppose that's 'cos he's a General.'

Jiggens set off again and we turned a corner. There wasn't a sound in the place, even the fall of our footsteps were smothered by the thick carpet. The corridor was dimly lit with shaded electric lamps standing on low bookcases. There had been a few windows too, but each had green velvet curtains drawn across them, shutting out the fading light.

'Here we are, sirs,' Jiggens whispered as we arrived at the end of the corridor and a sturdy oak door. He knocked, waited for a muffled response, then let us in and closed the door on himself.

'General Hackett.' The man behind the military desk spoke coldly. 'You're Major Lennox,' he said, then directed a hard stare at Swift. 'And you're the bag carrier.'

Swift had insisted on bringing his satchel with him and held it slung from his shoulder. He frowned at the remark.

'I am Detective Inspector Swift, retired from Scotland Yard,' he replied sharply.

'You're hardly old enough to retire,' General Hackett barked. 'What are you, thirty-two? Thirty-three? Barely learned your trade and you've already thrown in the towel.'

I bit back a sigh. 'May we assume you to be the Regent, sir?'

'*Humph*,' he rumbled in his chest. His black jacket was tailored to fit broad shoulders and fastened up to his neck in severe style. Thin hair, trimmed grey brows and dark eyes, which pierced us with a glacial stare. 'Retired from the Army after a lifetime of service to King and country. Didn't give up. Never gave up. Duty comes first.' He banged a hand on the desk making the ink pot jump.

Swift glowered, but held his tongue.

'Should we address you as General or Regent?' I continued.

'Sir will suffice,' he replied sharply. 'Sit down.'

We duly sat on the upright chairs facing him across the desk. I took the one nearest to the fire.

A collection of gleaming swords arranged on a far wall caught my eye. There were some old-fashioned flintlock pistols too, and a blunderbuss. I'd always wanted a blunderbuss – they were hopelessly inaccurate but jolly useful for frightening the life out of the unsuspecting.

There wasn't much else to the rest of the room; a few patterned rugs, a row of plain filing cabinets, a campaign cabinet, an oil lamp on the desk and a pair of lattice windows framing a dusky sky beyond snow clinging to the glass.

'Miss Cicely Sissinghurst advised I bring you in,' Hackett continued, his voice moderating as he spoke of the lady. 'Miss Sissinghurst is our Keeper of the Books, and an excellent administrator. She said she'd encountered you at Belvedere and informed me you were successful at bringing a murderer to heel. She recommended you; I trust her judgement. A notable lady…' he mused. 'Good ankles.'

'Right,' I said slowly, not having considered the lady's ankles given that she was old enough to be my grandmother. 'You are certain Sir Jasper was murdered then?'

'Don't take me for an idiot, Major, of course he was,' Hackett retorted.

'How?' Swift asked stiffly.

'Hypothermia,' Hackett replied.

'We were just informed he was sitting in front of his fire,' Swift countered.

'He didn't die there, he died in the morgue,' the Regent rapped. 'It was unfortunate, but they weren't to know.'

'Weren't to know what?' I asked, wondering just how many of the inhabitants were actually rational.

'Any of it, and why should they?' Hackett barked. Despite the belligerence, there was a gleam of disquiet in his eyes and I suspected his blustering manner was due to finding himself in unknown territory.

'Could you explain please, sir?' I asked.

'And may we take notes?' Swift added.

'You can listen, but I will not accept note-taking. This is an ancient order. Shrouded. Not to be bandied about in the outside world.'

'Fine.' I sat back in my seat. Swift did the same, and folded his arms.

'Yopo,' the Regent said. 'That was the real cause. Seeds and leaves taken from a tree in the Orinoco basin – nasty stuff if taken in excess. It can cause one to become catatonic… and it's hallucinogenic.'

'So he died happy,' I remarked, thinking of the smile he was said to be wearing.

Hackett fixed me with a sharp stare. He had a high forehead, straight nose, tightly compressed mouth and a granite jaw. He looked the tenacious type, with little time for idlers or fools. 'Let us hope he did, given the circumstances.' He stood up, went to the campaign cabinet and yanked open the top drawer. The sound of clinking bottles reverberated in the quiet. 'Drink?'

'Whisky,' I agreed.

'What?' Swift was surprised by the outbreak of cordiality. 'Erm…yes, a whisky, please.'

'Macallan?' Hackett held up a bottle of amber liquid.

'Swift's family is Braeburn Malt,' I mentioned.

Hackett swung round. 'Braeburn? Do you have any?'

Swift reached into the satchel, pulled out a half bottle and placed it on the desktop. 'There's more in my carpetbag.'

Hackett grabbed three shot glasses and returned in quick strides. 'Well, well.' He picked up the bottle to gaze at the black and gold label. 'Braeburn Malt… You may have retired as a detective, but it was obviously for a good cause.' The man sounded almost genial.

'Swift has extensive experience,' I said in his defence. 'In policing, I mean, as well as whisky.'

'Hmm.' Hackett poured the liquid into the glasses. 'You're going to need it. We've never had an incident of crime here. Members are Saints. Not real ones, naturally, but we're supposed to be on the side of the angels. What do you know about the Order?' He sat back down and took another drink.

DCI Billings had told us very little, other than to order us to Temple House and report to the Regent. That had been the intention, except for Lord Balthazar Cholmondeley's confused intervention.

'Almost nothing, sir.' I reached for my glass as he hadn't handed it over.

'Good, that's the way it should be. We're known as *Saints* and only to a select few. The Saints are an ancient Order of the high and mighty, each one the end of their lineage. It was set up by Bishop Nicholas of Bath and Wells in 1489. He's the founder – wanted to follow in the footsteps of old Saint Nicholas. Potential Saints are invited to join – sounded out first, of course. Can't have any Tom, Dick or Harry. There are only ever twelve. When there's a vacancy the next in line is summoned. Once they accept, they sign over all their worldly goods to the Order and their assets are liquidated. When the Saint dies, their funds go into our coffers.'

'Not before?' I asked.

'No,' he replied and knocked back the rest of his whisky.

'Why?' Swift asked, then added, 'Have Saints rescinded their positions in the past?'

'Precisely, well done that man.' Hackett topped up his glass from the bottle. 'That's why we don't take their money until they're dead. Two have backed out, both because they found lost heirs.' He frowned. 'Wrong side of the blanket, but better than letting the line die out, I suppose.'

'Presumably the funds are distributed to the poor and needy?' I said, because that was the Saint Nicholas tradition.

'Not individuals, not any more anyway,' Hackett replied. 'Nowadays, it's organisations: orphanages, hospitals, convalescent homes, old soldiers, that sort of thing.'

'Are there sufficient funds in the coffers now?' Swift asked, and earned a scowl from Hackett for the implication.

'Always. We are hugely wealthy. Only ever distribute ten percent. It's the rule.'

'And it's distributed at Christmas,' I said, just to be clear.

'Of course it is. That's the whole idea,' Hackett replied. 'We debate all year, decide who gets what, then off it goes. We have outside officials – three King's Counsellors. They receive the list, and send it to the right people.'

'These three officials – they aren't called the Wise Men, by any chance?' I asked without the hint of a grin.

He glared at me. 'Yes, and why not?'

Swift hid a smile behind his drink.

'If the Order is secret, what do the locals think?' I had the milkman, postman and all the rest in mind. The Saints may be covert but they were hardly invisible.

'They think it's a retirement home for the nobility,' Hackett replied, 'and that's the story we maintain. Now this incident could undermine the Order – even cripple us. I'm in charge and I'm responsible.' He drained his whisky again. 'Can I rely on you, gentlemen? Can I?' He banged his glass down on the desk. 'You cannot fail. The investigation must be dealt with competently. The tenor of this institution must flow as tranquilly as it has for centuries. It is your duty. Am I making myself clear?' His voice rose again.

Swift nodded. 'Absolutely, sir.'

I was inclined to tell him that we weren't duty-bound to investigate anything, but sipped my whisky instead.

'What happened to Sir Jasper?' Swift leaned back in his chair, one leg crossed over another, drink in hand, apparently relaxed and determined not to be goaded by the Regent's short temper.

'Ah, well.' He lowered his voice. 'It was rather macabre in the end.'

CHAPTER 3

Hackett poured himself another shot from the bottle, his features mellowing. 'Jasper liked brandy with his daily brew, whatever time of day. He was bored. Living in idle comfort suits some, but Jasper was used to the bustle of city life. He missed it. The brandy made him dozy…we believe someone threw Yopo seeds onto his fire sometime during the day. He inhaled the fumes and became comatose. The butler, old Jiggens, found him about four o'clock that afternoon. He raised the alarm and I was called to his room. Jasper gave every appearance of being dead. A doctor arrived; he pronounced his passing, and an ambulance delivered him to the morgue.' He paused to drink from his glass again, but hesitated, and continued talking. 'That was three days ago. It was cold, as cold as it is outside now.' He glanced toward the windows. 'Some hours later a morgue attendant was preparing the body for post-mortem and Jasper suddenly sat up, gasping for breath. Then he dropped back onto the slab – terrified the wits out of the attendant.' His lips twitched with what I'd swear was a grin. 'They tried their best to revive him, but that breath was his last. Nevertheless, he was moved to a bed in a quiet corner of the hospital. Next morning, after he'd turned stiff and blue, they carted him back to the morgue and he was examined under the knife. Fluids were taken, and all the usual unpleasantness indulged. Traces of unknown elements were found in his blood, which mystified them. I knew the source could only have come from here. I asked the Explorer to investigate the Chamber of Curiosities. He discovered the jar of Yopo had been emptied. That provided the answer to the riddle.'

'How could you be certain?' Swift moved into police mode. 'Was there any evidence of this?'

'There were some charred seed pods in the ashes of Jasper's fire,' Hackett replied.

'Were any kept as evidence?' Swift asked, predictably.

Hackett's gaze flicked to the fire. 'They disintegrated.'

'Could it have been suicide?' I asked.

'Absolutely not.' Hackett was adamant. 'Jasper may have been bored but he still had plenty of life in him. If you knew the man you wouldn't even ask the question.'

'Did anyone have cause to kill him?' Swift asked in formal tone.

'Obviously, or he wouldn't be dead.'

'Anyone in mind?' I asked.

'No.' Hackett's mood darkened. He drew the bottle of Braeburn towards him. 'Find young Jiggens, bed in, then scout about. Use discretion, no need for alarm. Find proof, flush out the bounder, then report back to me. Dismissed.'

We stood up, bowed respectfully, then filed out in silence.

'Best I show you to your rooms, sirs.' Young Jiggens was waiting for us in the corridor. 'Bedrooms are further along, if you'll follow me.'

'Who is the Explorer?' I asked.

'Mr Wilfred Rackham, sir,' Jiggens replied.

'We'd like to speak to him, please,' I said.

'He's out in the garden, sir. It's winter solstice today and he's gone to light candles in the graveyard.'

'Of course he has,' Swift muttered under his breath.

'What is the Chamber of Curiosities?' I asked, my imagination running to a room packed with strange and wonderful things.

'It's rather like the Ashmolean museum in Oxford, sir but smaller, and more peculiar,' Jiggens replied.

That was intriguing…

We turned a corner to find my cat sitting on the red carpet. I paused to scoop him up. 'Tubbs, you little rascal.'

'That's Nox, sir,' Jiggens said.

'What?'

'The cat, he lives here, he's called Nox.'

I held him up for a better look. He had green eyes, my cat had blue eyes. 'Ah, he closely resembles Mr Tubbs.' I would have put him down but he seemed quite content in my arms.

'Your kitty is with Mr Greggs in the kitchen, sir.' Jiggens grinned. 'Your dog's there too, Cook's giving them all snacks.'

'Including Greggs?' I guessed.

'With another drop of sherry, yes sir.' He grinned.

'We'd like to see Sir Jasper's room.' Swift's mind was still on the murder.

'Certainly, sir, here it is.' Jiggens swung open a door and stood back to allow us entry.

More dark panelling lined the walls. The room was hung with oil paintings of animals: dogs, cats, cattle, horses, even a lion. They were my type of pictures, and jolly well done.

An oak desk below the latticed window and two deep leather chairs were either side of a freshly lit fire. Plain woven rugs covered bare floorboards, dark antique furniture was set about the place, and there were two beds, one at each end of the room.

'Why are there two beds?' I asked, thinking I already knew the answer.

'Because you'll both be staying here, sirs.' Jiggens' smile didn't falter. 'We've cleaned it out and moved an extra bed in for you. And over here,' he walked to a narrow door in the panelling and lifted the latch, 'is for Mr Greggs. All the rooms have a servant's room off, just in case any Saint wants to bring one. Hardly any of them do, most of their servants just want to retire.'

The cat, Nox, leapt down from my arms and sauntered over to jump onto a large leather pouffe set before the fire. He began to delicately wash a black paw.

Swift looked around. It was quite obvious there wasn't any evidence left of Sir Jasper's death. He sighed and walked to an armchair. 'Which one was he sitting in?'

'That one, sir.' Jiggens pointed to the nearest.

Swift pulled a torch from his pocket, switched it on and

proceeded to slowly shine it over the dark brown leather. Nox thought this marvellous fun and dashed over to chase the beam, pouncing on it in kittenish play.

'I'll have this bed.' I strode over to the one by the window. It was furthest from Greggs' room, I knew how loudly he snored. Greggs and I had been through the war together, and spent any number of nights huddled at close quarters in bleak billets.

Jiggens pulled the heavy red curtains closed against the snow pattering onto the panes. 'I've left an oil lamp for you, sir, but you shouldn't need it unless the electric goes off. It's usually reliable.' He nodded at an elegant Tiffany lamp on the marble-topped washstand. 'Dinner's at half past six. The Saints like to eat early, it gives them time to play games before bed.'

'What sort of games?' Swift gave up with the torch and switched it off. The cat gazed at him in disappointment.

'Bridge, backgammon and chess, mostly. It's very competitive,' Jiggens said. 'I'll be off now. I'll tell Mr Greggs you're ready for him.' He gave another grin and left.

Swift was in investigative mood. 'Sir Jasper was found with *A Christmas Carol* on his lap.' He went to the bookcase opposite the fireplace. 'Lord Balthazar said he didn't usually read, so the book might have been left as a clue.'

I sat down in the other armchair by the fire, the one Sir Jasper wasn't found in. 'Why on earth would a murderer want to leave a clue?'

'As justification for killing him,' Swift explained as he scrutinised the shelves. 'He was said to be a miser.'

That didn't make sense. I noticed a book tucked down the side of the cushion. It was *A Christmas Carol.* I slid it out and thumbed through the pages while Swift kept himself occupied.

It was well read, the reddish-brown cloth cover and spine were crumpled from continuous use. A dedication and signature had been scrawled on the fly leaf; it appeared to be by Dickens himself. Apart from that, the book was unremarkable. I flicked through it then held it up. 'Swift.'

He frowned. 'You could have told me.' He came and took it, then sat down opposite. Nox climbed onto the arm of his chair and closed his eyes to snooze.

I yawned and stretched my feet toward the fire. It had been a long day and DCI Billings' orders to race off to Temple House had left me irritable. We'd originally planned to leave for London today – my wife, Persi, was an archeologist and had uncovered some intriguing artefacts from an ancient Long Barrow in our village, Ashton Steeple, some months earlier. Swift's wife, Florence, had helped her and they'd been invited to attend the British Museum and take part in a day of lectures. Swift and I had agreed to go along, and despite my usual reservations about the metropolis, I'd been looking forward to the lectures, and the visit to the museum.

After Billings had called, much debate had ensued. Swift naturally wanted to investigate; he'd never truly reconciled giving up the force, despite his contented life in the highlands with Florence, their toddler Angus, and the Braeburn Clan. Billings, Swift's ex-boss at Scotland Yard, termed us

'Detectives to the Toffs', and sent us off when members of the aristocracy were dispatched by unknown hands. Billings told Swift in no uncertain terms that we should uncover whatever was going on at Temple House and be quick about it. Everyone had been in favour, except me.

'It's made out to *Saint Euan, Keeper of the Books* and signed by the author,' Swift deciphered the scrawl.

'What year was it?'

'1843.'

'He'll be long gone,' I remarked.

'General Hackett referred to Cicely Sissinghurst as "Keeper of the Books".' He was still staring at the dedication. 'There's something written underneath it.' He squinted at the words. '*The Dead Reckoner*.'

I looked up at that. 'Really? Perhaps they keep the coffers filled by bumping off one of the Saints when times are hard.'

'Nonsense,' he objected.

'Sir Jasper died happy,' I replied.

'Cicely Sissinghurst recommended us. You can't consider her a suspect.'

'We should consider everyone a suspect, according to you,' I reminded him.

He gave a wry grin, then took out a magnifying glass to examine the pages.

Greggs arrived bearing a tray piled with sandwiches. 'Cook has prepared a light snack before dinner, sir,' he announced.

'You've finished yours then?' I turned to him.

'*Ahem*, it was merely a morsel, sir.'

'What are they?' Swift sat up.

'Beef and pickle, beef and mustard, ham and pickle, cheese and pickle, slices of game pie and apples. According to the staff, Sir Jasper kept an excellent claret in his room.' He put the tray on the leather pouffe in front of the fire and looked around with a gleam of expectation.

'I haven't seen any. Where would it be kept?' I stood up, ready for the search.

'Erm…' He looked about with some confusion. 'It was not specified, sir.'

'Right, well we'd best have a look then.' I glanced at the bookcase, it being the largest piece of furniture in the room.

Swift decided to join in. 'There aren't any bottles there, I've already inspected it.'

I turned around to scan the place. Greggs had gone to the marble-top washstand, but apart from the lamp it only held the usual ceramic basin, water jug, glass tumblers and whatnots.

'Where would he keep his clothes?' Swift asked.

'In the adjacent room, sir,' Greggs replied glumly. 'It is a dressing room, and has been allocated to me during our sojourn.'

'We know,' I said. 'Have you looked in there?'

'I did so earlier, sir, when I began to packed the carpet bags.' He let out a breath, causing his chins to wobble over the starched collar of his butlering togs. He was turned out in the usual black tailcoat, waistcoat, white dickie, and a bowtie slightly askew.

Swift had moved to the oak desk. It was large and unadorned, the sort used by money men, with multiple drawers and a cupboard each side of the knee-hole.

He opened and closed everything then called out, 'Nothing in here.'

I had been studying the dark panels on the walls. Temple House was early Tudor, it would certainly have gone through numerous changes. There would be servants' passages and doors hidden in the woodwork, because that's the way they did things back in the old days.

'There's an opening here.' I spotted a finely cut edge in a section of the oak.

We congregated to contemplate it.

'There's no keyhole,' Swift said. 'Don't touch it, there might be prints,' he warned as I reached to feel for a catch or some such.

'Oh, come off it, Swift,' I argued.

'Process and procedure,' he intoned, pulling his torch from his pocket and switching it on. Nox instantly awoke and came trotting over. He jumped up with paws padding the panel, trying to catch the beam as Swift played the light over the dark wood.

I doubt Sherlock Holmes had had to put up with this.

'Sir,' Greggs proclaimed, 'there's an indent.' He pointed.

He was right, there was a worn hollow in one of the panels. Swift picked the cat up, handed it to Greggs, then aimed the beam.

I reached to press it.

'Lennox, will you wait,' Swift instructed, then went to his discarded satchel by the fireside. 'Here.' He took out a jar of grey powder and soft shaving brush.

'Swift, why did you bring a detecting kit when we were

supposed to be heading for the British museum?' I asked, although I knew the answer.

'There's no harm in being prepared.' He spoke calmly while brushing powder over the wood. The cat's green eyes rounded in fascination.

I went to pick up a sandwich while he bent to peer through his magnifying glass.

'Interesting,' he muttered.

'What?' I said through beef and mustard.

'It's been wiped clean.'

'Hm,' I mumbled, unimpressed. 'Jiggens said they'd cleaned the room after Sir Jasper died.'

'Including the walls?' he remarked as he pushed on the indent, causing the panel to swing silently open.

CHAPTER 4

The top shelf was stocked with bottles of wine, whisky, brandy and a number of elegant glasses.

'Ah, and there's the claret,' Greggs almost purred. He put the cat on the floor and reached to remove a ship's decanter filled with a rich red liquid, and three wine glasses.

'Pour one for yourself,' I said.

'Thank you, sir.' He beamed and carried the booty over to the desk.

'There's a box.' Swift was still staring into the cupboard.

'As I can see,' I said.

The lower shelf held a large box of inlaid walnut with a fancy brass lock. There didn't appear to be a key.

'Shall I–' Swift reached for the powder and brush.

'No.' I cut him off and tried to lift the lid; it was locked. I squinted at it, which didn't help, then felt in my pocket for my lock picks.

'So you came prepared too?' Swift said.

I ignored him. I was particularly fond of the lock picks, having confiscated them on a permanent basis from a petty thief at Bloxford Hall. I carefully inserted a hooked end into the keyhole and turned it slowly, feeling for the pins within the barrel. I felt the first pin slide aside, then I had to insert another long slim tine, and another, until finally the catch gave way with a soft and satisfying *click*. 'Right, let's see what he's squirrelled away.'

It was a bit of an anticlimax, actually.

'Looks like a ledger,' Swift said as we regarded the black bound book. He reached in and picked it up.

I'd expected something far more exciting. A horde of golden guineas at least, given the implication that Jasper was a Scrooge. I ran fingers around the red felt sides and base of the box, but apart from dust, there was nothing.

'Would you prefer your claret by the fire, sir?' Greggs asked. 'Or should I bring it to you there?'

'The fire, please,' I replied.

Swift was already seated, the ledger open on his lap. He turned the pages. 'It's a diary of sorts. Sir Jasper Crawford has printed his name on the first page, followed by the year 1923. The writing is atrocious.'

I picked up another sandwich and bit into it, it was cheese and pickle. 'Can you make it out?'

He bent more closely over the thick pages. Each one had a few sentences scrawled over it in black ink. 'He's written the date at the top of each page, but he wasn't very consistent. There are only a few entries each month.'

'I don't suppose much ever happened,' I replied between bites.

'May I, sir?' Greggs had placed glasses of claret on small

tables at our elbows and held out his hand for the ledger. 'I am quite adept at interpreting the written word.'

That was true, he'd had to decipher my scrawl for years.

'Very well.' Swift handed it over and reached for a slice of game pie. Nox went to sit on the arm of his chair to watch him eat, one black paw occasionally extended when he fancied something tasty. Swift shared the goodies with good grace.

Greggs sat down on the pouffe and quietly turned the pages, pausing every now and then on a tricky scribble. 'It is mostly a record of his triumphs at chess, chequers, and cards,' he said. 'He appears to have had very little regard for Lord Balthazar. He won thirteen pounds and ten shillings one night from him, playing whist.' He took a sip of claret and turned more pages. 'There are accounts of the antics of cats, Nox and Furz. He seemed very fond of them and writes of toys he fabricated for them…Ah, here is a more recent entry. It is on the second of December. '*I heard news this day of a most satisfying nature. There is talk of a new Saint-in-waiting. The Regent is said to have nominated a lady – indeed it is our very own Keeper of the Books. She is mooted to join us at the next opportunity. What a delightful prospect – another fair maiden to colour this drab collection of dullards. We have the dazzling Lady Matilda, the charming Baroness Finch and the divine Miss Olivia Arbuthnot, who is as colourful as she is sharp. Now we await Miss Cicely Sissinghurst. A resplendent gem to admire in silent devotion.*' Greggs took a sip of claret and turned another page as we ate in bemused silence. 'The fifth of December,' he continued. *The rumour is confirmed! Miss Sissinghurst will join us at the next death,*' he intoned as Swift and I finished off the food. '*It should be Balthazar, the man will be no loss, indeed his passing would bring manifold benefits. He has been a nuisance, wandering about, talking of ghosts.*'

'Sir Jasper reverts to recording more winnings for a number of days,' Greggs continued. 'On the tenth he writes, *Balthazar is nothing but dead weight, his very existence is obstructing the admittance of the enchanting Cicely–*'

'Enchanting?' I repeated. 'Cicely Sissinghurst is many things, but hardly enchanting.'

'Beauty is in the eye of the beholder, sir,' Greggs intoned loftily, then carried on reading aloud. 'I am come to disdain the man further than ever. Miss C came today to instruct us upon our duty—namely the final list of distributions we must agree upon before Christmas Eve. Balthazar is still resisting the sanctuary for retired plough horses which I expressly submitted. I will not stand for it and so I told him. We parted after hot words.'

'Retired plough horses?' Swift said.

'The sanctuary must be one of the potential beneficiaries,' I guessed.

'I thought it was widows and orphans,' Swift replied.

'And old soldiers,' Greggs added.

'Well, I suppose they can't give it to the same lot every year,' I said. 'And he's clearly fond of animals.' I indicated the paintings on the walls.

'Indeed, sir.' Greggs bent over the book again. 'The entries sway from being positive about the lady's nomination to anger that her residency is obstructed. Most of the invective is aimed at Lord Balthazar.' He read a few more pages. 'He is again praising Miss Sissinghurst, apparently she has been attempting to calm the disagreement between the Saints.' He placed a finger under a sentence, trying to make it out. '*Miss C is the very epitome of womanhood, she reminds me of my dear Nanny. There can be no higher praise. Tomorrow is the day for the card. I will place it on the mantel shelf as my annual devotion to that revered lady.*' Greggs looked up. 'That is the last entry, sir, written three days ago. I believe it was the day of his death.'

'Yes,' I replied, then added, 'It wasn't what I'd expected.'

'No, and he didn't like Balthazar Cholmondeley,' Swift remarked.

'There is a card, sir.' Greggs had turned a page. 'It is an old Christmas card, inscribed, *To Jasper, my dear little one, all my love, your Nanny Prentice.*' He regarded it, then held up a faded card, yellowed with age.

We gazed at the picture of a nativity scene with Mary and Joseph gathered around the baby in a manger. An angel stood behind with wings outstretched over the little group.

'Should I place it on the mantelpiece, sir?' Greggs offered.

'Yes, please,' Swift replied quietly.

'I think you should,' I agreed.

He did so. It seemed rather sad actually.

We contemplated the unexpected turn in silence, then Greggs topped up our glasses again.

'I should make notes.' Swift dug out his notebook from

the satchel, then went to settle at the desk to write. Nox went with him, jumping onto the polished top to curl up and snooze.

'I believe I should finish unpacking the bags, sir,' Greggs offered.

'Fine,' I said and remained where I was, a frown on my brow, wondering what it all meant.

A rap on the door pulled me from my musings. Greggs opened it to discover young Jiggens.

'Just called with a fresh set of towels, sirs, in case you need them.' He came in with a cheerful smile and a pile of pristine white towels. 'Ah, I see you found the cabinet.' He indicated the hidden cupboard, its door still ajar.

'Claret,' I said. 'And an excellent choice of brandy.'

'Sir Jasper was very particular about the quality of his drink, sir.' Jiggens put the towels on the shelf below the washstand, then went to the cupboard. 'Oh, you opened his box, now that is impressive! We couldn't find the key anywhere, the Regent thought we'd have to force the lock.'

'He kept his diary in it,' I replied, then added, 'There was nothing of note.'

'But you found the key?' Jiggens brow creased in puzzlement.

'Not quite,' I said without explanation.

'Sit down.' Swift swivelled the desk chair around to eye the lad. 'There's a few questions I'd like to ask.'

'I'm afraid I can't stop, sir.' Jiggens began backing toward the door. 'Drinks are served in the drawing room at half past five, and I have to make ready. The Regent asked if you'd like to come down and join in.'

'Tell him we'll be there,' I replied.

The lad escaped before Swift could stop him. He turned back to his notebook, muttering under his breath.

'Swift, I'm going to find a telephone and call Persi.' I stood up.

'I'd like to talk to Florence…'

'Fine, I'll mention it,' I said and set off for wherever a telephone might be hidden. I didn't get very far.

'Young man,' a female voice called out in plummy tones. 'Who are you and what do you think you are doing?'

I had reached the staircase but not yet stepped down. 'Erm…greetings,' I offered.

The lady was of statuesque proportions with white hair in a fussy bun, arched brows, high cheekbones and mauve lipstick. Purple amethyst earrings hung in her ears, she wore a matching necklace and was dressed in stiff purple crepe with layered folds of lace covering an ample bosom. 'There are rumours of investigators in the house.' She advanced with a gleam of determination in grey eyes. 'I would wager that you are one of them.' She held a pair of gold lorgnette glasses on the end of a long handle, and prodded me with them.

'Major Lennox, and yes, I am,' I admitted.

She extended a white-gloved hand for me to peck. I did the honours as there wasn't much choice.

'As there's no-one to introduce us, I will do so myself. I am Lady Matilda Fettiscue.'

'Delighted,' I said.

'You're here about Jasper, I assume?' she demanded in a high voice. 'Another dry stick. Tongue-tied and dithering around us women, but if he got on his high horse about something he could be quite eviscerating. Very fond of animals,' she mused. 'What do you make of it, eh?'

'Erm, we're keeping an open mind.' I remembered we were supposed to be discreet. 'Nothing to worry about.' I gave her a reassuring grin.

'Well, hunting the cause of his demise will be a diversion, and I'm game,' she replied archly. 'Dull as ditchwater for the most part. How one craves amusement, particularly with such a fine specimen as yourself.' She eyed me sideways. 'I have a magnifying glass you know, as well as the bins.' She held up the lorgnette and gave it a twirl.

'Erm...right, excellent.' This wasn't what I'd expected. 'Don't happen to know where there's a telephone, do you m'lady?'

'A telephone!' she exclaimed in exaggerated tone. 'Ridiculous modern fripperies – gone within a decade, I guarantee it. Now, take me to the drawing room.' She suddenly grabbed my arm.

'What?'

'You can escort me,' she said, then laughed delightedly as she saw my expression. 'We haven't had any real men here in donkey's years. Dry old wrinklies. Come along, it's nearly time for drinks. I'm particularly partial to rum punch.'

I froze in horror. Swift came along at that moment.

'Lennox, I'll come with you...' he called out, then stopped as he spotted Lady Matilda.

'Swift.' I gathered my wits. 'This is Lady Matilda Fettiscue, she's keen to help with our enquiries.' I turned to the lady. 'Detective Inspector Swift of Scotland Yard.'

She lifted the lorgnette to examine him down the line of her long nose. 'Hmmm, an inspector are you? Hanged anyone recently?'

Swift was caught mid-bow, hand extended to take her gloved offering. 'I…not personally, no. But I'm delighted to meet–'

'I'll be off, Swift. See you in the drawing room.' I moved out of grabbing range. 'Lady Matilda is fond of rum punch,' I said as I trotted at speed down the stairs.

'Lennox,' Swift called after me but was too late, I was already approaching the hall.

I hadn't seen any sign of a telephone, but I stopped to check behind the Christmas tree, just in case. I leaned round it, there wasn't one, but I'd set all the brass bells tinkling. That attracted my little black cat, Mr Tubbs.

He made a leap straight for a wavering branch and batted a bauble off which fell onto the thick rug under the tree.

I picked the little blighter up to give him a lecture and realised he had amber eyes. It wasn't Tubbs, and it wasn't Nox either. I assumed it to be Furz, so I put him down and left him to it.

The spacious hall took up the centre of the mansion, with the staircase rising to all floors. Three doors led off. I turned about trying to decide which way to go, quite aware that Lady Matilda and Swift weren't far behind. I took the nearest route straight ahead.

It took me to the surrounding passageway, with even more doors set into the panelled walls. The first room I tried was a games salon dotted with circular tables and clusters of chairs. Sofas and wing chairs were gathered near the fire, and heavily carved sideboards were stacked with packs of cards, board games, paper, pencils and the usual whatnots.

It held a convivial air, but no telephone and I could hear Lady Matilda's voice. A servants' door was clearly evident in the panelling and I made an escape through it. The passage was typical of its sort, dimly lit by low-watt bulbs and a cold stone floor underfoot.

I followed it to some worn steps going downwards and arrived at a whitewashed junction. The most delicious scent of roasting lamb came from what must be the kitchens to my left. I was highly tempted to follow my nose, but noticed a thin black cable strung along the barrel ceiling. It was a telephone line!

Moments later I discovered the butler's pantry housing a candlestick phone on an ink-spattered desk.

'Ashton Steeple 451, please.'

'Where's that then?'

'It's between Oxford and Cheltenham,' I replied. 'Is this the operator?'

'It is. I'm Dottie.'

Isn't everyone, I thought but didn't say.

'Now, Oxfordshire's a long-distance call,' she continued, 'and it'll not be cheap. They never ring long distance from Temple House. It's only ever Bath, and even then it's a rare event. Is it another'un dead then?'

'No, why should it be?'

'That's all they ever call about. Only just lost one last week. Always come in threes y'know. Nothing for years then all of a sudden over they go, just like ninepins. Sure you don't want the doctor?'

'No, no-one's dead,' I said with as much patience as I could muster. 'I'm trying to speak to my wife. Could you put me through, please?'

'Alright, but if you want the doctor, you only have to say.'

'Thank you, but I'd like–'

'Putting you through now, duckie,' she cut in.

I sat down on the only chair and waited as the line clunked, clicked and hummed.

A cobweb clung to the top of the single light bulb hanging above the desk. The pantry was a small space and appeared little used. A white painted candle cupboard was fixed to one wall, red quarry tiles on the floor were scuffed, but swept. It was typical of most such places, although there wasn't a window of any sort as we were below ground.

''Ello, I don't know who y'want to talk to but there ain't no-one here,' a boy's voice replied. 'So ye'd best call back when they're home, bye–'

'Tommy,' I shouted before the line went dead.

'Oh, sir, is that you?' he said with sudden enthusiasm. 'Hello, sir. Did you get there alright? Was there blizzards an' snow drifts covering the road and you had to smash through them with the car goin' like the clappers?'

'Yes, I mean, no. It was fine.' I put my hand over my

eyes as I remembered that Persi was in London and I'd just called home. Tommy was our boot boy, and lived at my house with Cook, his aunt.

'Why'd you call, sir?'

'Erm...how are things?'

'Ah well, it's snowing here and me and Brendan have cleared the drive, then we built a big snowman out of the pile of snow we'd dug. We even had enough for a snow dog and a cat. How's Mr Fogg and Tubbs?' He didn't wait for an answer. 'Auntie says she's making shepherd's pie for supper and if the lane's blocked tomorrow I might not be able to go to school.' He chattered away, full of enthusiasm. 'But we're going to make paper chains and put up decorations in the church hall for the Christmas party, so I'm going to dig my way out even if I have to make a tunnel.'

'Fine, excellent. Well, I'll let you get back to it.'

'Right you are, sir. Oh, sir? Was he murdered then, because Mrs Craddock was asking?'

Flossie Craddock was our village telephone operator and I was surprised she wasn't listening in. 'No, no, it's all quite...normal,' I lied. 'Goodbye, Tommy.'

'But sir, why'd you call?'

'Just, erm...we'll be back home in a day or two. In time for Christmas, anyway.'

'Righto. Bye, sir,' he said and put the phone down to let the line go dead.

I waited a moment then rattled the hook.

'Hello?'

'Dottie, I'd like a London number please.'

'London! Well, you are a gadabout. This line must be red hot with all the chit-chat. Whereabouts in London?'

'Dukes Hotel, St James's, please.'

Some time later, after more tedious repetitions, Persi's voice came on the line.

'Lennox. Hello, my love.'

'Persi,' I sighed. 'I wish I was there.'

CHAPTER 5

Persi laughed, and after some soft words, I told her about Sir Jasper's demise, Temple House, and the few inmates we'd so far encountered.

'Sounds like God's waiting room,' she said.

I grinned at that. 'Precisely, and Sir Jasper Crawford has just been hastened through the pearly gates.'

'But, how?'

'Yopo, he inhaled fumes.' I explained what the Regent had said.

'Yopo…' she mused. 'Communing with the dead, or that was supposed to be one of its uses. Tribes in South America snort it. It can have psychotic effects. I hope he didn't suffer.'

'Well, he died…'

'I meant before that. Anyway, whoever gave it to him must have returned to put the book in his hands.'

'Yes, the implication being that it was some sort of vengeance for his miserly ways,' I mused. 'But his diary made him sound lonely, and he was very fond of animals. He admired the ladies from afar but didn't appear to have been able to talk to them.'

'You were just the same,' she laughed.

'I was not,' I objected. 'At least, not all the time. Anyway, I have you now.'

'Yes, and thank heavens for that, my love.' Her voice softened, then returned to the puzzle. 'What does Jonathan think?'

'Frustrated, of course. Billings warned us not to upset the residents, but to get a move on. And we want to be home by Christmas.'

'We will come to Bath if you aren't. It sounds rather fascinating,' Persi replied, laughter in her voice.

I grinned. 'How is London?'

'Oh, Dukes is utter luxury, and so quiet you'd hardly know we were in the middle of the city. We walked through the snow to Fortnum's, it was magical. Lights and decorations in the windows, people selling hot chestnuts and ginger cake in the street. Angus was mesmerised and when we went into a toy store his eyes grew as round as saucers. He's been drawing pictures of toy trains since we returned to the hotel.' Angus was Swift and Florence's little boy.

'What time do the lectures begin tomorrow?'

'At ten. I'm the third speaker and already quite nervous. The museum has quite a lot of the artefacts we found in the Long Barrow so I will focus on them during my talk.'

'I'm sorry we won't be there,' I said, and meant it.

'So am I. I'll just have to dig something else up, then you can come along to the next lecture.'

'You haven't arranged another dig have you?'

She laughed. 'No…well, not yet anyway.' She had a habit of teasing me.

The operator broke in. 'It's over two shillings now, duckie.'

'Right, thank you,' I said sharply.

We murmured our goodbyes after that until Dottie reminded us again. I sighed as I replaced the receiver back on its hook. Then I went in search of the drawing room because I was already late, and I didn't know where that was either.

'Lennox.' Swift extracted himself from a seat between Lady Matilda and another lady dressed in bright green silk and sporting unlikely looking black hair falling in ringlets from a braided topknot. He came over, a frown between dark brows. 'Will you stop disappearing. I've been trying to question people and I can't get any sense out of any of them. All they talk about is bridge and games. Where's the telephone?'

'Go toward the kitchen and follow the black cable on the ceiling.'

'Where's the kitchen?' he demanded.

'Downstairs.'

He huffed and stalked off. I took a few more steps into the room, reluctant to enter the fray, not that there was one; those present were murmuring among themselves or quietly reading newspapers.

The room was high-ceilinged, the walls papered in floral style, roses and carnations and the like – more feminine than the few other rooms I'd seen. Cushioned chairs and sofas in various shades of rose pink and lilac were arranged in groups about the place.

A white-bearded chap sitting reading, with slippered feet up on a stool in front of the blazing fire, leaned forward to peer at me through round spectacles. I spotted Greggs and diverted over. He was pouring punch into glasses on a long rosewood sideboard. Old Jiggens was slowly stirring a jug of yellow liquor beside him.

'Ah, sir, Mr Jiggens senior is feeling the strain,' Greggs explained. 'He has been mixing, and I have offered to serve while young Jiggens prepares the dining room. There is a range of most excellent choices. May I recommend the eggnog? Mr Jiggens has made it to his own recipe.'

Jiggens stopped stirring and looked at me with a spark of expectation in his faded eyes.

'What's in it?' I regarded the glass jug. It was darker than the usual pale cream colour and had bits floating on top.

'Thick Jersey cream, coconut milk, eggs, brown sugar, vanilla and nutmeg, sir, with a plentiful measure of spiced rum from the Caribbean,' Jiggens said in his thin voice.

'Hmm, I'll give it a try.'

'Mr Greggs, would you?' Jiggens asked.

'It would be an honour, Mr Jiggens.' Greggs reached for the jug and poured the mix into a shallow cocktail glass, then reverently handed it over.

I took a sip. It was absolutely phenomenal! And with a kick I hadn't expected.

'Does it agree, sir?' Jiggens asked.

'It agrees, Jiggens. Actually, it's sublime.'

A smile lighted the old fellow's face.

'If you will excuse me, sir. I must go to the kitchen and help Cook.' Jiggens made a shaky bow, then tottered off, beaming happily.

I took a longer drink of the heavenly nectar then held the glass up. 'Top up, Greggs.'

He duly obliged. 'If you would excuse me, sir, I must attend the ladies. Baroness Finch has just arrived and I would like to ensure she is well catered for.' He simpered and went off, tray in hand, paunch to the fore, and white napkin over his arm.

I watched as he wound deftly around chairs and sofas to where three women now sat. I assumed the dumpy lady with white hair and wearing a dreadful mustard-coloured frock to be Baroness Finch. I knew the statuesque lady in purple to be Lady Matilda, so the animated lady with black ringlets and wearing the bright green frock must be Miss Olivia Arbuthnot. Jasper had described her in his diary as "as colourful as she is sharp" and she looked it.

'Hello there. You're one of the investigators, I take it.' A young man raised a glass in my direction. He was standing alone, next to a display case full of fussy china ornaments. 'The Regent – I mean General Hackett – said you wanted to speak to me.'

I went over. 'Greetings, I'm Major Lennox.'

'Wilfred Rackham, better known as the Explorer.' He grinned and shook my proffered hand.

'Does everyone come with an epithet?'

He laughed. 'Not really, although poor Jasper was known as the Miser behind his back.'

'What about Balthazar Cholmondeley?' We both looked over at the old fellow, who was blinking owlishly at Greggs as he fussed over the three ladies.

'Often referred to as the Duffer, although not by me,' Wilfred Rackham said. 'I was taught to respect my elders.' He raised a wry brow.

I was surprised to find a chap not much older than me here. 'Thought this was a terminus of some sort,' I said.

'Ha.' His grin turned to a grimace. He raised the chestnut cane he'd been leaning on and banged it against his leg. It clanged tinnily. 'Lost a leg, and more, to frostbite in the frozen north. Fingers gone too.' He turned his hand holding the glass to show a shrivelled forefinger and thumb. 'Along with the left eye. My sight is failing in the other.'

'Sorry,' I said, there not being much else to say.

'At least I made it back. I was the only one who did.' His one good eye turned to me, the other stayed where it was. 'Mind if we find a seat?'

'Lead on.' I raised my glass.

He limped but was quick, swinging the tin leg in an arc as he strode forward, leaning on the cane for support.

'Here, this chair's mine, it's upright and easy to get out of.' He dropped down in a dark leather wing chair, with an embroidered cushion to support his back.

I sat opposite in a similar type. We were some distance from the fire but its warmth emanated our way, and it was also out of earshot of the white-bearded chap next to the hearth.

'Right, ask away,' Rackham said, then grinned. The right side of his face showed a pleasant chap with even features and a ready smile. Fairish hair, grey-blue eyes, straight nose, square chin – the usual features. The left side of his face was puckered, the mouth drawn upwards and the cheek shrunken. The socket seemed unaffected but the eye, which I now knew to be false, appeared paralysed.

'What happened?' I asked and took another sip of eggnog.

'To me, or Jasper?'

'Both,' I replied.

He lifted one brow, the other refused to move. 'I'll begin with Jasper,' he said. 'I didn't see his body before he was taken away, there was no reason why I should. Hackett called me to the Regent's Room at around…' he glanced over to the elegant grandfather clock, 'ten o'clock that night. A police constable had come to the door and asked to speak to whomever was in charge. They think we're a retirement home, you see,' he threw in with a grin. 'We heard him out: Jasper had apparently "woken up". I think it was literally his last breath…it can happen like that.' He grimaced.

I nodded. I'd been with my father when he died, and friends during the long days and nights of the war. Death doesn't always come as quietly as one would wish.

He carried on. 'The hospital realised Sir Jasper's death wasn't due to natural causes, and that there was something seriously amiss. I asked the constable to describe Jasper's state and he explained that he'd appeared dead and was freezing cold – that was hardly a surprise as he'd been deposited in the morgue. Anyway, I didn't say much but as soon as the chap was shown out, I told Hackett I'd best go and look in the Chamber of Curiosities. It didn't take long to discover the jar of Yopo had been emptied.' He took another sip of eggnog, adroitly manoeuvring the glass with his shrivelled forefinger and thumb. 'I'd guessed it must be that. We have an extensive collection of botanical samples, including poisonous ones, but most need to be injected and he wasn't reported as having any injury or needle marks. Poisons causing paralysis, such as curare, are harmless if ingested.'

'Isn't curare taken from frogs?'

He smiled at that. 'No, curare is made from a mixture of different plants, the poison frogs you're thinking of secrete toxins. The effect is much the same if the quantity is sufficient; the muscles relax to cause an effective paralysis, which causes the diaphragm to cease functioning and death through asphyxiation follows. Yopo is far kinder; it's psychotropic and isn't necessarily fatal.'

'Do you think the intention was to kill or merely stupefy?' I asked, turning the information over in my mind.

'I've been trying to determine that myself. I even wondered if he'd tried inhaling it as an experiment or some such. But I don't believe he had, the jar was washed clean, and I mean really clean – someone had used carbolic on it. I smelled it the moment I picked it up. Even the cork lid had been wiped. It seemed too deliberate, too well-thought-out for Sir Jasper. He was an impatient man, and a very rich one; I doubt he'd ever cleaned anything in his life.'

'Is the carbolic kept in the Chamber of Curiosities?' I sipped my eggnog slowly to savour the taste. Greggs was still in conversation with the ladies and not serving drinks at all.

'Yes, under the sink. Not the first place most of the residents would think to look. None of them are the practical sort.' He tipped his head back and emptied his glass. 'I truly believe someone was up to no good.'

'And you found the residue of Yopo in the ash of Sir Jasper's fire,' I added, watching him from the corner of my eye.

He nodded. 'Yes.'

'Why are poisons kept in this house?'

He shrugged. 'They're just specimens, and regarded as Curiosities. Temple House is a very private place. There's no reason to suppose they'd be put to any misuse.'

'How would anyone here know about Yopo?' I asked the obvious.

'Ah, well that would be my fault,' he said gravely. 'Unintentionally, of course – I give lectures every so often about my expeditions, and what we discovered. I'm actually a botanist, you see. They've merely given me the sobriquet of the Explorer. I was the leader of a team dedicated to finding and collecting plants believed to have medicinal properties.' The grin returned. 'It was quite dangerous at times, there were any number of local tribes who didn't take at all kindly to us traipsing through their territories. We got pretty fed up of being attacked, and eventually discovered they were far more friendly if we handed out clay pipes. Extraordinary.' He shook his head. 'They just couldn't get enough.'

That surprised me. 'I'd have thought they'd want knives.'

'The blades rust with alarming speed in the jungle. I've heard there's a new stainless steel around now, but I haven't seen it. Besides, the tribes make their own stone arrowheads, they don't depend on our technology.'

'What else have you covered in your lectures?'

Greggs had finally dragged himself away from the ladies and meandered towards us with the jug of eggnog. I drained my glass and held it up. He paused at the white-bearded chap by the fire who had been joined by Lord Balthazar Cholmondeley and they were in deep discussion about something or other. Greggs was just about to turn in our direction when Swift arrived.

'I'll have one, please, Greggs,' he called in amenable manner then strolled over with a smile softening his sharp features.

'Florence and Angus are having a marvellous time. Angus is obsessed with trains; he saw a model set in a toy shop, you know the sort, cottages, snow, steam trailing from the funnel.' His smile widened. 'We've arranged for Santa to bring a set for Christmas. I can't wait to see his face.'

'Excellent,' I remarked, and returned the grin. I remembered my first train set and the endless hours my father and I had spent playing with it.

'Swift, this is Wilfred Rackham.'

They introduced themselves and Swift sat down as Rackham began another explanation of his botany credentials. Greggs had gone to fetch a glass for Swift and brought it with the jug. He made a fuss of serving, then poured the remnants into my glass.

'The best is at the bottom, sir,' he told me sotto voce.

I took a sip. He was right, it was utter heaven. 'Well done, old chap.'

'Thank you, sir.' He chortled then went off for another jugful.

'That was in the Orinoco,' Rackham was telling Swift when I turned my attention back to the conversation. 'Simply seeking medicinal plants didn't sound quite as exciting to the press, hence the puff about us being explorers, although our patrons were only paying for us to find plants. They didn't care what we were called.'

'Who were these patrons?' I asked.

'There was a group of them,' Rackham replied, suddenly serious.

'Anyone from here?' Swift's eyes narrowed as he watched him.

The damaged side of his face lost some colour. He nodded, his lips turning down. 'General Hackett and Sir Jasper were majority investors. Baroness Ginny Finch, she's the lady in the mustard dress, and Pastor Peabody, he's the chap with the white beard sitting by the fire.'

'Santa Claus,' I muttered as we all glanced at him.

'Not quite,' Rackham said. 'But a kindly soul nonetheless.'

'Were they a consortium, or shareholders in a limited stock company?' Swift felt in his pocket for his notebook. I frowned at him and he let his hand drop.

'A consortium.' Rackham lowered his voice though I

doubt we could be overheard. 'Medicine is big business, as you must realise. Nature holds all manner of secrets locked in her bosom. If we can discover a few decent phyto-medicines, there's potential for tremendous benefit to mankind.'

'And very profitable,' Swift added.

'Everyone prospers.' Rackham raised his chin. 'Look, these discoveries come with huge risks, they're speculative, and you can't expect charities to fund them, or hospitals. They could lose a fortune and their patients would suffer.'

'Are you saying that an Order such as this,' I waved a hand to indicate Temple House, 'would not invest in one of your expeditions?'

'Precisely,' Rackham confirmed. 'The Saints donate to good causes, not hazardous undertakings, however high-minded their intentions may be.'

Swift wasn't entirely happy with that. His socialist tendencies cleaved toward good intentions heedless of cost. A distinct defect in every socialist's ideology.

'What happened to your team, and your leg?' I switched tack to the far more interesting topic.

'Ah…' he began, and then young Jiggens came in with a gong and banged it three times with a bonger.

'Lords, Ladies and Gentlemen. Would everyone like to make their way to the dining room, please. Dinner is served.'

CHAPTER 6

Damn, I'd been looking forward to hearing Rackham's tales of derring deeds and disaster. I knocked back my drink, which improved with every drop, and followed the shuffling crowd.

'I've claimed you! There's no escaping now.' The lady in green, with the unlikely black ringlets, slipped an arm under mine and clung on.

'As it would seem,' I replied with as much enthusiasm as I could muster. 'You wouldn't be Miss Olivia Arbuthnot, by chance?'

'My reputation betrays me!' She laughed gaily. 'Yes, 'tis I, and by no other shall I be known,' she added with a flare of drama, then turned a tad more serious. 'I don't always attach myself to young men, but I understand you are here to delve into Jasper's death.' She raised a quizzical brow.

'Major Lennox, and yes I am. I'm with him. He's a real detective.' I nodded towards Swift who had been hijacked by both the other ladies. He was looking resigned as they chattered to him, one in each ear.

We were making our way along the wide passage towards the front of the house.

'Well, it's jolly nice to have two handsome young men about the place,' Miss Olivia Arbuthnot continued, undeterred. 'Perhaps a few more of the obsolete excess needs to be bumped off, then we would have no end of gallants to admire.'

'But then you'd probably end up with Scotland Yard's finest and there aren't many gallants among them,' I replied lightly. 'You believe Sir Jasper was bumped off?'

'Of course he was. You wouldn't be here otherwise, and besides, there was nothing wrong with him.'

'We're here to ascertain the facts.' I tried a policeman's intonation. 'It's possible his death was an accident.'

She laughed at that.

We entered the dining room; I almost stopped on the threshold. It was one of the most agreeable rooms I think I'd ever been in.

A candlelit chandelier hung over a long table set with damask linen, silver cutlery, crystal goblets and gold-rimmed china. Red candles were set in antique candelabra along the centre of the table, each surrounded by a circlet of glossy green holly with red berries. The gleaming chestnut panelling reflected a myriad burning candles and glowing flames from the fire blazing in a magnificent carved fireplace. There was even another Christmas tree in the corner; smaller but decorated just as prettily as the one in the hall.

'Come on, there's an extra place set for you,' Olivia

Arbuthnot insisted. 'It's next to me. I told young Jiggens to arrange it.'

'Miss Arbuthnot…' I tried to protest.

'Call me Olivia.' She was almost pulling me along. 'Here you are. Sit!'

I helped her be seated first, as was the custom, then waited as the white-bearded chap, Pastor Peabody, shuffled past to take the seat at the tail end, which was the other side of me.

Foggy suddenly dashed in and came bounding over, woofing with delight, and jumped up at the side of my chair.

'Ah, a dog!' Pastor Peabody exclaimed, his eyes lighting up. 'Good dog.' He extended a gnarled hand, trying to stroke Fogg's head but the dog was far too excited.

'Sit,' I told him firmly.

He did nothing of the sort. Olivia started cooing over him, as did most of the others in the room, and he raced about in excitement before finally returning to sit by me with his tongue hanging out.

'He's called Mr Fogg,' Lord Balthazar said loudly.

'Are you acquainted?' Baroness Finch in the mustard-coloured frock asked in a soft voice.

'I am, and we shared shortbread. He belongs to… erm…' Balthazar stuttered to a halt and raised a finger to point at me.

'Major Lennox,' I reminded him.

Various murmurings rumbled about the room.

'I'm Jonathan Swift, and we're very pleased to meet you all,' Swift said formally.

'The writer?' Pastor Peabody asked.

'No, I'm–' Swift began.

'Gulliver's Travels!' another man spoke up, a chap with a weathered face and a ready smile. 'Exceptional book. First-class poetry too. Here's a good one for Jasper: Threescore, I think, is pretty high; 'Twas time in conscience he should die! This world he cumber'd long enough; He burnt his candle to the snuff; And that's the reason, some folks think. He left behind so great a stink.'

'He's a detective, silly.' Lady Matilda waved her lorgnette at the weathered chap. 'The writer died centuries ago.'

'I am quite aware, dear lady,' he replied with a twinkle in his eye. 'I may have washed up on the shore, but my brains are still attached.'

'Detective?' Balthazar looked shocked. 'Are you really?'

'Didn't you say you took tea with them?' Pastor Peabody asked.

'Yes, but nobody mentioned detectives.' Balthazar blinked at us. 'And the dog?'

'Trained bloodhound,' I said and spread my napkin across my lap.

'Lennox.' Swift frowned.

'You jest, Major!' The weathered chap laughed. 'I'm Captain Philip Lockhart, ancient mariner at your service.'

'Marinaded more like,' Olivia Arbuthnot remarked.

I gave the chap an informal salute across the table. Dressed in navy blazer, red cravat with a crisp white shirt, thick silver hair and deep lines carved into a mature, handsome face.

'I'm Santa Claus,' Pastor Peabody said, then chortled. 'Better known as Pastor Peabody.' He held out a wizened hand to shake mine. 'They just call me Pastor. You can too, if you wish.'

'Thank you, Pastor. I answer to Lennox.'

'Now hush everybody.' Lady Matilda banged a spoon on the table. 'The game is afoot – if I recall my Holmes correctly. These detectives are here because there is a madman in our midst. A murderer no less! Who is it, I say?' she demanded, then raised her lorgnette to the end of her nose. 'Reveal thyself, infernal thief of souls!'

'She's always been keen on amateur dramatics,' Olivia said to me, a ringlet falling over her shoulder.

'What's all this? What do you mean "thief of souls"?' General Hackett stalked in, dressed as before in buttoned-up black. It hadn't occurred to me that we should change for dinner as it was so early, fortunately no-one else wore formal rig either, although the ladies were in colourful style.

'The murderer, Regent, who else?' Lady Matilda expounded.

'Gentlemen,' Hackett barked, meaning Swift and I obviously. 'Is this your idea of acting with discretion?'

'Oh, do sit down, Gregory,' Olivia told him. 'They have been discreet. The Major told me they were merely ascertaining the facts. Everyone's embellished the tittle-tattle, and why not? It's the most excitement we've had in years.'

'Is it true? Poor Jasper's life was taken from him?' Baroness Finch asked, her pale blue eyes rounded. She was short and round with fine wrinkles etching plump cheeks, her thick white hair in a cottage loaf bun.

'Now my dear Ginny,' Captain Lockhart was sitting next to her and put his hand over hers, 'this is exaggerated nonsense. Old Jasper just keeled over of his own accord and these chaps were sent to satisfy the pettifogging authorities. Matilda has been dramatising events as usual, haven't you old girl?' Lockhart gave her a gimlet eye.

'Possibly.' Lady Matilda lifted her chin. 'If that is the *official* line.'

'It is, thank you,' General Hackett growled. 'And we'll have no more talk of murder.'

Balthazar Cholmondeley looked utterly baffled.

Greggs and young Jiggens entered bearing laden silver platters which they placed on the long refectory table next to the fire. After some muttered debate, they began to serve in unison.

'Cream of leek and potato soup,' Jiggens announced.

'Garnished with chopped bacon and chives,' Greggs added. 'Accompanied by hot Turkish rolls.'

'Oh, how accomplished.' Lady Matilda played the coquette as Greggs whipped the napkin from her place setting and let it fall across her lap. It took deft skill to do it properly – he was just showing off.

'You can do mine too, if you want,' an effeminate voice from the top of the table called out. A man with wavy blond hair, sporting a blue cravat and fancy embroidered waistcoat under a cream wool jacket, sat up in his chair, hope on his primped face.

'Roger, you do not need help!' the man seated opposite answered in a high voice. 'You can do it perfectly well yourself.' He leaned over, grabbed the napkin from in front of the blond chap and tossed it at him.

'Norman! There is no need for such boorish behaviour,' Roger hissed back. 'You jealous little cat.'

'Enough,' General Hackett rapped. 'Be quiet for grace.' He bowed his head. Most of the Saints did the same. 'May the Lord bless this food for the nourishment of our bodies and minds. May we be granted humility and compassion in all our endeavours. Amen.'

'Amen.' The word rippled around the table.

'Now we may begin,' Hackett said and picked up his spoon.

The soup was superb, thick and creamy with salty cubes of fried bacon. The Turkish rolls were soft and airy in a buttery crust sprinkled with seeds. I hadn't had Turkish rolls before but they were as first-rate as everything else.

Jiggens came round with a Chateau La Tour Blanche. This too was excellent; if nothing else we would be jolly well catered for while we were stuck here.

'Major Lennox,' Hackett barked. 'Your uncle is Lord Charles Melrose. You're his heir.'

I was inclined to say I knew but decided against.

'Ah, yes, the name...Lennox.' Captain Lockhart turned to me. 'That's the old Melrose family line. I knew Sir Hugh Lennox. Met him in Burma; he was in charge of the Army Artillery. I was a lieutenant on the man-o-war, The Woodlark. We ferried him and his regiment up the

Irrawaddy to Mandalay. There was a bit of a ding-dong, then we were all dispatched to Rangoon. He was a good man, he knew what he was about. Invalided out I heard, then married an heiress.'

'Yes,' I agreed. 'He was my father, and injured by cannon fire.'

'So you're an heir?' Olivia Arbuthnot eyed me speculatively.

'I'm married, and there's no money left and we're…' I began to babble, then shut up. Babbling was a bad habit when nervous, particularly around women, although that had improved since I'd married.

'I have heard of you, you are Sir Heathcliff Lennox.' Baroness Ginny Finch spoke up. 'A pilot during that awful war. I read about it in the newspaper, they said you were a hero.' She suddenly beamed, her round cheeks crinkling into dimples. 'So like my boy. Marvellous boys, all of you. And a lovely name – Heathcliff.'

I particularly disliked my name. I've no idea why people insisted on going on about it.

'Heathcliff? Well, how romantic.' Lady Matilda arched her thin brows. 'I am organising the Christmas repertoire and you are just perfect for a leading role.'

'What?' Roger put his soup spoon down with a bang in his dish. 'But I am the lead. I am always the lead,' he objected in a high voice.

'We're here in an official capacity,' Swift cut in. 'We are not playacting.'

'It's mostly singing,' Olivia said.

'I can't sing,' I said. 'Greggs is a leading light in the local Gilbert and Sullivan group.' I offered him up in sacrifice.

'Oh, he's just what we need.' Roger gave Greggs a glad eye. 'And what a fine figure! I'd say he would be perfect in any role.'

Greggs stopped in his tracks, bottle of wine in hand. '*Ahem*…in what manner, sir?'

'It's a seasonal medley of light-hearted entertainment.' Lady Matilda had finished her soup and lifted the lorgnette once more. 'Are you game, Mr Greggs?'

'I…I…' he stuttered, then bowed. 'Indeed, m'lady, it would be an honour, and I am a noted tenor in certain circles.'

'If it is the nativity,' Lord Balthazar quibbled, 'I don't think there were any ladies in the stable, except Mary, and she was a virg– Oh!' He put his hand to his lips. 'I do apologise, ladies.'

'Don't worry, Balthazar, we are women of the world,' Baroness Ginny said kindly.

'It's singing, just as it is every year,' Roger told him. 'Christmas carols and a few modern songs.'

'I'm going to sing "I'm Just Wild about Harry!"' Norman started singing in a fine baritone. 'I'm just wild about Harry, and Harry's wild about me. The heav'nly blisses of his kisses, fill me with ecstasy. He's sweet just like choc'late candy–'

'Norman, stop that!' Roger scowled at him. 'It's going to be "Jingle bells".'

'Oh, don't be tedious, Roger. We should do something

completely fresh this year. We all need someone fresh every so often to liven things up,' Norman replied, a gleam of mischief in his dark eyes. I realised his thick head of brown hair wasn't all his own. In fact I doubted any of it was.

Olivia laughed delightedly, while Roger flushed and launched a minor tirade.

Hackett banged his spoon on the table again. 'Enough. We shall have the repertoire then a gramophone and dancing.'

'Dancing! Oh what fun!' Olivia clapped her hands.

'Are you inviting Cicely?' Lady Matilda directed that at Hackett.

A faint flush rose to his cheeks. 'Why would she not be invited?'

'Dancing?' Balthazar repeated as though the idea had just sunk in.

'What sort of dancing?' Pastor Peabody asked.

That began a long and quite amusing digression between the inmates. I listened with half an ear as I polished off the next course; it was prime lamb in mint butter with mash, gravy, greens and carrots. Utterly sublime. Pudding was even better; treacle sponge and custard. I must admit, it improved my mood and I actually considered entering into the hubbub of chatter around the table.

Fortunately the Regent announced a digestif would be served in the games room and they all rose to troop out. I waited till the coast was clear, picked up my dog and headed for the snow-covered grounds to breathe in some fresh air and clear my mind.

I found Tubbs on the way, or rather he found me, and bounded up as though we'd been parted for weeks. He was closely followed by the two other cats: Nox and Furz. It was quite a sight, the three of them gambolling along the red carpeted corridor together.

They tumbled outside in a flurry of black fur, despite the cold. Large flakes were still falling and the snow was already above my calves and deepening by the hour. I'd stopped to pick up my hat and coat from the boot room, but pulled my collar up around my neck all the same.

The animals ran about as though they'd never seen snow before. I spotted a trodden path trekking along the front of the mansion, and followed it.

Slits of yellow light escaped between drawn curtains. I glanced up at the house, not having had time to take it in on our arrival.

It rose two tall storeys with attics under the eaves, the windows iron-framed with diamond panes held between lead muntins. Huge upright timbers formed the structure, supported by cross beams in corners and bracing spanning the centre. Creamy white plaster filled areas between the black timbers. It was typically Tudor, redolent of the great age of seafaring; a time when mighty oaks were felled to build majestic galleons to fight whatever invaders were threatening our small island at the time.

The trail led around the side of the house, the animals strung out in a line behind me. Light shone from lanterns hanging from the eaves to throw glowing halos across the blanketing snow. The grounds were more extensive than

I'd thought. Trees, shrubs and a number of graceful statues stood shrouded in white. It was beautiful, and silent and so very, very peaceful.

Amber flames flickering somewhere in the distance drew my attention. Wilfred Rackham had been out lighting candles in the graveyard, according to Jiggens. I could make out gravestones as I approached, some humped and squat, others simple crosses and one or two tombs were topped with angels in solemn prayer. A pretty chapel stood further away in the distance, a single lamp burning above its dark door.

Three gravestones bore glass bowls at their base; the snow had melted in hollow basins around each. Stubby white candles were lit within, all of them guttering at the wick.

I stopped at the first gravestone to brush fresh flakes from grey granite.

Benjamin Mortimer Hackett, 1880 - 1914. Brave, steadfast and true. His courage knew no bounds.

The next read, 1882 - 1914 Peter Michael Finch. A loving soul, a man of worth. Too short a time upon this earth.

The last was, 1881 - 1914 John Henry Peabody. His name is written in letters of love on the hearts he left at home. Rest in peace in God's gracious love.

Hackett, Finch, Peabody; The Regent, the Baroness, and the Pastor. Rackham's consortium. And the only one to survive was Wilfred Rackham himself, the Explorer.

CHAPTER 7

I trudged back to the front door, dog and cats crowded about my feet, apart from Tubbs who had insisted on being carried.

'Lennox.' Swift stood up as I walked into the games room. I'd been inclined to go to bed and read a book but decided I should put on a show of support before turning in.

'Took Fogg out,' I gave by way of excuse.

All the pets had come in with me and were greeted with cooing and saved tidbits. Nobody gave me a second look.

'Can you play bridge?' Swift came over. He was obviously the dummy.

'No.'

There's chess, chequers, and mancala, which is an interesting game. I used to play it in South Africa. I've never seen it in England before.' He grinned. I realised he was actually enjoying himself.

'I can play fox and geese,' I said.

'Hum.' He didn't seem impressed by that. 'Try mancala, it's quite simple but needs clever tactics to win. It should appeal to you.'

He was suspiciously chirpy. 'Swift, is there something you're not telling me?'

A flicker of unease crossed his hawkish face and he suddenly became quite serious. 'It's something Billings wrote to me last week. Scotland Yard might want to put us on a retainer…I hadn't wanted to mention it until you'd stopped sulking.'

'I wasn't sulking,' I retorted.

He raised a cynical brow. 'It's just something to consider, that's all.'

'What sort of retainer?'

'A fixed amount each month. It wouldn't be a great deal, but it's a regular income.' He suddenly grinned. 'And we'd be on the Yard's books, Lennox. Officially!'

'Does that mean we'd have to drop everything and race off whenever they say so?'

'I doubt it will be very different from what we've already been doing.'

I gave him a wry eye. 'Then why are they prepared to pay us?'

'To recognise our competence and professionalism, and to give us some official capacity – only as consultants,' he added hastily. 'We're not going to be regulars or anything.'

I sighed. I knew what it would mean to him, but as much as I enjoyed hunting down murderers, I wasn't keen on being caught in an institutional web. Scotland Yard had strict rules: processes, chains of command – the same claustrophobic constraints I'd endured in the RAF. 'Let me think about it, Swift.'

'Persi thought it a good idea.'

'You mean you've discussed it without me?'

'Erm...it just came up in conversation...'

Greggs came over bearing a decanter of dark red wine. 'Lafite Rothschild, sir?'

'Very well,' I agreed. That lightened my brows but I was still rather confounded by the Yard's request, and Swift's explanation was exactly the sort of thing he'd want to hear...there was more to it.

'I will bring a glass, sir. Where will you be seated?' He looked about at the crowded tables.

'Pastor Peabody hasn't got a partner at the moment.' Swift nodded in the chap's direction. He was on a sofa by the fire, a wooden board game set out in front of him on the low table.

'Right.' I nodded. 'I'll ask him about his dead son.'

'What?' Swift asked.

'Cooeee,' Olivia Arbuthnot called out from a round table. 'Inspector, you're needed.' She waved a hand.

'Lennox...' Swift began.

'We'll talk later,' I said and headed toward the sofas by the fire.

'Ah, the detective!' Pastor Peabody brightened as I sat down. 'Mancala.'

'The game?'

He giggled. 'Indeed, and mancala is Arabic for count and capture. A most appropriate game for a man of your profession.'

He really was reminiscent of Santa Claus, even his voice

resonated with warmth and kindness. 'Swift's the professional, I merely tag along.'

'Ah, now I doubt that is true. A man like that would not suffer an amateur at his side.' His eyes twinkled behind his spectacles. 'We play for sixpence a game.' He waved a hand at the board. 'Cash.'

The image of Santa Claus suddenly vanished.

'But I've never played before,' I objected.

'Very well, thruppence for each of the first two rounds,' Peabody said in all seriousness.

Greggs placed a large glass of red at my elbow and a plate of cheesy roundels. 'I have change of a crown, sir, if required.'

'That won't be necessary, thank you, Greggs,' I told him.

The game was fairly simple, a board with six hollows scooped out on each long side with larger hollows at each end.

'The easier game,' Peabody explained, 'is played with three pebbles, but we prefer to play with four.' He dropped four colourful pebbles in each hollow on his side of the board.

I followed suit.

'Now, each player takes all the stones from one hollow and drops them one at a time in the subsequent hollows…' He went on to demonstrate.

There weren't many rules, it was in theory a simple game. He proceeded to thrash me.

I took another drink as we set up the fourth or fifth or whatever game we were on.

'Rackham led the team of explorers, I believe…' I spoke amiably, intent on catching him off-guard. That was one of Swift's tactics and it quite often worked.

Peabody's hand froze over the board. 'It wasn't his fault, they…they were caught in the open. The weather turned.' His voice wavered, then he gathered up his pebbles with a shaking hand.

'I'm sorry,' I said, feeling a heel for distressing the old fellow.

He played his round without speaking. 'My boy…he was all I had left…I came here afterwards. No point in retaining the estate with no-one to continue.' His mouth was barely visible beneath the white moustache and beard, but I noticed his lips tremble. His blue eyes dulled too. The pain of loss was still raw.

'He's buried in the grounds,' I said quietly.

He nodded. 'I was invited here, so were the other parents. Obviously we had to await a vacancy, but we were all acquainted…' He was staring unseeing at the game. 'Our boys went to university together, then after they'd graduated, they devised their exploration team. They had such high ideals, you see. We supported them by forming a consortium. It was to find herbal remedies, all they needed were the funds. They wanted to save lives. We never thought, not for a moment, that it would be truly dangerous. We didn't know what to do after they were lost… and then they were found.' He closed his eyes before continuing. 'I agreed to come here if my boy came too… his body I mean. The old Regent agreed, and so they were interred in the chapel grounds and we followed one by one. It has been a blessing.' He ended on a sniff.

'Who was the old Regent?' I moved some pebbles along the board. He didn't appear to notice.

'The late Lord Brentwood, he was a friend of Wilfred Rackham's father.' He looked up. 'Wilfred was believed to have died with the others. They were in Finland, they'd set up an expedition to search for a variety of reindeer lichen known to a native tribe. It is found in many northern regions, but there was talk of a variety growing in a forest in Lapland, one with specific properties…' He paused for a sip of wine, his hand shaking as he raised it to his lips.

'Would you like to call a halt?'

'No, no.' He put the glass down.

'What benefits did they think the lichen held?' I asked.

'An antidote to sepsis,' he replied gravely. 'They considered it worth the risk, although it was a little late in the year when they arrived in the country. The trail was difficult and hazardous, slowing them further.' He leaned contemplatively over the board.

I waited as he played his turn. He was hesitant and distracted, but continued talking. 'I believe it was further than anticipated, they became lost…' His voice petered out but he took a breath and continued. 'Well, they struggled on, they were determined young men, but a storm caught them. They were found by the merest chance. Wilfred was alive, although terribly afflicted.' He glanced briefly over to Rackham. He and General Hackett were playing bridge against Swift and Olivia Arbuthnot. They were all absorbed in the game, bent over their scorecards. 'The hunter took him back to his settlement. His tribe nursed him, but he was too badly injured for their limited skills and they eventually delivered him to civilisation.' He struggled with the explanation. 'They kept him in the hospital through the winter, doing what they could. They'd had to amputate his leg, the Finns' medicine was advanced and they were used to dealing with frostbite and that sort of injury. They pulled him through where others might not have been able to. Despite their advancements, they had no telephones or even telegraph. The weather destroys the lines, you see. We'd heard nothing, except that the team had failed to return to their base and were reported missing…naturally we feared the worst and so it was confirmed when the thaw came and a message could be sent to London.'

I took my turn and managed to capture some of his pebbles, although my focus was on the old man's story. 'Sir Jasper was part of the consortium with you and the parents.'

'He was.' His moustache and beard drooped. 'Jasper was an odd sort. He had supported the boys' efforts, possibly through altruism, although he always had a mind to profit. When he heard the team was lost, he withdrew his funding. Jasper was a speculative financier, you see, and he was very good at calculating risk. Well…Hackett was incensed. He had been organising a rescue party, we were all suffering and Jasper just seemed to be washing his hands of it.'

I frowned. It sounded a pitiless act. 'Had he withdrawn merely to save money?'

'No.' Peabody stared at the board then moved to capture a pile of pebbles I'd been building up. 'There was an article in *The Times* about a certain medical company using dogs as part of their tests. Jasper was deeply upset and swore to have no more to do with any of it. We understood his objections, he was very fond of animals, he preferred them to people. But we thought he should have maintained his support of us and the boys.'

'The remainder of your consortium were all very wealthy though,' I said. 'I can't imagine Jasper's withdrawal prevented setting up a rescue party.'

'No, it didn't. We had sufficient funds, of course, but it was thoughtless in the midst of our distress.' Peabody shook his head.

I dropped my remaining pebbles into their hollows. He took a turn and I lost again.

'I do hope you are better at detecting than you are at playing games, Major Lennox,' Peabody said mildly.

'So do I,' I said with a frown. 'I think I owe you three shillings and sixpence.'

'It's four shillings, actually,' he said.

Swift came over.

'Ah, is it time?' Peabody asked. 'Are you willing for the challenge?'

Swift grinned as he eyed the board. 'I am. Lennox, they rotate the games. I'll take over mancala, what do you want to play?'

'I'm turning in, Swift,' I said then stood up. 'Thank you Pastor Peabody.' I gave a nod of the head, called my little dog and left. Swift didn't try to stop me, although he looked rather rueful, but there was something niggling away in my mind.

The fire had died down in our room, or rather Jasper's old room. I tossed a couple of logs onto the burned remains, gave it a good poke to knock out the ash, then settled at the knee-hole desk with Foggy at my feet.

Persi had insisted I take a notebook with me. I admit I'd got out of the habit of taking notes during the last couple of investigations Swift and I had made. This was because he wrote more than enough notes for both of us – but my mind was churning with the names of all the people I'd just met.

I opened the blue leather bound journal and began with "Temple House, Bath" in large letters, and the date, *December 21st 1923. Winter Solstice.*

There were twelve Saints. I was already beginning to confuse the names of the women in my mind so I wrote *LADIES* at the top of the next page.

1. Lady Matilda Fettiscue. White hair, purple jewels, crepe frock, statuesque, lorgnette, high-handed manner. Given to Dramatics.
2. Miss Olivia Arbuthnot. Black hair (probably dyed), spinster, sharp, loud – but good fun.
3. Baroness Ginny Finch. Hair in bun, short and plump, grandmotherly. Part of the Consortium supporting the exploration team. Son, Peter Michael Finch.

I didn't really know much more about any of them. I turned a new page and wrote *MEN* at the top.

The Regent was the chap in charge, and I started with him.

1. General Gregory Hackett. Typical army type. Stiff-backed, buttoned-up, grey hair, fond of whisky. Consortium member. Son: explorer, Benjamin Hackett.
2. Pastor Peabody. Santa Claus in appearance, kindly, wizened, likes to win. Consortium member. Son: explorer, John Henry Peabody.
3. Lord Balthazar Cholmondeley. Known as the Duffer, woolly minded, genial enough. He'd opposed Jasper in their debate to donate funds to retired plough horses.
4. Captain Philip Lockhart. Navy, knew my father from Burma campaign. Good chap
5. Wilfred Rackham. The Explorer. Leader of a team of young men, all perished in Finland, bar him. Youngest of the Saints. Badly injured, presumed non productive, losing sight.
6. Roger…colourful.
7. Norman…also colourful.

I couldn't think of anything more to add about them, or not that I wanted to write down anyway.

I turned to a new page. I was doing rather well, I thought, it made me feel quite the professional.

Victim: Sir Jasper Crawford, known as the Miser. Very keen on animals, and the ladies, though he admired from afar. Pulled out of the Consortium because he thought animals were used in medical trials and the explorers were searching for medicinal plants (was that really true, or had he fabricated the excuse?) Discovered his private journal in locked box. He loved his nanny, and hoped Miss Cicely Sissinghurst would soon be joining the Saints. Believed to have inhaled an overdose of Yopo, a psychotropic which causes coma-type sleep. Found with the book A Christmas Carol open on his lap. The killer must have returned after tossing the Yopo on the fire and left the book there. Jasper died later in the morgue of hypothermia.

Then I sat with ink drying on the nib. What had been niggling me?

I ran my eye back over the names. I counted them, then did it again. There were only eleven – that was it! So who was missing?

'Ah, sir.' Greggs came in. 'I did wonder if you may be here. *Ahem.*' He cleared his throat. 'Your absence was noticed among the Saints, sir. The Regent remarked upon it.'

'I told Swift I was going upstairs. Actually I've been working.' I turned to face him. 'There's someone missing, Greggs. Who is Saint number twelve?'

He frowned, brows drawn together. 'Erm…' He began counting on his fingers, mumbling under his breath. 'I'm afraid I do not know, sir.'

'Go and find out, would you?'

He sighed, making his chin wobble. 'Very well, sir.'

'Oh, Greggs.' I stayed him a moment. 'What happened to the middle Jiggens?'

'The war happened, sir. He lost his life at Mons.'

'Ah, thought that might have been it. Thank you, old chap.'

He bowed and left.

CHAPTER 8

The door banged open some time later, waking Fogg and making him bark. I looked up from *A Christmas Carol* which I'd settled to read by the fire.

'Hah! So, you are Nemesis!'

'Actually, I'm Major Lennox,' I replied.

'You know what I mean,' the man growled, then moderated his tone. 'Is that his claret?'

'Yes, it's jolly good.' I had the decanter at my elbow, having been topping up my glass as I turned the pages.

'*Hmph*,' he muttered, then came over to plonk down in the chair opposite. He was a large man of considerable width and height. Six foot at least and would have made a fine rugby prop in his youth. He wore an old-fashioned nightgown under a thick red dressing gown, and a white cotton cap, complete with long tassel, upon his head. I assumed him to be the twelfth Saint.

I let him pour his own glass of claret.

'Justice St John,' he announced and took a long draught. 'They call me the Judge.'

Thick grey hair, neatly trimmed beard and brows, bright

blue eyes, ruddy cheeks, a drinker's nose and a mouth twitching with a smile, which he seemed to be trying to suppress.

'Greetings, Your Honour.' I raised my glass.

He did the same. 'Nice dog. Yours?'

'Yes, he's called Mr Fogg.'

St John bent to pat the dog's head. 'You think Jasper was murdered?'

'It sounds plausible,' I remarked, thinking he must have known better than I.

'We want no cause to make a stir.' He leaned back and ruminated, glass cradled in a large hand. 'Play cricket?'

'Used to play for Oxford.'

'Ah.' The topic turned to games and players and we spent half an hour in pleasant chat. I realised he was taking the measure of me, which was no great surprise if he were a Judge.

'Jasper's death.' He swung abruptly back to the subject. 'What are you doing about it?' His voice had a rumble to it, like thunder on a distant horizon.

'Investigating,' I replied, refusing to be intimidated.

'Now look, Major.' He slammed a hand onto the armchair. 'This could undermine the Order, even destroy it. There's something rotten here. You must extract it, and quickly! Accusations could be aimed that Saints are hastened to their grave to expropriate their funds. How do you think that will play? We are under scrutiny of the Monarch and his most trusted counsellors. What do you say? Eh?' He leaned forward, a thick finger pointing.

'Had Sir Jasper threatened to withdraw from the Order?' I made a guess.

He froze for a moment then leaned forward, anger in his eyes. 'So they told you about that, did they?'

'No, I deduced it,' I replied. 'Was it because of the plough horses?'

'You know about that too, *humph*,' he snorted.

'And he changed his mind when he heard Miss Cicely Sissinghurst had been nominated as a Saint-in-Waiting?' I watched him, his expression changing but unreadable.

'She lost her nephew and heir at Belvedere. Nasty business. Miss Sissinghurst has been our Keeper of the Books since the war ended. Very able administrator.'

'Her nephew was Jack Dutton,' I replied. 'Swift and I investigated his death.'

'I know, she told me.' He nodded. The tassel on his nightcap swung about his left ear. His conversation ricochetted around in erratic fashion.

'Was she nominated with the intention of encouraging Sir Jasper to remain here?'

'No.' His denial was too quick. 'The circumstances were merely propitious. We were all agreed she is the perfect candidate. Trusted, hard-working, a good woman,' he rumbled, a gleam in his eye that hadn't been evident before.

'Sir Jasper appeared to have had little regard for Lord Balthazar.' I switched tack.

'Why should he, the man's an idiot.' He drained his drink, then eyed me again. 'But he's no killer. Don't think old Balthazar would do anyone mischief. He's a muddled fool, but a harmless one.' He put the glass down on the table at his elbow. 'Now, I'm off to bed. This was my day of fast, I have not eaten. Damned quack says I need to lose weight. Ha, it's Christmas, I'm going to spurn the regime now until twelfth night.' He stomped off towards the door.

It opened just as he reached for the handle. Swift entered.

'Lennox, I–' He almost walked into the Judge. 'Sir… I…I…Your Honour.' He stopped in his tracks.

'Policeman, are you?' Justice St John bent to peer at him. 'Attended my court, I suppose?'

'Yes, Your Honour, a…a murder…' Swift was almost babbling. 'I had no idea you were…'

'Retired. Well, I am and here you find me. You'd better catch this blighter, and be damned quick about it.'

'Yes, Your Honour…erm…I mean, my Lord, we…' Swift was left talking to the door as St John stalked out and slammed it behind him.

'He was taking a day of fast,' I said by way of explanation.

'What?' Swift came to drop into the seat the Judge had just vacated.

'He was fasting, it was the reason he wasn't at dinner.'

'Justice St John was one of the most highly respected judges to sit in the Old Bailey. I had no idea he'd retired.'

'Well, he has, and he's going to be breathing down our necks all the time we're here.'

'Oh, hell,' Swift said and slumped back in his seat.

I poured him what was left of the claret and told him what St John had said, and about the consortium, the tragic fate of the expedition to Finland, and the graves outside. 'There's a chapel as well,' I added.

He'd taken out his notebook and was writing quickly as I spoke.

I reached to put another log on the fire. 'What did you learn?'

'Erm…' He glanced up. 'Well, we were playing bridge and it's quite intensive, you know.'

I raised a brow. He looked a little sheepish.

Greggs arrived with all three black cats. The cats jumped onto my bed in a game of rough and tumble. Tubbs was easier to pick out when they were all together. His stubby legs and fat tum made him a roly poly next to the sleek perfection of the other two.

'Ah, sir,' Greggs began. 'I imagine you have encountered Lord Justice St John? I was erm, introduced, and he announced he would come and discuss matters with you. I couldn't stop him, sir. He expressly said he wanted to talk far from the tittle-tattlers.' He sounded quite sober, but there was a rosy glow to his cheeks and he was swaying slightly.

'You've been making merry, Greggs.'

He simpered, twiddling fingers together over his paunch. 'The ladies wanted to arrange their Christmas recitation and we rehearsed one or two songs in the games room, sir. We were very well received.'

'You do know there's a murderer in the house?' I reminded him.

'*Ahem.*' He straightened up. 'Indeed, sir, and I am maintaining eyes and ears at all times.'

'Your rendition of "O Holy Night" was very well done, Greggs,' Swift said to him.

'Thank you, sir.' He puffed out his chest. 'And your duet with Miss Olivia Arbuthnot was excellent.'

'What?'

'It was only one song,' Swift replied.

'Just marvellous,' I muttered under my breath.

* * *

I slept squished among cats and dog. Apparently the cats had always slept with Sir Jasper, the only beings in the house he had affection for, besides his admiration of the ladies, of course.

It was still dark when I awoke to all three cats sitting on my chest, staring at me. It's amazing how heavy a cat can be when it wants to. I was trying to reach for my dressing gown when young Jiggens put his head around the door. He was holding his hand around a candle, trying to dim its light.

'Sir,' he whispered. 'Sir Jasper always let the cats out at six. Then they come down to the kitchen for breakfast.'

'Fine, take them with you,' I whispered. They dashed out of the door before I'd even finished the sentence.

Swift was still asleep, and Greggs was snoring in the room next door. I decided on some quiet ablutions in the bathroom across the corridor before either woke.

A simple night light was burning on the top shelf of a low bookcase in the corridor and I picked it up en-route.

The bathroom was freezing; it had a hearth but the kindling was unlit. It was probably too early for anyone to have started the fires yet.

I found a match and put it to the screws of newspaper under the sticks. Jasper would have used this bathroom, it was the closest. I rummaged about in the cabinet but it only contained talc, foot powder, scented hair oil and that sort of thing.

Dressed and shaved some time later, I retrieved Fogg from the bedroom. The others were still asleep so I headed for the great outdoors with my dog at my heels. Apart from a ticking grandfather clock the place was silent as the grave.

A haze of icy mist hovered over the snow-layered grounds. Frozen crystals sparkled in the light of my torch as I waited on the doorstep for Foggy to snuffle about in the snow. Despite the cold he seemed to be in no hurry. After a circuit around the pristine white lawn, he came back to me with balls of ice fringing the end of his long spaniel ears. I took him to the boot room, rubbed him down with the blanket I'd brought for the very purpose, then followed my nose in search of my favourite meal of the day.

'Swift?'

He was already seated in the breakfast room looking spruce and alert.

'I've ordered tea and whatever they've got,' he replied, seeming to be perfectly at home.

I took a seat opposite; the chairs were comfortably padded in cosy chintz, the room papered in lemon and white. The fire was lit and woodsmoke mingled with the scents of fresh-baked bread and fried bacon. Yellow curtains had been drawn back and the first rays of dawn could be seen beyond frosted panes.

General Hackett marched in, spotted us and stopped. 'My room, nine o'clock sharp.'

'Right–' I replied, intending to continue, but he turned on his heel and marched out again. He was wearing black canvas shoes without socks, which I thought odd.

'They're all bonkers, you know.' Swift sipped his tea.

'The word is *eccentric*.' I poured my own tea as no-one else was around to do it.

'If they're toffs.'

I glanced at him above my cup. He seemed in a genial mood, no socialist sneer on his lips. 'They're going to die for a good cause.'

He grinned at that. 'Having lived out their days in luxurious comfort. I heard them discussing the Christmas donations. Seems they're considering setting up a permanent home for retired plough horses in Jasper's honour.'

That made me smile. 'At least the chap received his wish, even if it was his last one.'

'Hum,' Swift agreed. 'They're having a meeting later, which Miss Cicely Sissinghurst will be attending.'

'Now, sirs, I've included everything.' Young Jiggens came in with two covered plates lightly steaming. 'Here you are, one each.' He raised the lids with a touch of drama to reveal all the very best an English kitchen could provide. Devilled kidneys, black pudding, thick pork sausages, bacon, eggs, and mushrooms, all cooked to perfection. 'And here's my Auntie Essie with the fried bread.'

A lady had followed him in holding a silver rack on a platter.

''Ello,' she said shyly. 'I'm Essie. Bread's been fried in best beef drippin' and a bit o' butter.' She put the rack in front of us, then bobbed a curtsey. 'And if you be wantin' sumthin' more, I'll be right pleased to be fetchin' it for ye.' A Somerset accent. Essie was short, rather too thin, a face lined and wrinkled, but with the kindest, sweetest smile I think I'd ever encountered. Her long navy dress was covered by a white apron reaching her ankles – and a white cap on grey curls.

We both greeted her and thanked her politely. That made her giggle for some reason and she went out with her hand to her mouth and brown eyes twinkling.

'She's very shy,' Jiggens explained as he poured us another cup of tea each. 'But always willing and a hard worker. She looks after the ladies mostly.'

'I'm sorry about your father, Jiggens,' I said.

His young face fell. 'One among too many, sir, but he was always keen to do his duty.' He went off, empty teapot in hand.

We ate in silence for a while, sharing tidbits with Foggy. The cats came in and sat in a row beside the dog, waiting for slivers of bacon and sliced sausage.

'We'll go and look at the Chamber of Curiosities,' Swift said as he cleared his plate and put his knife and fork down neatly. 'That's where the Yopo came from.'

'Hum,' I mumbled.

'The consortium seems the most obvious motive for Sir Jasper's murder,' he continued.

'Why now, though?'

He raised his brows and smiled. 'That's the question, isn't it!'

He was enjoying himself among the Saints. I suppose it appealed to his socialist conscience, the accumulated wealth of the old aristocracy being dispersed to the sick and deserving. I admit, I rather liked the disparate group of eccentrics too.

We left the room and made our way quietly upstairs, aware that most of the rest of the house was still sleeping.

'It must be up here somewhere.' We'd arrived at the very top floor to find ourselves in a large square area formed around heavy bannister rails guarding the stairs.

Like most attics, it looked older than the rest of the house because such places were rarely renovated. Old panelled walls, dull with age and lack of polish, surrounded us. Simple plank doors were apparent in the panelling. The boards creaked beneath our feet as we opened one door after another. We found disused storage rooms and redundant servants' quarters. These still held old truckle beds divided by canvas sheeting hung from beams between each servant's "room".

'Mediaeval,' I said.

'In more ways than one,' Swift muttered.

'Ah,' I said, as we walked through the door at the very end marked: 'The Chamber of Curiosities'.

CHAPTER 9

The Chamber of Curiosities took up the whole section above the west end of the mansion. Black rafters with rough lime plaster between each formed the ceiling. A long row of windows let in the pink light of a rising dawn. The walls held glass-fronted cabinets filled with many wonders. In the centre, a desk designed in the shape of a pentagon, with space enough for three or more people to work comfortably in the middle.

'This is a form of catalogue.' Swift had gone to the desk to peer at the pages of a huge black bound book, almost two feet in width and longer in length. 'It lists medicinal herbs and poisons, as well as other items.' He turned thick pages slowly as he leaned over it. 'Including the contributor and where it came from.'

'Dodo.' I read the label of the stuffed bird I'd paused to gaze at in one of the cabinets. '1667, Port de Warwick, Mauritius Island. Donated by Bishop Beaune (Regent).' It had the look of an overgrown pigeon, with grey down and a stumpy bunch of tan feathers on its tail. It looked the sort of bird to make an excellent roast. It was a shame they were extinct.

'Why do they have so many deadly samples?' Swift was still turning pages of the catalogue.

'It's a question of dose, isn't it?' I replied. 'They won't all be deadly unless someone takes too much.'

'I suppose so, but a lot of these are dangerous at any dose.' I stared at a gruesome mask from New Guinea, and decided not to ever go there…or anywhere excessively exotic.

'Here's the items from the Amazon basin.' Swift was still poring over the ledger. 'Donations made by the expedition led by Wilfred Rackham. There are also items from Benjamin Hackett.'

'General Hackett's son, although the General wouldn't have been here whilst his son lived.'

'No, but they obviously had close connections to the place.' Swift continued reading. 'Underneath is written "Sponsor: Sir Jasper Crawford". Olivia told me last night that he'd been a resident since 1916.'

'So you did actually learn something while you were playing cards,' I needled him.

'Bridge is an intellectual challenge,' he huffed. 'And there's an extremely high level of skill amongst the Saints.'

'So they're clever then,' I remarked.

'And devious,' he replied, running his finger down the page. 'This is listed for Yopo. A dried mix of leaves and seeds from the tree Anadenanthera Peregrina, donated by Wilfred Rackham.'

'Hmm…' I stared at a fossilised dinosaur egg. Tiny embryonic bones could be clearly made in the exposed interior.

There were a great many fossils including the skull of something called a Timurlengia. It was the size of a horse's head, but with a huge jaw full of long sharp teeth. Someone had written on the label, *Here be dragons.* These kinds of finds had probably led to myths and legends about monsters of all kinds.

Swift was staring at the page. 'I've never heard of most of these.'

I'd moved from fossils to a cabinet of ancient weapons of torture, then realised they were actually surgical instruments. 'Where are the poisonous samples kept?' I asked.

He stopped reading and looked about. 'That cabinet marked "poisons".' He pointed then walked over to it. I decided I should probably join him and crossed the width of the room to where he was staring at a key in the lock.

'It's not secured in any way,' he said.

'Why would it be, the place is full of Saints,' I replied dryly.

He unlocked it to open the glass door and eyed the blue and white ceramic jars, each neatly labelled. 'Indian Hellebore, Nicotine, Thallium, Tetrodotoxin, Kratom, Mistletoe, Ayahuasca…ah, here we are. Yopo.' He reached for the jar and pulled it from the shelf.

'What on earth is Tetrodotoxin?' I asked as he sniffed the cork lid of the jar, then opened it.

'Extract of puffer fish, they're keen on it in Japan.'

'The poison or the fish?'

'The fish. The poison is in its liver, it's deadly. This is empty.' He showed me the jar of Yopo. 'The lid smells of carbolic.'

'Just as Wilfred Rackham described,' I said.

He took out his magnifying glass and scrutinised it carefully, including the underside. 'Nothing,' he muttered and put it back on the shelf before grasping the jar marked Tetrodotoxin. He prised off the lid and gazed into it. 'Hum.'

'What?' I leaned in to peer over his shoulder.

He turned the jar upside down and banged it. A small dried fish fell out, entirely round and covered in thorny spikes; it had pouting lips, a broken tail and ragged fins.

'Well it doesn't look as though it's harmed anyone,' I remarked and prodded it with my finger.

'Assuming there was only one in there,' he replied, then took tweezers from his pocket to carefully lift it by the tail and drop it back into the jar. 'There's enough poison in here to kill the entire city of Bath twice over.'

'As with most pharmacies,' I said.

He muttered something to himself, locked the door and slipped the key in his pocket.

I moved away to wander about in fascination, gazing into other cabinets. There was an intriguing mix of oddities. Glass phials holding ancient Egyptian cosmetics, an Aztec game described as 'Patolli' consisting of a carved board and beads made of pure gold. A display of terrifying Inca masks also in gold and inlaid with precious stones.

Conical glass containers held strange sea creatures in a thick liquid. Fish with mouthfuls of teeth, colourful octopuses and squid, striped lion fish, tiny frilled sea slugs called blue dragons, a jellyfish labelled a Portuguese man o'war, balloon shaped with a sail on top, mantis shrimp and moray eels among many others.

Another cabinet held ancient objects, ivory needles, flint knives, Saxon torcs, obsidian axes, Roman shields, an imperial eagle and treasures of every imaginable kind. Persi would be utterly entranced, and she didn't even have to dig them up.

'Lennox, I found the carbolic soap.' Swift was rooting about below the large stone sink set in the central work desk.

'Marvellous,' I muttered as I ran fingers over a narwhal tusk propped in a corner; the ivory tusk had been carved with galleons, whales, dolphins and all manner of strange sea creatures.

'I could fingerprint the cupboard–'

'No. We have to go, General Hackett ordered us to meet him at nine.'

He sighed. 'Right, fine.'

We made our way to the floor below and entered the Regent's office to find a lady sitting in front of the desk with a pretty maid standing at her side.

'Ah, there you are. And about time too!' Miss Cicely Sissinghurst aimed a steely glare at us. 'And the Regent is late, which is most unlike him.'

'Greetings,' I said and made a formal bow. We had encountered Miss Cicely Sissinghurst at Belvedere earlier in the year.

Swift bowed, then asked, 'May we sit?'

'Please do, or I must crane my neck to look up at both of you,' Cicely replied. 'This is Freya.' She waved towards the fair-haired maid, who bobbed a curtsey. 'She is of great help to me. I am afflicted with arthritis, it stiffens my bones in the cold and is a dratted nuisance.'

Swift sat in the only vacant chair this side of the Regent's desk and pulled his notebook out. Cicely frowned but didn't object. I went to fetch a stool from near the crackling fire. The curtains were drawn back and rays of sunshine seeped through the snow-etched panes.

'Do you mind answering a few questions while we're waiting for General Hackett?' Swift asked politely.

'I suppose I must, given it was I who recommended you come and investigate,' Cicely replied sharply.

'You are the Keeper of the Books for the Order?' Swift made a note of the date on a fresh page.

'Yes. It is a role I have filled since I returned from the war,' she replied. 'I informed you when we last met, that I administered the largest hospital in Flanders. I have a long acquaintance with the Order and should not need to remind you that this is strictly confidential.'

'It is also a murder enquiry,' Swift replied evenly.

'Doesn't the Keeper of the Books need to be a Saint?' I asked.

'It's preferable.' Cicely eyed me sharply. 'But if no-one has the requisite skills, then a trusted outsider may take the role. It is without remuneration, of course.'

'But you have recently been invited to become a Saint when opportunity allows.' Swift wrote as he spoke. 'Which, with Sir Jasper's death, it now has.'

Her brows almost met. Cicely Sissinghurst had steel

grey hair swept back from a high forehead, a sharply intelligent face, blue eyes and an indomitable air. She wore a dark wool jacket over a high-necked russet dress in the old-fashioned style.

'Inspector,' she almost growled, 'I do hope you are not suggesting I was in any way involved in Jasper's death.'

'No, I'm merely ascertaining facts.' Swift spoke smoothly.

'How well did you know Sir Jasper?' I sought to divert her.

She switched her gaze to me. 'Only since I took the role of Keeper of the Books. And even then, our relationship was distant.'

'He was rather keen on you,' I said.

That took her by surprise. She stared, then laughed. 'Good heavens, the man must have been defective.' The frown returned. 'How do you know this?'

'It's our business to know.' Swift didn't look up from his notebook. 'Were you here the day he died?'

'Yes, we arrived at…?' She turned to her young maid, Freya.

'Nine of the clock, ma'am, now four days gone,' Freya replied. Her accent held the lilting cadence of Scandinavia. She was tall and slim, her fair hair plaited and coiled, clear blue eyes, skin so pale as to be almost translucent, a fine-boned face and a determined lift to her chin. 'We came here for to speak with the General. He was barking loud, as always.'

I laughed. She looked at me in confusion. Swift grinned too.

'You mean shouting, Freya,' Cicely corrected. 'I'm afraid Freya takes her lead from me and I am given to speaking my mind.'

I was quite aware of that.

'Why were you here that day?' Swift continued.

'I came to discuss this year's list of donations with the Regent,' Cicely answered. 'Donations must be made on Christmas Eve. Usually there is agreement well in advance of December, but this year there has been dissension, unfortunately, and we cannot have that.'

'Retired plough horses,' I said.

She eyed me narrowly. 'You are remarkably well informed.'

I gave her a grin.

'Why did you bring Freya on your last visit?' Swift asked.

'She often comes, and as I said, I sometimes have difficulty moving when it is cold. She assists me. And as I have been nominated as a Saint, I believe it will help her decide if she wants to move in here with me.'

'This is correct,' Freya said. 'It is a nice house. Warm. More warm than Bath townhouse we are living in now. And no noise is here. I like it better.'

Swift glanced at Freya, then continued addressing Cicely. 'Your visit to the Regent was to settle the dispute over donations. Sir Jasper was the cause of the dispute.'

'Correct,' she replied.

'Was the situation serious enough to motivate murder?' Swift stopped writing and looked at her.

'Don't be ridiculous,' she rapped. 'It was aggravating, but hardly momentous. And it was quite typical of Jasper. He was insular, he disliked his fellow man quite intensely. His nominations were always for charities supporting distressed and abandoned animals.'

'Sounds like a good chap,' I said.

They ignored me.

'If he disliked his fellow man, why did he choose to live here?' Swift continued.

'He was lonely and miserly,' Cicely answered. 'He was loath to spend anything, even on himself. Living here was comfortable and he was well cared for without cost.'

'He was making the threat to depart, madam,' Freya spoke up. 'You said it to me, and it made an upset to the house here.'

'Thank you, Freya. Please do not talk unless I ask you to,' Cicely spoke firmly; the girl didn't seem perturbed by the reprimand and Cicely continued. 'Jasper's threat was a humbug. I did not believe him and neither did the Regent.'

Given what we'd heard, and read in Jasper's diary entries, I thought they were right.

'Was there any romance between the residents?' I asked.

Freya giggled, then straightened her face.

Cicely's brows drew closer together. 'Certainly not, the idea is preposterous.'

'But there was jealousy,' I persevered.

'Well, a little, but it was mere posturing. Typical male behaviour. The ego, you know,' Cicely admitted.

'Norman and Roger is not typical,' Freya said. 'They are both very jealous, but only for the other.'

'That's simply the way they are,' Cicely replied. 'But Jasper wasn't. He had nothing to be jealous about.'

She was wrong about that.

'Are you moving in now?' I threw in the question.

'No, I am not. The Regent advised that I delay any move for the moment,' Cicely explained. 'He actually thought it better to wait as there is another candidate in the wings.'

'Who?' Swift asked.

'A judge, an acquaintance of Justice St John,' she replied. 'I informed the Regent that I was perfectly content at home and was in no hurry.'

'Not so, madam,' Freya said. 'We should move to be warm and in comfort here.'

'Freya–' Cicely twisted round to address the maid.

'Now I shut my lips, madam,' Freya promised meekly.

If the girl did come to live here, I thought, she would cause chaos.

A knock sounded on the door. Young Jiggens came in bearing a tray with teapot and all the usual. Freya went to help him.

'Oh, no, no, miss. Please don't disturb yourself.' The lad's cheeks blushed pink.

'I like to be of help,' Freya insisted.

He could barely look at her, seemingly overcome by shyness. 'I brought you a cup of the green tea you like,' he said quietly.

'That is nice, young Mr Jiggens,' Freya said in a formal tone. 'I am thanking you kindly.'

I noticed Cicely's stern face soften; she wasn't quite the martinet she pretended.

Jiggens served tea to each of us, and placed a plate of chocolate biscuits on the desk. 'I'm not sure where General Hackett is, Miss Sissinghurst, it's not like him to be late.'

She glanced at the clock on the mantel shelf above the blazing fire. It showed quarter past nine. 'Have you tried his room?'

'I knocked on his door, ma'am,' Jiggens replied earnestly. 'He didn't answer, but I think he was getting dressed. There was a light showing under the door and I could hear movement.'

'He was already dressed when we spoke to him this morning,' I said.

'What was he wearing, sir?' Jiggens asked.

'Black rig, buttoned to the neck,' I replied.

'Did it have black buttons or silver ones?'

'Erm…no idea.'

'Black,' Swift supplied the answer.

'Then he was going for a swim, sir. That's his early suit, he dresses more formally for the daytime.'

His jacket had looked just the same to my mind, but it explained why he'd worn canvas shoes without socks. 'Where does he swim?'

'The Roman Baths below the house,' Jiggens answered as though it were entirely commonplace.

'Go and knock on his door again, perhaps he's mislaid something,' Cicely ordered.

'Yes, ma'am.' Jiggens nodded.

'I come with you.' Freya made to follow.

'No, no, you can't come – it's his bedroom!' Jiggens'

cheeks turned red again. 'Now you just stay here, miss.' He made a rapid escape, but had barely gone when he returned.

'General Hackett is–' he began.

'Coffee, Jiggens.' Hackett marched in behind him, irritation in his eyes, deep furrows across his forehead.

'Yes, sir, right away, sir.' He dashed off again.

'Dust on my shoes. I had to polish them,' he said and stopped, his cheeks suddenly flushing purple. 'It's too hot in here.' He raised his hand to the neck of his black jacket to tug at the collar. It had silver buttons.

'Sir. What is become of your hand?' Freya moved from behind Cicely's chair.

Hackett stared at it: red weals were forming along his forefinger and thumb; more were visible on the back of his hand.

There was a jug of water on a filing cabinet. Cicely went over to it as we sprang to our feet.

'Hold your hand out,' she ordered. 'Freya, fetch more water. There's a bathroom across the corridor.'

'Yes, madam, I go now.' Freya made a dash for the door.

Cicely began washing Hackett's hands with a wet handkerchief, dipping it in and out of the jug. He struggled to hold his arms out for her.

'It stings, quite painful,' Hackett said through gritted teeth. 'And my feet…'

'Sir.' Swift moved beside him. 'You should remove your shoes.'

Hackett didn't seem to hear, he started trembling, but fought to control it, baring his teeth, his outstretched arms slowly sinking. The shaking became more violent, his whole body swayed, then his knees buckled.

'Gregory!' Cicely dropped the handkerchief and tried to hold on to him, but he suddenly collapsed, sinking in jerking convulsions to the floor.

'Sir.' Swift sprang forward the same moment I did.

'Oh Lord,' Cicely cried out. 'Gregory.' She tried to lift his head but his eyes rolled back and he convulsed again.

'We need to remove his shoes,' I shouted.

'Lennox,' Swift said. 'I'll do it, you lift his leg.'

Every fibre in Hackett's body seemed to be jolting, as though shot through with electric shocks, he let out a groan from deep within his chest.

'Help me,' I told Cicely and we gripped each leg tightly as Swift fought to pull off his shoes, then socks, using his handkerchief wrapped twice around his hand.

'Don't touch anything,' he ordered.

Jiggens came in with a pot of steaming coffee and cups on a tray and almost dropped it. 'Aaagh! What's happened to the Regent?'

'Call a doctor,' Cicely shouted.

'And the police,' Swift added.

CHAPTER 10

Jiggens put the tray on the Regent's desk and ran out.

Freya came in carrying an enamel bowl of water, faltered on the threshold, then rushed to the General lying on the floor. Swift and Cicely were kneeling over him, his shoes and socks thrown aside, his bare feet swollen and blotched with bulging red weals running criss-cross all over them.

'It looks like there's something in his socks,' Swift said. 'And on his shoes – he must have got it on his hands.'

'The trembling seems to have lessened,' Cicely said, trying to calm her voice. She was right, his muscles seemed to have relaxed, his breathing quietened although he was still unconscious.

'Madam, I put water on him?' Freya asked.

'Quickly, over his hands first,' Cicely told her.

Freya tipped some of the water from the bowl onto Hackett's right hand, then stepped deftly round to do the same to his left.

Hackett gulped a deep breath. Swift unbuttoned his collar.

'Now his feet,' Cicely ordered, and Freya moved lithely to comply, but Hackett suddenly clasped his chest, his mouth gaping wide.

'Urghhahhh,' he gave a gasping groan as he fought for breath, his spine arching upwards.

'Gregory…Gregory…' Cicely leaned over, calling out to him.

Hackett groaned again, another spasm contorting his body. He tried to gulp air but his jaw contracted, his lips drawn back from teeth and gums. Tendons tightened like cords in his neck, his chest filling with air, a strangled cry gurgling in his throat, then he slumped, all muscles suddenly flaccid.

'Gregory,' Cicely called his name again, her face showing panic. 'Gregory…can you hear me?' She put her hand to his damp forehead, then knelt closer, listening for his breath.

'We give kiss of life, should we, madam?' Freya moved to kneel beside her, her blue eyes focused on the General's face, his skin mottled purple and grey.

'No,' I spoke harshly. 'Whatever killed him was too dangerous.' I stood up from where I'd been kneeling, cursing under my breath.

Cicely desperately felt his wrist for a pulse, then sighed a groan. 'It's too late…' Her shoulders shuddered, she sniffed, tears forming in her eyes.

'He is dead?' Freya asked. 'But how? It is not normal. Has someone done this?' She looked up at me.

I frowned but didn't answer.

'Let me examine him, please.' Swift leaned over, trying to find a pulse in the man's neck. He kept trying, then sat back on his heels before pulling back his cuff to check his watch. 'Nine thirty-eight a.m.,' he said, then sighed sharply.

Nobody spoke for a moment. It was hard to accept a man so vital and strong had just died in front of our eyes.

Freya broke the shocked silence. 'Evil is in this house.'

Jiggens ran in. 'Doctor's on his way, should be here any–' He stopped suddenly. 'Is…is General Hackett…?'

Freya stood up. 'No more. He is dead and gone.'

Jiggens turned ashen then fainted to the floor.

'Oh, come now.' Freya picked up the bowl. 'This is not manly.' She promptly emptied the remainder of the water over him.

'Arghh!' Jiggens sat up, eyes wide in shock.

'Now, young Jiggens, you are to be of help,' Freya ordered.

'Why did you…? I'm all wet!' Jiggens looked down at his spattered waistcoat.

'Jiggens go and lock the Regent's bedroom. Freya, you go downstairs and wait for the doctor,' Swift ordered.

'I…I… yes, sir.' Jiggens wiped water from his eyes.

'Find the Judge,' I told him, 'and tell him to come here.'

'Yes, sir. Right away, sir,' he said, and shoved a strand of dripping hair back from his face.

Freya marched past him, her head held high. He followed; whispered bickering broke out between them.

'Would you like to take a seat, Miss Sissinghurst?' I asked her.

She rose stiffly to her feet, then stood still, unable to take her eyes from Hackett. 'Oh, dear lord.' She raised a hand to her cheek. 'This is terrible.'

I encouraged her to sit in the chair by the desk she'd vacated.

Swift picked up one of Hackett's shoes with his handkerchief and began to examine the leather upper. The smell of fresh polish was quite distinctive, even from where I was.

'Tweezers, Swift,' I said.

He felt for them in a pocket then held them out. 'Careful how you handle things, Lennox. Whatever was used is deadly.'

I plied the tweezers to pick up a discarded black sock. There was a line of blue-grey residue visible on the toe, and more on the underside. It appeared to have come from inside the sock. The enamel bowl Freya had brought in was now empty and I reached for it.

'Let me,' Cicely said in a hoarse voice. She dug into her handbag for another handkerchief and wiped the bowl dry, then gave it back.

I held the sock with the tweezers and shook it very carefully. A small amount of powder, like bluish talc, fell into the bowl.

Swift put the shoe down and advanced with a magnifying glass in hand.

Cicely came to stare through the lens with us. 'We must turn it inside out. I have gloves…' She rooted in her handbag and pulled out a pair of black leather gloves. 'Let me.'

She turned the sock inside out. Clumps of damp powder were stuck to the underside and toe. She carefully knocked them free of the fine wool fibres to fall into the bowl.

'It seems to be made up of tiny particles,' I said.

Swift aimed the lens in closer. 'Like flakes of skin, or flesh.'

'Could it be dried mushrooms?' I hazarded.

'Give me the tweezers,' Cicely demanded.

'Fine.' I obeyed, because she could be quite assertive.

She picked up the other sock. Swift and I leaned backwards as she shook it over the bowl.

'It must be from the Chamber of Curiosities,' Swift replied.

'One of the poisons,' Cicely said.

The door suddenly flew open. 'What devilry is this?' Justice St John barked, then stomped in, dressed in a black suit with a grey silk waistcoat straining across his considerable paunch. 'Is the Regent truly dead?'

Cicely turned to him, her face pale. 'Humphrey, he's been murdered. It's appalling. He died in front of us not fifteen minutes ago.'

'Outrageous!' St John shouted, fury in his face. 'This is absolutely outrageous.' He advanced on us, his voice raised to explosive volume. 'You were here to stop this, and the man is murdered quite literally under your noses. Is this the best Scotland Yard can do? Is it? Because I'll have you–'

I had been growing rather tired of being ordered about, and Justice St John was the last straw.

'We are not answerable to you.' I raised my voice to parade ground level. 'Now sit down.'

They all stared at me. St John tottered a little then sat on the nearest chair, his eyes rounded. 'Well, there's no need to shout.'

'You will take charge,' I told him firmly. 'This house will need reassurance and a steady hand.'

He harrumphed and drew himself upright. 'I intend to take command, and you, sir, will not raise your voice to me.'

'Fine, then don't give me cause,' I retorted.

Swift frowned at me, then addressed St John. 'Sir, it may put you in danger.'

'The danger is equal to each of us,' St John replied, reverting to his usual loftiness. 'Now describe to me how he died.' He nodded toward Hackett. Cicely had placed his hands across his chest and closed his eyes. He appeared relatively peaceful although his face was blotchy with an undertone of sickly yellow. I considered checking if he were only comatose, like Jasper had been when assumed dead. But then I decided the doctor could do that.

Swift made a succinct explanation of events, showing him the clumps of strange powder in the bowl.

'The Chamber of Curiosities should be locked,' I said.

'Absolutely,' Cicely agreed. 'And at once.'

'Stable door and horses,' St John rumbled. 'But Rackham will do it. He's our curator, along with Captain Lockhart.'

'Does Captain Lockhart give lectures about the Curiosities too?' I asked.

'He does, and they're very interesting,' St John replied with enthusiasm. 'Man of the world y'know. Rackham's the dry sort, academic. Lockhart's an adventurer!'

'Has Lockhart included any poisonous powder in his lectures, sir?' Swift asked.

'Believe he mentioned something some time ago,' St John ruminated. 'Memory not what it was.'

Cicely glanced at him but didn't comment.

A knock sounded at the door. Jiggens came in followed by a smartly dressed young man – a doctor judging by the medical bag in his hand.

'Dr Moule,' he said, a smile on his pleasant features. The smile vanished when he spotted the body. 'Good Lord, it's General Hackett! I only saw him four days ago when I attended Sir Jasper.'

'These deaths are not a coincidence,' Cicely told him.

The doctor widened his eyes. 'What? You mean he was mur–'

'I'm Inspector Swift of Scotland Yard.' Swift stepped forward. 'I'm investigating with the help of my…erm,' he waved a hand at me, 'my colleague.'

'Hum,' I replied. I've never been keen to shake the hands of doctors, given the sort of poking about they do, but he looked the fastidious sort so I took the risk. 'Major Lennox.'

'Delighted. Dr Peter Moule.'

'He had poison powder in his socks.'

He stopped shaking my hand. 'Erm…Really?'

'Doctor, come.' Cicely took charge. 'You will need gloves, please ensure you put them on before touching anything.'

He dug a pair of rubber gloves from his bag and went and knelt by the General with Cicely, the doctor trying his best to appear professional and not perturbed at all. Swift went to join them.

The pot of coffee was still on Hackett's desk. I poured myself a cup and sat down.

'I've called for an ambulance too, sir.' Jiggens addressed St John. 'The rest of the residents are in the breakfast room. They've been asking questions, but I don't know what to say to them?' He ended plaintively.

St John rose slowly from his chair and threw out his chest. 'I will convey the news to them. Lead the way, lad.'

'Wait,' Swift said. 'Please do not declare the means of murder, sir.'

'Very well.' St John nodded. 'Should I state, "died by hand unknown" or "under suspicious circumstances"?.'

'Can't you just say he died and the doctor is examining him?' I said.

He raised thick brows at that. 'You mean tell the literal truth and no more? Ha! I believe that will suffice.' He went off, his mood quite jolly.

Freya came in as the Judge and Jiggens went out. She made a face at the young man then came to the desk and lifted the lid on the teapot.

'Madam, the tea is all cold now. I shall take and warm it, if you please.'

'The coffee's hot,' I said. 'Jiggens brought it for the General.'

'The General cannot enjoy coffee when he is dead.' She picked up the pot. 'Who is wanting some?' She looked at the group around the dead man.

The doctor had sat back on his heels and was staring at her. 'I…erm…hello.'

'Hello, my name is Freya,' she replied. 'You would like coffee?'

'Yes. No. I mean no, sorry,' the doctor stuttered. 'I can't. I have to, erm…' He indicated the body. 'I'm the doctor.'

'A doctor is a most clever person.' Freya curtsied. 'I am a mere maid, but I am clever too.'

'I'm sure, and very…erm…' Dr Moule looked rather dazed.

'*Ahem.*' Swift cleared his throat meaningfully.

'The body, yes, of course.' Dr Moule returned to examining the welts on Hackett's bare feet.

I ate a biscuit, thinking that I'd like to telephone Persi, but she would be giving her lecture this morning at the British Museum, so I'd have to wait.

All three cats came bouncing in, full of mischief. I picked Tubbs up, then the other two. It was too dangerous for them to stay. 'Swift, I'll see you later.'

He looked up. 'You could start the interviews.'

'I could,' I agreed, and with an armful of cats, made an exit.

If there was a Roman Bath under the house, all I had to do was keep going down until I found it. I let the cats jump down, they followed me, playing skittishly. My little dog was downstairs in the hallway sitting in front of the Christmas tree, apparently mesmerised by the baubles, or possibly the bells. He came to greet me, rather subdued, with his ears down and tail low. He would have sensed the death; dogs had a way of knowing and Foggy disliked all things dead. He wasn't much of a gun dog, and he wasn't very bright either, but he had a good heart and that was all that mattered.

I fussed Foggy, trying to reassure him, then gave him a treat from my waistcoat pocket. This perked him up and he came with me and the cats to the games room and we all entered the door in the panelling.

I hesitated at the delicious smells emanating from the kitchen, then resolutely continued onward. The cats raced along in a game of rough and tumble, passing the Butler's Pantry and onward to find a narrow passageway with worn steps winding downwards.

The walls were hacked out of stone and reddish in colour. Some areas were rubbed smooth where people had skimmed their shoulders against the sides, presumably for more than a millennia, if it really were Roman. Small bare bulbs were strung along the ceiling, giving off a low light. The damp rose to meet me about halfway down, but it was warm and slightly sulphurous, not like the usual mouldy dank so typical of old cellars.

The passage wound around a corner and suddenly I'd arrived.

CHAPTER 11

I'd half expected to find a body in the pool, given the number of deaths in the house, but the water was perfectly clear, apart from a haze of steam rising from the surface.

Oval shaped, quite deep by the looks of it, tiled in pale blue and surrounded by slim columns painted to look like marble. There was a set of shallow steps leading into the water, which looked warm and inviting. Beads of moisture glistened from every surface, including the ancient marble tiles beneath my feet. The place was hacked out of red sandstone, rising like a cave above me and lit by glass lanterns suspended by chains attached to hooks in the roof.

There was an antechamber just off; I wandered over with hands in pockets and stood to gaze. A continuous marble shelf ran around the walls just above head height, stacked with folded white towels. Wooden slatted benches were situated below and there were pegs fixed to one wall for clothes. I wished I'd brought some bathing togs.

Hackett had swum here this morning. The place seemed immaculate, nothing indicated he'd even been here – or that anyone had, actually. He'd asked to see us in his office, and it was clear Cicely Sissinghurst had been invited too. We should have asked why, but I'd thought he'd simply wanted to question us.

I made a slow circuit of the pool, which was quite large. The cats had galloped twice around it then settled down next to a slender column to watch me. Fogg dogged my footsteps, then stopped to gaze at the water. There was an inlet pipe made from copper just below the overhanging edge of the pool. An outlet pipe, covered by a metal filter was set in the tiled wall opposite, at the same level. As I pondered how it all worked, I noticed something at the bottom of the pool. Something small and white, barely visible amid the slowly rising steam.

Damn it, I'd have to go in.

There didn't seem to be anyone about, so I stripped off in the anteroom and walked down the shallow steps. The warmth of the water added to the buoyancy; I floated effortlessly for moments and then dived to the bottom, some twelve feet down. I scrabbled about, felt with my fingers, and brought the object back up to the surface.

A bone needle, as fine as any steel one, but much, much older. The pointed tip was smeared with a dark, sticky substance. I pushed wet hair from my face and noticed something else: the glistening marble-tiled floor was covered in cat and dog paw prints from where they'd scampered about. My footprints were there too, and those left by my bare feet.

I moved about the pool, my eyes and nose just above the water, to make out others that were barely visible. A set of prints made by ribbed soles came from the entrance and went to the antechamber. Hackett had been wearing black canvas shoes this morning when he'd spoken to us in the breakfast room. The ones we'd pulled off him as he died were formal leather. And he hadn't been wearing socks earlier either.

His bare footprints came and went to the pool just as mine did, but there was a different set of prints in the layer of moisture on the floor. They came from the winding stone stairs and stopped near the edge of the pool, then went straight back to the stairs without diverting to the antechamber. They were made by smooth rubber soles, such as slippers. The edges had been blurred by tiny droplets of moisture, but I'd have said the size was smaller than I took, but impossible to tell if they were man's or woman's. I tried to make out something more useful, but couldn't, so I swam over to sit on the steps and lifted the needle up in front of me to stare at the dark, sticky substance. Perhaps a blowpipe had been used, and the killer had missed…?

'Sir?' A voice came from the passageway. 'Sir?'

'Greggs?'

'Ah, sir. Inspector Swift said you might have come down here…Good heavens, sir, this is remarkable!' He stopped to gaze about.

'Couldn't get me a towel, could you, old chap?'

'Um, indeed, sir…'

'Anteroom, over there.' I pointed.

He went to fetch one and placed it on the floor next to me. I held the needle up.

'Take that to Swift, tell him I found it in the pool and I'll be with him shortly. And don't touch the sticky stuff on the point, it could be deadly poison.'

'Poison, sir!' His brows shot up.

'Just take it by the blunt end, here.' I offered it to him.

'Oh, sir, this is like that grenade.' He took it gingerly and held it with arm outstretched as though it were likely to explode.

'Nonsense, you only had to stick the pin back in that. Now off you go.'

He made a rapid retreat and up the steps as quickly as he could muster. The cats decided to follow and ran in a bundle behind him, tails held high in excitement.

I towelled off and dressed unhurriedly, humming to myself. Swimming in the warm water had been really quite relaxing. I wondered if there were any ancient Romans Baths near my home.

Foggy had remained sitting by the pool, his long ears drooping and looking as sorry as only a sad spaniel can. I picked him up, gave him a cuddle and carried him back to the hustle and bustle of the house.

I could hear the chatter as I approached the games room; I guessed they must have congregated in there.

'Lennox,' Swift called from a bridge table he'd settled behind. 'We're taking fingerprints.'

Cicely Sissinghurst was standing next to him, and there were a number of Saints lined up waiting. Others were washing inky fingers in a bowl presided over by Freya. Young Jiggens was helping them dry their hands with white towels.

Olivia Arbuthnot was wearing a striking Chinese-style dressing gown; she glanced over at me, distress clear on her long face. Lady Matilda was with her but was in close conversation with Pastor Peabody and didn't look up.

I put Foggy down; he went to stare at Balthazar who was nibbling a biscuit on a sofa by the fire.

'Oh, it's the doggie. Hello doggie,' he burbled happily.

'Could you arrange for them to make statements, please?' Swift said as I went over to join him. 'And start the interviews.'

I held back a sigh. Swift was thrilled with any sort of police procedures, but I liked to be on the hunt – taking action not notes. 'Fine,' I said then went to young Jiggens.

'Jiggens, give each of them a pen and paper and tell them to write down everything they did this morning since they got up.'

He glanced up at me. 'Erm…righto, sir…Isn't that police work?'

'Yes, consider yourself deputised,' I told him and went in search of a victim. The two colourful characters caught my eye. Roger and Norman were seated together on the sofa opposite Balthazar. 'Which one of you is Roger?'

'Me! I am.' The blond one wearing a pale blue jacket jumped to his feet.

'Come with me,' I said and walked towards the door.

'Oooh, my lucky day,' he said. 'Lead on, handsome.' He sauntered past Norman, who crossed his legs, then his arms with a huff of indignation.

I headed for the library, which was mercifully vacant.

'Sit down.' I took the chair behind a green leather-topped reading table, which put some distance between us. There were pens, paper, ink and all the usual whatnots – I drew out my notebook and opened it on the blotter.

'You're very stern, Major,' Roger said. 'Am I in trouble?'

'Name, please,' I said as I shook my pen to set the ink running.

'Roger Nesbit, dealer in rare and unique books.' He tugged the peacock blue silk handkerchief from the top pocket of his jacket and wafted it about. 'I was in partnership with Norman. We had many years together, wheeling and dealing, wining and dining – only ever with the very top clientele, of course. We were terribly well-known in the most exclusive circles. Nesbit and Keene. Have you heard of us?'

'No.' I wrote his name down. 'Did you know General Hackett, or Sir Jasper, before you came to live here?'

'Not personally, they're hardly our sort, you know.' Roger held the handkerchief between finger and thumb. Wavy blond hair, a lean face, creased but not wrinkled, blue eyes, a firm chin and a look of ascetic refinement. His fingernails were immaculate and I doubted he'd done a hard day's labour in his life. Despite his well-preserved appearance, I reckoned him to be close to seventy.

'There's a signed Dickens in Sir Jasper's room.'

'Is it *A Christmas Carol?* Because if it is, we've been searching all over the house for it.' Roger sounded peeved. 'It's worth an absolute fortune.'

'Did Sir Jasper often take books?' I was acting stern and businesslike, just as Swift would.

'Oh, he took whatever he liked. Everyone found it most annoying.' He waved the handkerchief again.

'Cut the play-acting,' I growled. 'This is a murder enquiry.'

That made him sit up. He shoved the handkerchief back in his top pocket. 'Were they truly both murdered? Because there's a lot of silly talk around the place and no-one's really sure.' He dropped his voice an octave, placed his hands on his lap and looked me in the face.

'Yes, and everyone's life is in danger until we discover who did it, and why this is happening.' I eyed him. 'What were your movements this morning?' I'd just thought that phrase up – it sounded the sort proper detectives would use.

He blinked. 'You mean getting dressed and all that?'

'Obviously.'

'Well, I awoke around seven, I think… one doesn't always keep track.' He put a couple of fingers to his chin as he pondered. 'Snoozed a little, then got up, washed, shaved and chose my outfit for the day. Then I came downstairs to the breakfast room, and was just finishing my porridge when the hullabaloo broke out.'

'Did you see anything or anyone acting oddly?'

'When?' he asked.

'Any time at all.'

'No, it was rather quiet actually. Didn't you notice anything? You're the one who's supposed to be detecting.'

'I was busy looking into things,' I said tersely. I wrote: *woke, dressed, ate porridge,* then carried on with the interrogation. 'Do you have any idea what's behind it?'

He pursed his lips. 'No, but I can understand someone becoming angry with Jasper. He was a difficult man, and terribly argumentative. He bullied poor Balthazar, it was mean of him, and of course he had threatened to sue Lockhart.'

'Sue Lockhart?' That was the first I'd heard of it. 'Why?'

'Jasper said Philip was here under false pretences and wouldn't have enough money to contribute to the funds if his debts found him out.'

'What debts?'

'No idea. Something from his past, I suppose, he was quite the buccaneer,' Roger said, then sighed. 'But if it's true, then Jasper had a point, because if Lockhart hasn't any money, he'd be guilty of taking a wealthier person's place, and the beneficiaries would suffer accordingly.'

I decided I'd better write this down in more detail. 'How are potential Saints chosen?'

'Well, I can only speak for myself,' he began, obviously enthused by the subject. 'When Norman and I decided to retire from book dealing, we held an auction of our stock. It was in all the papers, and simply everyone who was anyone came.' He reverted to type, legs crossed, hand circling as he expounded. 'People were utter darlings. Afterwards, we went for a little round the world jaunt, as one should after a lifetime of labour. Anyway, we encountered the most appalling poverty.' His voice rose, then fell. 'There was mud and dust, and ordure, and children – just little tiny children – living in the dirt. No shoes, barely clothed, and their parents were thin and ragged. I know one is aware such things exist, one reads the newspapers after all. But to see it for oneself was just...' He looked genuinely upset. 'Well, we were quite distraught and we vowed we would do something. When we returned home we discussed our desire to save these poor little souls. We talked to friends and asked for suggestions. A short while later Miss Cicely wrote to us, asking if she may rendezvous to discuss matters of philanthropy. We invited her to our London abode, and she arrived with Justice St John. We all took tea together, and she was most diplomatic in her approach. St John sat in silence, rather like Buddha, on the sofa. He listened, and... well, he's a judge, you know, so he was obviously judging us.' He sketched another circle in the air with his hand then let it drop and leaned forward. 'Then he finally spoke, and all he said was, "you will do." And that was virtually his whole conversation. Then Miss Cicely, who is an absolute brick by the way, asked if we would like to consider joining a very select group dedicated to philanthropy. She allowed us to ask questions and she explained all about the Saints, and the wonderful history of the Order, and the need for secrecy of course,' he added sotto voce in case anyone ignorant of the fact was listening. 'Well, after much consideration and debate between Norman and I, we decided we would accept the offer.' He ended with a smile and recrossed his legs.

I'd been writing through most of his animated discourse, but put my pen down and leaned back in my chair. 'Your lives sounded quite sociable before retiring here, don't you miss it?'

'Oh, yes at times.' His face fell, and he looked down at his nails. 'But Norman isn't very well...he had fits on our cruise down the Nile. Epilepsy. It was quite frightening, actually. We don't know what caused the fits, but we cut our big trip short. We consulted all sorts of experts and they advised that he must avoid potential triggers. Too much noise and over stimulation could set him off again. So we were already contemplating a quiet retreat to the countryside when Miss Cicely approached us.' He let out a loud sigh. 'We thought this little enclave sounded as though it would suit us. Not too isolated, you know, and we are very well looked after. It's really quite fun.'

'There must be some falling out,' I prompted, thinking him just the sort to thrive on gossip.

'Oh, all the time,' he giggled. 'But that's just part of the fun, isn't it? And despite the minor tirades, we actually rub along perfectly well. Gregory Hackett was good at managing men, and the ladies.' He closed his eyes and raised his hand to his smooth cheek. 'It's such a shock to think we've lost him…' He sniffed. 'The captain of our ship…a sure hand on the tiller…a–'

'Yes, right, understood.' I cut him off before he ran out of cliches. 'I assume Miss Cicely, as Keeper of the Books, is aware of the value of each Saint's worth?'

'Well, yes, that's her job isn't it?' Roger pulled a proper cotton handkerchief from his trouser pocket and blew his nose noisily. 'She's called the dead reckoner, you know. All the Keepers were. She'll be sequestering Jasper's funds now, and Hackett's. That's the rule – when someone goes to their coffin, their funds go to the coffers.'

'It has been explained to me.' I nodded, then pondered a

moment. 'If Miss Cicely knows exactly how much everyone is worth, she could have put a stop to Jasper's threat to sue Captain Lockhart.'

'Oh, she tried, but Jasper accused Lockhart of having hidden liabilities she didn't know about. He said the pigeons would come home to roost. And Jasper involved Hackett too.' He nodded emphatically. 'Even threatened to bring him forth as a witness to the fact.'

'You're accusing Lockhart of having a motive to murder?' I said in the sort of stern tone Swift would have used. He had a habit of throwing accusations around and it often caught people off guard.

'No! No, you must not twist my words. I am merely trying to be of help,' he said in indignation. 'I mean really! One goes out of one's way to explain the…the facts of the case, and the reward one receives is a nasty insinuation. Major, I protest!' He threw his nose in the air, folded his arms and waited for an apology. I realised this was probably a practised tactic.

I was of a mind to say what I thought but it would see him stalk out of the door. 'Apologies, old chap.' I spoke laconically. 'I appreciate your candour and thank you for providing a new lead to consider.'

'Hum,' he pouted. 'It was likely just one of Jasper's little spats, anyway. He was terribly prickly, it didn't take much to set him off.' He paused to gaze at the yellow and orange flames of the fire, then turned abruptly to face me. 'Jasper was a well-known money man, he knew what he was talking about. There truly may have been something in it, you know.' He suddenly bounded to his feet. 'Now, I really must go and see how Norman is. He truly might have a fit if I'm away too long.'

I sat back and let him leave without a word.

CHAPTER 12

I contemplated going to find Swift, but instead decided to jolly up the fire and settle in a comfortable wing chair in front of it. I was just adding a few more details in my notebook when Freya came in.

'Your man Greegs is most good,' she announced and for some reason started to tidy up. 'Miss Olivia is weeping in buckets, and then m'lady Matilda did begin to do the same, because she is always wanting to be looked at the most. Pah, these ladies are silly. Justice St John was shouting, this was not of use, and then Greegs brings them hot chocolate with good whisky in it. And he is talking with them, making them be seated and giving kind words.' She came to plump cushions on the sofa next to me, knocking dust in the air and making me sneeze. 'And your Inspector Swift is telling them to be careful, but not to worry. How can this not make them worry?' she demanded. 'Now it is for you to correct all in this house, Major Lennox, and you must be quick in doing it. There must be no more killing.' She stopped and put her hands on her hips. 'Well? Are you sitting there all the day?'

'I have just–'

'*Humph*,' she blew out her breath in indignation. 'So, you are now ready for taking action?'

Good Lord, the girl was an absolute tartar. 'Right. I'll go and find Swift. But,' I stood up, towering over her by almost two feet, 'we will be using this room as our headquarters, so you cannot simply walk in whenever you feel like it.'

'I hope I have not need to,' she retorted.

I stalked off, muttering under my breath. I'd just interviewed a suspect, I'd even taken notes, and now I was being harried by a slip of a girl. I should have simply ordered her out, or demanded she bring coffee or something…

'Lennox,' Swift was coming from the hall, 'it's getting a bit fraught.'

'So I understand.'

'Think we'll use the library as our incident room.'

'I already was, but Freya is in there,' I replied.

'Ah.' He hesitated. 'She's very blunt.'

'Huh,' I agreed. 'Viking blood, I expect.'

'I suppose so. Rackham has locked the Chamber of Curiosities, by the way.'

'Good.'

'We'll go and investigate as soon as–' He stopped.

Freya had come out of the library and walked up behind us. 'You are still not investigating yet?'

'Yes, we are,' I retorted, stung.

She arched her brows.

'We are having a private conversation,' I said, thinking she might take the hint.

'In the passageway?'

'Would you please ask Jiggens to come to the library?' Swift said.

Her brows came down. 'Very well, but acting with urgency is required.'

'So you have said,' I replied heavily.

'Pah,' she said and went off.

We went to the library and I closed the door firmly behind us.

'Why do you want Jiggens?'

'I didn't, I was just trying to divert her.'

That made me grin. I sat in the fireside chair I'd just vacated and he slumped down in the one opposite.

He carried on talking. 'The Saints were all quite calm to start with, then the doctor asked if everyone was feeling fine and they all broke into a panic.'

'There have been two murders in the house,' I remarked as I pulled my notebook from my jacket pocket.

'I know,' he said dryly. 'And it's hardly a surprise they're worried one of them might be next.' He eyed me. 'Greggs gave me a bone needle. Where did it come from?'

'The Roman Bath in the basement. It's where Hackett was swimming. Jiggens told us about it,' I reminded him.

'It's really Roman?' He sounded astonished.

'Yes, well I assume it is. It looks like a Roman temple deep below the house. I suppose that's why it's called Temple House,' I said, then explained what I'd found, including the footprints on the damp floor.

He wrote it all down of course. 'Describe the prints.'

'Slippers.'

'Size?'

'Too indistinct to be sure, but smaller than mine.' I waited for him to finish writing. 'What did you do with the needle?'

'Put it in an evidence jar and gave it to the policeman. He's sending it to the Yard for analysis along with the powder from Hackett's socks.'

'Right...jolly good.'

'Someone may have tried to kill Hackett with a blowpipe and missed,' he mused.

'That's what I thought. The powder must have been a backup plan.'

He considered that. 'The killer went down to the pool, presumably carrying a blowpipe, tried and failed to hit Hackett while he was swimming, then went up to the Chamber of Curiosities and fished out the powder to put in his shoes.'

'Possibly...No, we were in the Chamber. They must have already taken the powder.'

'Good point,' Swift said and wrote it down.

I was thinking of Hackett's buttons, and wondering why he had different outfits when we were interrupted by a knock on the door and the entry of young Jiggens with a tray.

'It's all falling apart, sirs.' He sounded anxious, his face pale. 'They've been working themselves into a lather.' The tray rattled as he put it on the low table.

'Freya mentioned the same,' I replied.

'Oh she's been here, has she?' He put cups on saucers

in front of us, then lifted the coffee pot to pour. 'She's a right bossy boots, she is. Ordering me about as if I'm just a lackey. And no-one says a word, neither. They just smile at her and say how pretty she is and how nice it is to have a young face around here. I've been here most of my life, working hard, day in, day out, but not a dickie bird about that.' He put the pot down and clattered teaspoons onto the saucers. 'And that doctor's fallen for her. He looked like a soppy puppy dog, staring at her every time she came anywhere near him. I almost had to shove him out the door after the ambulance was loaded up.'

'Jiggens,' I began, 'did you mop the floor of the Roman pool today, or yesterday?'

'I…erm, not today, sir, nor yesterday. It's just that with–'

Swift cut in. 'Did the General wear canvas shoes without socks when he went down to swim, then return to his room and dress for the day, including socks?'

'He did, sir,' he replied.

'Did he swim yesterday?' Swift continued.

'I…I think so, sir,' Jiggens stammered. 'Sorry, I've been awfully busy.'

'Has anyone else been down there other than General Hackett?' I asked.

'Not that I know of, sir.'

'Did Mr Jiggens Senior see or hear anyone going to the pool?' Swift rattled out questions. 'Or any of the staff?'

'Pretty sure they didn't, sir, or they'd have said something.' Jiggens took a breath. 'Grandad is awful discombobulated now. He likes routine, and things kept simple, but it's all a ruckus and he's…well, he's had to retire to his room, sirs.' His shoulders sagged. 'He did the same when my father was lost in the war. I can't blame him, but it's hard to shoulder it all.' He sighed then made an effort to straighten up. 'Auntie Essie's been with Cook, baking. That's what she does when she's worried. There's tons of cakes now, so I brought you some slices of chocolate cake, mince pies and toasted tea cakes.' He lifted the silver lid from a bone china plate. There were two of everything, fresh baked and smelling heavenly.

'Just leave it and we'll help ourselves,' I told him, feeling sorry for the lad.

'Right you are, sir, and I'd best be going. It'll be lunch in a while, and I have to make the preparations all on my own. Unless Freya "helps" and starts bossing me about again…' He went off muttering to himself.

'Good thought about when the floor was last mopped, Lennox,' Swift said. 'You might make a detective, yet!'

I didn't rise to the bait. 'Here.' I held out my notebook. 'Interview with Roger whatever-he's-called.'

'Roger Nesbit.' Swift took it as I bit into a warm mince pie. I could taste rum in the filling. I had a toasted tea cake to follow, thickly spread with butter, then drank my coffee and gazed about the room as Swift deciphered my notes.

The library was stuffed from floor to ceiling with books bound in varying tones of leather. Some of the shelves were labelled; I could see history, travel, antiquity, myths, lost civilisations…every sort of topic. Persi was on my mind, it was still too early to call her. She'd said there would be a lunch following the lectures, and a chance to meet fellow archaeologists. We'd all been invited to attend. I probably wouldn't have had a clue what they were talking about, but the museum would have been fascinating. They had Egyptian mummies in real sarcophagi. I'd never actually seen one in the flesh, or bandages, or whatever they looked like.

'Lennox.'

'What?'

'Jasper intended suing Captain Lockhart and bringing General Hackett in as a witness.'

'I know, I wrote it down.' I nodded at my notebook in his hand.

'But it's a motive, we need to interview Lockhart.'

'Yes,' I agreed. I don't know why he was so excited.

'I'll go and find him, and ask him to come in.' He jumped to his feet.

'Fine. And you should take a look at the Roman Bath too.'

'Good idea.' He made for the door, then hesitated. 'You're not going to disappear, are you?'

'No, no. I'll be here.'

He knew I was lying. 'Right.' He sniffed, then cleared off. Why he thought I would just sit around kicking my heels for no good reason was a mystery.

A clear blue sky beckoned beyond the lead-framed windows. I finished my coffee and what was left of the goodies, then found my little dog and headed once again for the great outdoors.

Pristine snow sparkled in bright sunshine, white frost clung to black twigs and branches. Holly, ivy, mistletoe and sharp pine needles lay green glazed under thin layers of ice. I took a deep breath of crisp air and strode out to follow the fresh tyre tracks heading to the real world beyond.

Foggy was thrilled to be outdoors, he ran along the drive, nose to the ground and tail in the air.

Silence settled around me as I tramped behind him and out between ornamental gates to pass below snow-laden trees. We rounded a bend and suddenly found the full panorama of the city held below us in a valley circled by seven hills. I stood to stare; it was only a half mile away, with a fine collection of slender church spires, handsome edifices, Georgian crescents of elegant houses and white-coated rooftops. I wasn't keen on cities, but it beckoned with the promise of shops, inns, restaurants and all the usual temptations of civilisation.

Fogg had started digging frantically in a virgin snowdrift smothering the verge. I remained motionless, hands in pockets, my eyes on the city and mind elsewhere.

Two men dead. Why?

The Saints were mere mortals. They hadn't been chosen because they'd led virtuous lives, they were flawed and most certainly had erred along the way. What were their sins? And who had they sinned against?

The killer must have planned to murder Hackett and our presence hadn't inhibited him… or her? Why Hackett? He was an army general – a man practised in the way of warfare – surely if he'd been guilty of something, or suspected someone, he'd have been more alert to the dangers? But then who the devil expects to be killed by powder in their socks? Or poison darts?

I sighed, a stream of white clouding my breath.

Foggy gave up delving. He'd dug down to the frozen grass beneath the snow; no doubt he'd heard a mouse, or shrew. He shook his ears, covered yet again with balls of ice. I picked him up, put him under my arm, and carried him back to Temple House.

I dried him off in the boot room as best I could then went in search of Swift. I found Greggs instead, a hangdog look about him.

'Sir, I think this situation most undesirable.'

That sort of statement begs all sorts of questions, so I merely raised an eyebrow.

'There's a murderer in the house, sir.' His chins wobbled above his stiff collar.

'Yes, Greggs, that's why we're here.'

'But the ladies are most concerned. We had rather…' he searched for a tactful word, 'an upset earlier, sir. I have assured them of your, and the inspector's, breadth of experience, and, *ahem*, aptitude, but they did question how General Hackett could be killed whilst you were actually in the room with him. I have to say, sir, it did not inspire confidence.'

Words of reassurance failed to form in my mind. 'We'll get the blighter, old chap,' I said, having nothing more concrete to offer.

'But will it be before he takes another life, sir? And why is this evil being perpetrated?'

'Greggs…'

'Could we lock them up, sir?'

'Who?'

'The men. It must be one of them, sir.'

I hesitated. It was a tempting idea. 'No, we've had the Chamber of Curiosities locked, and everyone will just have to be vigilant.'

'But, sir–'

'And Jiggens Senior is having a hard time of it, so you'll have to stand in for him.'

'But, sir–' he tried an objection.

'It'll keep your mind off things.'

'Very well, sir,' he sighed and trudged off, shoulders stooped and a frown of fretful worry on his forehead.

Swift was in the library leaning on the reading desk, notebook open. Miss Olivia Arbuthnot was sitting opposite. Neither turned around when I entered, but the atmosphere was tense.

CHAPTER 13

'I am not over-dramatising, Inspector,' Olivia said stiffly. 'We are all frightened by what has happened in this house today and nobody has told us the cause.' Her high cheekbones were flushed with anger in her long face, but she was clutching a handkerchief and her green eyes were glazed with sorrow.

'And I'm saying that stalking in here,' Swift responded, 'demanding that I arrest the culprit or face the wrath of His Majesty's high counsel is hyperbole.'

She shrugged. 'Perhaps, but it's clear the Regent's death was not natural or you would not be taking statements. All I am saying is that if you do not act quickly, you will lose the support of the Saints. They will seek your removal, and it will be done surreptitiously. You will know nothing of it until you are literally escorted out of the door.'

Swift let out a sigh of irritation, but there was an element of unease too. Olivia was right, we would be unceremoniously replaced if the Order lost faith in us.

'Greetings,' I said as I went to sit near Swift.

'Major Lennox, I was trying to explain–' Olivia spoke tersely.

'Thank you, it's not necessary.' I held up my hand to stop the flow. 'Perhaps you'd care to shed some light on why someone has murdered two of your fellow residents.'

'If only I could! We're all racking our brains.' She'd changed into the green silk dress, and tied her long black ringlets into a loose knot. 'Is someone offended? Has there been a threat to expose some terrible secret? I simply don't know, and neither does anyone else.'

'Someone does,' I remarked. 'There's a rumour that Sir Jasper was going to sue Captain Lockhart for misrepresenting his wealth.'

'Oh, for heavens' sake, Major,' she retorted. 'It was nonsense, all the Saints are thoroughly appraised before they are invited to join the Order. Jasper's accusations were merely to gain Cicely Sissinghurst's attention. She had to interview Jasper and investigate his allegations. It was simply a clumsy attempt to communicate with her.'

Swift glanced at me. We'd both read his journal, we knew how keen he was on Cicely.

'Jasper threatened to call General Hackett as a witness,' Swift stated. 'I doubt he'd have done that if the allegations were baseless.'

She shrugged. 'Then you must talk to Cicely.'

Swift made a note in his book. The clock on the mantelpiece above the fire chimed half past eleven. I regarded Olivia; an interesting lady, to my mind. Her black hair was obviously dyed; she was angular and thin, which exaggerated the lines and creases of her long face. She was fun though, with a sense of humour that bubbled not far beneath the surface. And intelligent, engaging and direct.

'What do you know of the expedition led by Wilfred Rackham?' I asked.

'Ah, now, that was tragic. We prefer not to speak of it.' She turned her eyes to mine, gazing from below dark-pencilled brows.

'When did Rackham come to reside here?' I was fishing, not having a clue if any of it was relevant.

'Oh, two years after his rescue. He was in hospital in Finland for many months.' She lowered her voice. 'The amputations were complicated, and there was infection. I don't know all the details, and I'd rather not, actually. It was all rather…' she pursed red lips as she searched for the word, 'delicate. Particularly for a young man. When well enough, he travelled to Switzerland in the hope of saving his left eye. They couldn't, and I'm aware the sight in his other eye is failing. Pastor Peabody knew the old Regent – the one preceding the General – and he badgered him to admit the boy. I'm sure you are aware that the Pastor's son was one of those who was lost. We thought it heroic, in the circumstances. The parents all knew each other, and the boys were close…' She looked up suddenly. 'You don't think there's a connection with the murders, do you?'

Neither of us replied to that.

'What brought you here?' I asked with a reassuring smile.

'Oh, how I wish we'd met in our youth, Major Lennox, you really are everything a man should be,' she declared, then laughed when I sat up, startled.

'I…erm, I'm married. Persi, she, erm…' I babbled like an idiot.

'Could you just answer the question, please, Miss Olivia.' Swift frowned.

She pulled at a stray tress, curling it between her fingers. 'Oh, don't be such a stuffed shirt, Inspector. Let an old lady have some fun,' she countered. 'Anyway, what relevance can it have? I've been here five years and nothing has happened until now.'

'Why did you come here?' I asked again, relaxing back in my chair.

Her green eyes clouded as she gazed into the distance. 'Everyone I ever loved was dead. I was left alone, and I hated it. When this house was suggested to me, I said yes without hesitation.'

Swift put his pen down and clasped his hands together. 'You must have made some close friendships here,' he spoke kindly.

'I have,' she replied. 'They have become my family. We bicker and gossip and have our differences, but none of it is any different to most families.'

'Most families don't have a murderer in their midst.' Swift's words were a policeman's, but his tone was sympathetic.

It brought tears to Olivia's eyes nevertheless. 'We're utterly devastated. I know we appear to be silly old people, but we're not. We donate huge sums of money to organisations which are a lifeline for many in need. We take our responsibilities very seriously, and what happened to Jasper, and now General Hackett, has put everything in jeopardy. Everything,' she repeated, and dabbed her handkerchief to her eyes.

I felt sorry for her and sought a distraction. 'Did you know anyone here before you came?'

She nodded, blew her nose and put the handkerchief firmly away. 'I knew Matilda. We were childhood chums. Our nannies were related and they'd meet in Greenwich Park in London and chat while we played on the grass together. We went to the same school and were determined to remain pals afterwards. It didn't turn out that way, of course. She met a man and married. I met a man and he jilted me, the rotter.' She suddenly laughed. 'I thought it was the end of the world, but it was actually the start of my great adventure. Matilda had read a magazine article about voluntary work, and she suggested I go and do something to help the poor and unfortunate. So, I went to America!' She wagged a finger. 'Now I know that sounds ridiculous considering how advanced America seems to us here in fusty old England, but poverty is to be found in even the most advanced civilisations. I joined the Women's Depository and Exchange in New Brunswick, which I'm certain you will know is in New Jersey?' She aimed an interrogatory glare at us, suddenly quite serious.

We duly nodded, although I hadn't a clue where it was.

'The Woman's Exchange was begun in Philadelphia early last century and spread across the States. Each branch established a retail outlet, which was actually a consignment store,' she explained enthusiastically. 'Women who had suffered hardship were encouraged to use their skills to create clothing, or quilts, and even hats. These were sold through the stores and most of the profit went directly to the creator herself.'

'Was this for any woman or just gentlewomen?' Swift was listening attentively. I expect it was the sort of thing to appeal to his socialist nature, and I found it interesting too.

'Initially it was just for gentlewomen.' Olivia turned to him. 'You will realise that society was embarrassed by such a situation, and these ladies couldn't take jobs. But eventually the movement was expanded to include women from any background. There were tearooms and libraries as well as the sales departments – all run on the principle that the charity helped those who helped themselves. I believed it to be a marvellous enterprise and offered my services.'

'Sewing things?' I suggested.

She laughed. 'No, Major. I inherited a great deal of money. The stores were unable to support themselves financially and I was both patron and governor. I spent almost forty wonderful years there and became responsible for setting up training workshops across the whole of the north east. We organised classes each morning and afternoon for ladies who wanted to learn additional skills. We even expanded into baking and preserve making.' She smiled broadly, obviously enjoying herself. 'It saved so many families from poverty and gave women dignity and independence. I was terribly proud of our work there.'

'Why did you return to England?' I asked.

'Oh, many reasons, and Matilda had long been widowed,' she sighed. 'Neither of her children had survived infancy. She was alone, and old, and so was I. And I missed England; I adored America, but this is my home and it called to me. Matilda had been invited to Temple House and wanted me to come too – she was the only woman at the time and you can imagine the tedium.' She made to stand. 'Now if we're finished, I must go and freshen up, it's been a truly awful morning.'

'One question,' Swift said. 'The ladies making hats, did they use mercuric nitrate?'

'No, absolutely not.' Olivia's eyes flashed. 'We knew how dangerous mercury vapours were. Erethismus mercurialis. All the manufacturers were aware of it, so were most of the poor souls who worked for them.' She settled back down in her chair to lecture us. 'Poverty, you see. They were driven to sacrifice their health for the sake of earning a living. Our organisation did all they could to persuade the local Board of Labor and Industries to legislate, but they were resistant, and said mercury was used in many manufactories and not all workers fell to the disease.'

Swift had grown tense, his face taut, his gaze dark and distant.

'Swift?' I said.

He didn't reply.

'Inspector,' Olivia spoke kindly, her voice softened. 'Do you have experience of this?'

He nodded slowly, tears suddenly springing to his eyes,

which he blinked away. 'My mother,' he muttered under his breath.

Olivia reached out to take his hand. 'What happened to her?' She leaned across the desk. 'Tell me in your own time, there is no rush.'

I felt almost frozen in place. Swift had never confided in me about his mother. I knew he had returned to London with her when he was about seven, but that was all he'd said. I'd occasionally wondered what had become of her. She hadn't been at his and Florence's wedding, so I'd assumed her dead.

'They couldn't find the marriage certificate. It was kept at the Office, in Johannesburg. After Papa was killed in the battle of Ladysmith, Mama went to the Regimental Office at Headquarters for our documents. We'd been ordered to leave. She took me with her because I was too young to be left alone. I didn't understand why she was so upset about "papers". They insisted she must have the certificate, but she said she didn't. She repeated over and over that army headquarters held all official documents and they knew this. She pleaded with them to find her certificate.' He glanced away. 'They gave her our passports, then a soldier came and we were marched out of the building and through the gates…' He came to a stop, took out his handkerchief and blew his nose. 'I apologise. I haven't spoken about this before, except to Florence, my wife.'

'It's difficult to express words that have so much emotion and pain wrapped within them.' Olivia continued to hold his hand. He didn't resist. 'But by relating this terrible episode in your life, you will eventually exorcise the pain. Talking can bring acceptance and peace.'

He nodded mutely. 'Without the marriage certificate, my mother couldn't receive my father's Army pension. I think they knew that. The authorities were always trying to cut costs; she was one widow among many. She had no influence and very little money. My father was a captain from a good family, but only his mother survived, and she was barely able to provide for herself. We lived with her… GanMa, my grandmother.' A catch in his voice made him pause to clear his throat. 'It was a tiny house in Blackfriars. We had a room of our own. Mama found work in a hat-making factory. She went every day, and I went to school, or stayed home with my grandmother.' He took a breath, then carried on with more determination. 'Her hands had taken an orange tinge. I asked her why but she laughed it away. When I was ten, her behaviour began to change. She didn't want to leave the house, but had to go to work… there was no choice. She'd cry for an hour before she left, I heard her, weeping under the stairs trying to hide herself away. Grandmother was very frail by then, and I cared for her, fed her and…whatever was necessary. Then she died, and Mama's illness grew worse. I didn't know what it was at the time, and it was never acknowledged. Sometimes she'd simply seem very shy, or frightened. If someone glanced at her in the street, she would lower her head and put her hands over her face. Then the tremors started – her hands would shake, or her head, it varied, but grew gradually worse. Any loud noise would frighten her, and she barely slept, pacing her room for hours at night. The madness eventually took over; confusion, delusions, hallucinations. I tried so hard to keep her at home, care for her and make her feel safe. I took any job I could, except at the hat factory. I was sixteen when they took her to Bedlam. She died two years later.'

'Mad Hatter's disease,' I said, having heard of it.

'Yes,' Swift replied, still far from his usual self. 'But Lewis Caroll's Mad Hatter was quite different from the actual illness.'

'I'm so sorry,' Olivia said. 'Thank you for sharing your story, Inspector. I have seen too many examples of Erethism. It is a terrible neurological disease caused by mercury poisoning.' She sighed. 'We did not succeed in convincing the legislators in America to stop the use of mercuric nitrate, but the Order of Saints was instrumental in restricting it in England. The Felt Makers Guild was finally convinced some years ago to replace mercury with hydrochloride, which is known as the French method.' She lowered her voice. 'We donate to certain legal firms who are "persuasive" among those in power. It may not be quite as one would expect, and we are very cautious about our "causes".'

Swift squeezed her hand then gently extracted his. 'You're very kind, Miss Olivia.' He let out a long sigh. 'I apologise, I don't usually allow personal feelings to enter my professional life.'

'Of course you don't.' She smiled warmly. 'But I'm grateful you had enough trust to confide in me. I wish you peace, Inspector.' She stood up, we did likewise. She left the room, closing the door quietly behind her.

We dropped back into our seats, neither of us speaking. I broke the silence after some minutes.

'It can't have been easy to speak about your past.'

'No,' he agreed. 'My mother was kind, and unsuited to the harsh realities of life, like the women Olivia was trying to support, I suppose.'

'And the reason for your socialism.' I tried a slight tease.

One side of his mouth turned up. 'Possibly, but it's a balance, Lennox. People can get rich at the expense of another's labour. It's called providing employment, but without a balance formed by intervention of state, it becomes exploitation.'

'Not in all cases. There's a house full of people here who are wealthy and they only want to give back.'

'There's twelve of them, or there were. How many people do you think prefer to take, rather than give?' He waited for an answer, which I didn't have, so I stood up. 'Come on Swift, let's find out who's been killing them off.'

CHAPTER 14

'Actually, I thought you'd intended interviewing Captain Lockhart,' I mentioned as we went in search of prey.

'I couldn't find him.'

'Didn't anyone know where he was?' We were almost at the games room, muted voices could be heard within.

'There was mention of the chapel.' He opened the door; the voices grew louder, then stopped as we entered.

Young Jiggens, Freya and Greggs were seated at a circular table near the window, Cicely Sissinghurst was leaning over their shoulders. Papers were spread about in front of them. I could see some were the fingerprint papers, others were written in various hands. I assumed them to be the statements.

Jiggens and Greggs instantly sprang to their feet. Freya remained seated, Cicely straightened up.

'Where are the Saints?' Swift asked.

'Gone to their rooms to prepare for lunch,' Cicely replied in a high voice.

'Greggs, what are you doing?' I asked.

He flushed from wobbling chin to hairline. 'Ah...*ahem*, I am assisting, sir, at the request of Miss Sissinghurst.'

'We make inquires for ourselves, in case you fail,' Freya said without the hint of a blush.

Jiggens gulped, his Adam's apple bobbing.

'Freya, one does not accuse people of failure, or at least not to their faces,' Cicely reprimanded lightly. 'Gentlemen, we were merely observing remarks made by the Saints in their statements. We felt that we might be of some use to you.' She raised a steely brow, daring us to protest.

'Certainly.' Swift fixed a smile on his face. 'And we appreciate your help.'

I glanced sideways at him. 'What?'

He continued in an even tone. 'Jiggens, do you have time before lunch to help Major Lennox and I search General Hackett's room?'

'Yes… Yes, sir, absolutely, sir,' he stuttered. 'We didn't mean to read your papers, sirs.'

'Yes, we did,' Freya contradicted. 'We were agreed on it.'

Greggs' eyes widened in horror before he closed them.

'Freya and I will deliver these documents to the library.' Cicely indicated to Freya she should gather together the papers on the desk.

'The library is locked,' I said sternly, then took the key from my pocket and put it on the table. 'Lock it behind you and keep it hidden until we see you at lunch.'

'Very well,' Cicely agreed, her cheeks pink, but her face firmly set.

'Greggs,' I said.

'Sir!' He threw his shoulders back in military fashion.

'There is a killer in the house. You will keep the kitchen

safe, and ensure no-one other than the staff go in there,' I ordered. 'You will also make sure the food is never left unattended.'

'Indeed sir. I will do everything within my power to keep the residents safe, sir,' he replied in clipped manner, then went off quickly, head down.

'Come along, Freya.' Cicely set off. Freya followed with the papers in hand and her chin firmly raised.

'Right,' Swift said. 'Come on.'

Jiggens manoeuvred sheepishly around the table.

'Swift,' I said. 'I'm going to find Lockhart. It doesn't take three of us to search a room.'

'Good idea, Lennox.' He was almost genial. 'I'll see you on return.'

I nodded, then waited as he and the young footman went off. I'd left Foggy to his own devices after we'd come in from our walk, and he'd scooted off towards the central hallway where the Christmas tree stood. It had become a source of entertainment for the animals and I'd seen them there playing with a ribbon they'd tugged off the tree, having great fun.

There was no sign of any animal of any sort until I noticed the lid of the large log hamper was askew and the end of a mangled ribbon caught in the wickerwork. I lifted the top to see not only three cats cuddled together in contentment, but my dog had climbed in there with them. He blinked wearily, yawned and settled back to sleep, his head on a tartan blanket that had been folded and placed there by some kindly soul. At least it explained why the logs had been piled up on the other side of the hearth.

I left them to it and headed to the boot room to find my coat, hat and gloves and then the chapel – assuming Captain Lockhart was indeed there.

'Lennox.' Lockhart was seated on a pew at the very front, nearest the altar. 'I was expecting you.'

'Really?' I strolled along the short aisle; there were only four sets of pews each side. Built of Bath stone in rather austere style with a whitewashed interior, the apse lit by a single large window, with twelve haloed saints formed in pale coloured glass. Dark green tiles formed the floor, beams and pews were of black oak, and the altar was of plain stone with a brass cross upon it. I'd expected something fussier, more ornate, but its simple unadorned elegance was perhaps more suited to its surroundings. 'Why's that?'

'Your father,' he replied without turning around. 'A good man; understanding, compassionate, the type one sought to emulate, if only one didn't have feet of clay.'

'Are you saying you're stuck in the mud?' I sat down next to him.

He grinned. 'Stuck, in a way, yes.' The smile faded, lines deepening in his craggy face, his blue eyes fixed on the cross. 'You will know there's talk of a financial threat hanging over my head?' His gaze shifted momentarily to me, then back again.

'There was some mention of it.'

'It's nonsense, an old accusation made many years ago.' Irritation sharpened his voice. 'It had no foundation then and it doesn't now.'

'Was it a business deal?' The fact that Jasper had been involved in investment made that likely. 'I thought you were in the Navy?'

'I began in the Navy. It was terribly glamorous back then, everyone aspired to be an Officer of the Line.'

I knew that expression came from the old days of lining warships up in formation to blast cannon fire into enemy galleons. 'Presumably that was a first career?'

He gave a rasping laugh. 'Saw out the third war of Burma, helped extract the despotic little king the country had been saddled with, then went off to set my own course. I'd always wanted to build ships – elegant, streamlined racing yachts,' he sighed. 'And I succeeded. I bought a shipyard in Southampton, was given contracts from my fellow sea-dogs. After decades of hard work, I ended up with five shipyards around the country. We even refitted Navy frigates. Then I had to retire – the ticker was failing, according to my physician.' He tapped his chest lightly with two fingers. 'I sold up, moved into my old family house in Cornwall overlooking the bay, and grew bored of my own company. Hackett and I go back to our Burma days, he came to see me. He'd just joined the Order and thought I might be a suitable candidate. I allowed him to persuade me, and when a place arose, I came here and rather liked it. It's my home now, and will be until I die.'

'Jasper threatened to sue you, and bring General Hackett in as a witness.' I let the words hang.

He was sitting relatively relaxed in the upright pew, his legs crossed, hands loosely resting on his lap. Dressed in the smart blazer, blue silk cravat and cream trousers, he looked as though he should be heading for the Yacht Club. 'The Burma prizes.' He spoke quietly. 'We took the country, or the capital anyway, in a matter of weeks. There was little resistance, the British had sent out rumours that we were going to install a rival prince to the throne, a chap called Nyaungyan. It wasn't true, the man was actually dead, but the diplomats knew it for a seductive lie and the locals fell for it. Their Minister of Defence told the Burmese Army not to offer resistance, a few refused and put up a spirited fight but we soon had them whipped.' He mused for a moment, eyes gazing into the distance. 'The king ordered his army to lay down their arms, and most of them did. We took the Royal family prisoner and moved into the palace.' He gave a half smile. 'Your father had been invalided home by then. Hackett was involved in trying to round up the remaining dissenters. I was given the task of selling off the royal treasure.'

'What happened to the king and queen?'

'King Thibaw Min had a number of queens and concubines. He and his court were offered luxury accommodation in India under the gracious protection of Her Majesty Queen Victoria, Empress of India.' He glanced at me under a raised brow. 'Don't feel too sorry for Thibaw Min, he'd murdered a hundred of his fellow princes and princesses when he came to power. His own flesh and blood; it was rather a medieval place in some ways. The treasure on the other hand was very sophisticated, and there was an enormous amount of it. There were a group of us commissioned to sell it off, that way we could all keep an eye on each other. Well, we did a pretty good job of it. Part of the deal was to give us a percentage of the sale.' He grinned. 'It was standard practice – honouring the old tradition of sharing prizes among the officers instrumental in bringing about the victory. That's how I gathered enough funds to buy my first shipyard. As part of our series of lectures, I related this tale to the Saints. Everyone was suitably enthralled.' His tone grew colder. 'But the following week Jasper went to Hackett with allegations that I'd stolen some of the treasures.' He lapsed into silence, his lips tightly clamped together.

'I assume there was no truth in his allegations,' I prompted him.

'Absolutely not.' He spoke harshly. 'It was merely done so Jasper could find a reason to spend time with Cicely. He was pitifully shy around women but one could see the yearning, and he was particularly keen on Miss Sissinghurst.' He let out a pent-up breath. 'There had been a number of articles in *The Times* about the treasure, and the usual insinuations of theft and looting from political agitators. Jasper was ensconced in the business world, he'd read about it and heard more stories through the grapevine. I knew he had no intention of going through with his threats to sue me, and would never have succeeded if he had. But it left a question mark over the foundation of my wealth, and a slur on my good name. I was very angry with him.' He turned to me. 'But I had no reason to kill him, nor Gregory Hackett. I'm really terribly sad that Hackett's gone. He was a good man.'

'I assume Hackett stayed in the Army?' I was becoming quite cold, my back stiffening against the hard, upright pew.

'Yes, and spent a long time in Burma, actually. The lie told about installing Prince Nyaungyan backfired when he didn't turn up and the betrayal was exposed. Guerrilla warfare broke out. The British annexed the country, which added fuel to the fire, and the remaining opposition joined forces and organised themselves into a proper rebellion. Hackett was part of General Roberts' force to quell them – it took ten years to bring the country to heel. I doubt the Crown would have bothered had it not been for the ruby and sapphire mines in Mogok; the value of those made the palace treasure look like small change.'

I recalled quite a lot of the history from school, including the mines. I hadn't heard much about the palace treasure though, and thought that far more interesting. 'Were you allowed to keep any of the treasure, apart from your percentage?'

'Yes, we were permitted to choose a token each. I had a miniature jewelled horse; it was very pretty, pure gold inlaid with tiny gemstones. I used it as part of my lecture on the downfall of King Thibaw Min. I noticed it had disappeared from the Christmas tree a few days ago.' The frown between his brows deepened. 'I tie it on there every year, just below the angel. A pretty bauble…'

'Nobody mentioned it had gone missing,' I said casually.

He let out a sigh. 'No, well, we didn't want you getting over excited and dashing off on the wrong track.'

'Hum.' I nodded. 'When was the last time you were in the Chamber of Curiosities?'

'About three weeks ago. I was giving my latest lecture – a presentation on box jellyfish.' He glanced at me. 'Powdered box jellyfish.'

'Ah. Powdered box jellyfish. A bluish powder?'

He nodded, his lips folded in a thin line.

'You know how Hackett died?' I continued.

'I heard talk,' he replied.

I nodded. So much for trying to keep the means of murder a secret. 'Where did the powder come from?'

'A friend of mine brought it back from the islands in Torres Strait last summer. Box jellyfish, or rather Chironex fleckeri, thrive in the warmer waters there. Their toxin is one of the deadliest on earth, and remains potent even after death.' He glanced down at his hands. 'I informed the Saints of this in the lecture about three weeks ago.'

'Did everyone attend?' I asked.

'Yes, including our much admired Keeper of the Books, but none of the staff.' He clasped his hands more tightly together. 'It was quite fascinating. The Islanders catch the jellyfish and dry them in the sun, then grind them to powder. They stuff it in bait, or mix it with tree sap and smear it on harpoons.' He glanced at me. 'Was it quick?'

'It was,' I confirmed.

'The Chironex fleckeri sting can be intensely painful, and invariably fatal. It stops the heart, so I suppose it reduces the suffering.'

'Was the powder in one of the poisons jars?' I asked.

'It was,' he replied.

'Strange way to kill someone,' I remarked.

'Strange way to die.' Lockhart shook his head.

'Why keep the stuff if it's so deadly?'

He gave me a wry look. 'It's on a par with other Curiosities. Who'd have imagined anyone would want to murder anyone with it,' he said then swore. 'Damn it. We'll miss Gregory Hackett. I suppose Justice St John will take over as Regent now.'

'Temporarily,' I agreed and stood up. 'Best go and make ready for lunch, are you coming in?'

'I will.' He rose stiffly. 'Lennox, I want to live my life out here. I'm too old to change tack now, and I didn't kill Jasper or Gregory.' He smoothed his blazer down, then looked me in the eye. 'It's down to you and Swift; we sink or swim by your proficiency. Tell me truthfully, are you likely to nail the culprit? Because if you have any doubts we need to bring in the professionals.'

I bit back a sigh. The chapel bell chimed a single resonant clang, then died away. 'Yes, Lockhart, we'll find whoever it is, and we'll see them hanged for their deeds.'

'Good man.' He grinned. 'I knew Hugh Lennox's son would never let us down.' He clapped me on the shoulder and we walked out into the snow together.

CHAPTER 15

'All rise.' Justice St John took the top seat in the dining room as we arranged ourselves around the table for lunch. 'We will mark the passing with prayers.'

Everyone lowered their heads, including Cicely Sissinghurst, who had joined us.

'We offer prayers for those we have lost and those you have gained, dear Lord. We pray that the soul of Gregory Hackett finds safe haven and everlasting peace in your presence. For ever and ever, Amen.'

'Amen,' was muttered in response.

'Now one minute of silence,' St John demanded in an overloud voice.

We duly remained quiet. Fogg and all three cats wandered in, looked about in mild curiosity, then decided a game of tag was in order. No-one said a word but there were a few stifled giggles as the animals ran rings around our feet with as much noise as they were capable of.

'All be seated,' St John bellowed. 'Jiggens, you may proceed.'

Greggs and Jiggens had been hovering on the threshold with tureens of soup. They entered in suitable pomp, chins raised above stiff collars. Greggs proceeded to serve the soup into bowls arranged on the sideboard while Jiggens rushed to place them in front of each of us. Two bread rolls each were under napkins on our side plates. I whipped mine off, then picked up my spoon and waited politely for a lady to make the first scoop. No-one did. We all sat with spoons poised, glances flicking one to the other, but mostly at us.

'Right,' I muttered under my breath and took a mouthful. They watched me in morbid fascination, including Swift. I frowned at him and he quickly started eating.

'Excellent oxtail soup,' I said loudly. 'Please pass our compliments to the cook, Jiggens.'

'Will do, sir.' The lad forced a grin, pretending that everything was entirely normal. 'And the bread…?'

I duly took a roll and broke it open, then dipped it into my soup and took a bite. 'Perfect,' I mumbled through the crust.

Swift and I were almost finished before the rest of them took their first sip of soup. I was of half a mind to grab my throat and pretend to gasp for breath, but decided against.

'The library key, Inspector.' Cicely made a show of handing the key to Swift. 'I trust you will make good progress in your endeavours.'

'So do I,' Swift muttered.

We'd been a little late in arriving because we'd dashed up to the Chamber of Curiosities after I'd told Swift what Lockhart had told me. Rackham had the key and wanted to come, but we forbade him. All these locks and keys were becoming a damned nuisance and made me realise why things were left open.

The jar of jellyfish powder was indeed empty, and smelled of carbolic. It was impossible to tell when the contents had been purloined. We'd examined the curare at the same time, thinking it may have been smeared on the bone needle. The jar and contents appeared untouched, which had given us pause. We fingerprinted it anyway – it showed a few smeared prints, none clear enough to identify, and hadn't been cleaned in an apparently long time. That fairly flummoxed us and we'd gone down to lunch with long faces.

Freya came into the dining room with fresh jugs of water and glanced about at us all. 'Not finished? It is good food, no poison. We look after it very carefully. No worries for the food, nor the wine.' She frowned at Jiggens.

'We weren't going to serve until…' Jiggens began then lowered his voice as we all looked at him. 'Until we knew everything was fine,' he hissed.

'As you see, it is fine, and the wine is still in its cork. Hurry along now, I bring small salad and cut meat pie next.' She went out, her chin in the air and lids lowered. Jiggens' cheeks burned red.

'Great girl, that.' Justice St John smiled as she passed him.

'A model of perfection,' Pastor Peabody said. 'Although rather forceful, I have noticed.'

'It's just her way.' Lockhart finished mopping the soup with his roll. 'And a girl as pretty as that can be any way she wants.'

Neither Roger nor Norman said anything, they barely seemed to be listening, and Wilfred Rackham appeared lost in thought, his gaze on the fire – or Justice St John, it was difficult to say given the false eye.

Talk was muted throughout the salad course, and the trifle which followed. Cicely Sissinghurst made an announcement as the dessert dishes were removed.

'A meeting of the Order is required, and I suggest we commence over tea,' she said, then turned a steely eye on us. 'The meeting will be held here, gentlemen. I imagine you will be adjourning to the library.'

I was first on my feet. 'Yes, thank you, we are.'

Swift rose too, although he was frowning and seemed none too pleased his investigation was expected to play second fiddle to their meeting. He bowed politely nonetheless and muttered something inaudible under his breath.

'I suppose they'll have to reorganise themselves now that they are without the Regent,' I said as we headed along the passage.

'Fine, but they're telling us to get on with it, that they could be next, and then they obstruct us.' His benign mood seemed to have evaporated.

'It's hardly an obstruction.' I waited while he unlocked the library door. 'Who's been putting pressure on?'

'Justice St John, of course, and even Pastor Peabody asked that we 'expedite matters'. They were keen to remind me of my duties while you were with Lockhart in the chapel. St John was worried about the ladies, he seemed to think them the most vulnerable. I didn't respond, but I think he has a point; this could be a power struggle between the men.' He slipped the key back into his pocket and went straight to the reading table where the statements were stacked neatly next to the blotter and ink stand.

I sat down and took out my notebook. 'You think one of them wants to run the show?'

'The Order holds hundreds of thousands of pounds, Lennox, Justice St John told me.' He sat down too and drew the statements toward him. 'The Regent has the final say in where the donations go if there's a tie.'

'St John doesn't have authority.'

'They will take a vote today, so he soon will have, although it has to be ratified by their legal counsel.' He picked up the first statement.

'The Three Wise Men?'

'They're called "King's Counsellors", Lennox.' He looked about the room. 'Do you think there might be a blackboard in the house?'

'You always ask that, and no, why on earth would there be?'

'The Saints give lectures, perhaps they use one to demonstrate things.'

'The lectures are merely entertainment, and we don't need a blackboard.'

He sighed. 'Fine, shall I read out the statements?'

'No.'

He frowned. 'Lennox, we're supposed to be doing this properly. It's part of learning police procedure.'

'I don't want to learn police procedure.'

His frown deepened. 'Right, well I'll summarise, and you can make notes in your book so that we both have the same information.' He turned pedantic.

I would have quibbled, but we'd just be there all day. 'Right, fire away.'

'Statement by Baroness Ginny Finch,' he read out then quickly scanned the page. 'She was dressing in her room when Lady Matilda came to inform her of the news around nine forty-five.'

'Is that it?'

'In short, yes.'

I muttered under my breath, then said, 'Go on.'

'Lady Matilda stated she had been told by Pastor Peabody.' He turned pages over. 'He had been on the way to breakfast when old Jiggens told him.' He peered to decipher a tightly written page. 'Wilfred Rackham was already in the breakfast room when he heard voices calling out. He went into the hall and found Freya and she told him before she ran upstairs.' He turned another page, covered in flourishing handwriting. 'Roger and Norman were still in their rooms and only heard about it when they came downstairs… and Lord Balthazar wrote that he'd like bacon and eggs for breakfast rather than his usual marmalade and toast.'

'Oblivious, as usual.'

Swift grinned, then he stretched his arms above his head. 'I agree, it hardly helps, but we should have a disciplined approach.'

'Was there anything untoward in General Hackett's bedroom?'

'Nope, no fingerprints other than his and Jiggens'. Nothing relevant at all. He appeared to live a spartan life.'

'What about his office?'

'He kept a log of events but they mostly revolved around the official meetings of the Order.'

'Cicely Sissinghurst was here the day Jasper died.'

'There wasn't a meeting that day, but she came to discuss the list of donations with Hackett,' he confirmed.

I made a note of that; so did he.

'Lockhart gave a lecture about the box jellyfish three weeks ago,' I told him. 'Cicely attended, although none of the staff did.'

'Where did the jellyfish come from?'

'Somewhere called the Torres Strait.' I told him how they'd been brought here, and then regaled him with Lockhart's story of the last Burma war and how the royal palace fell to the British forces.

'So we stole the Burmese crown jewels.'

'And sold them to the highest bidders, yes.'

'Nothing new there,' he said wryly, then thought for a moment. 'According to what I understand of Jasper's accusations, he believed Lockhart could be liable to a legal prosecution if he sold any of the treasures without authority, or stole any?'

'It's nonsense. You know how the system works. Lockhart was a Naval officer, and the Army formed part of the disbursement team alongside him. There would have been inventories made and intense scrutiny of everything they did. Lockhart wasn't high enough in the ranks to siphon anything off for himself, even if he were inclined to.'

'And General Hackett would have told Jasper that was clearly the case.' Swift made a note. 'Unless he didn't, of course.'

'I find it hard to believe Hackett would have acted with anything other than absolute integrity,' I replied.

'We should keep an open mind.' Swift wrote something else, then looked up. 'But I agree.'

'Do you really think it was a power struggle?'

He sat with pen poised before replying, 'Only if there were some compelling reason to be Regent, but that doesn't explain Jasper's death.'

'Then it's love or money,' I said.

'Hum...love seems unlikely.'

'Jasper wanted Cicely to join the Order, he adored her from afar,' I said.

'He adored them all from afar,' he replied.

'He was quite willing to sacrifice Balthazar Cholmondeley,' I reminded him.

'Implying Balthazar killed Jasper to save himself, and then killed Hackett because he'd acquired a taste for murder? You don't believe that any more than I do.'

'No,' I replied, and decided to stop goading him. 'It's more likely to have risen from Wilfred Rackham's failed expedition.'

'Precisely,' he said, then stopped writing to lean back in his chair. 'Jasper, Hackett, Peabody and Baroness Ginny Finch. Two of the patrons are dead and Rackham is the most likely culprit.'

'How the devil do you come to that conclusion?' I demanded.

'Logic.'

'By deduction – like Sherlock Holmes?' I wasn't convinced.

'Are you demanding evidence?' He grinned wryly. 'You're in danger of becoming a professional, Lennox.'

'No, I'm not,' I protested. 'It's merely that we don't have enough information.'

He grinned. 'Precisely, so we need to gather some.'

'There's the bone needle,' I said.

'Scotland Yard has it,' he reminded me.

I ignored him and began writing a list. 'The empty jar of Yopo, the empty jar of jellyfish powder, and a description of the footprints in the Roman Bath.'

'You're convinced the footprints were a man's?'

'Yes,' I replied, then sighed. 'Probably. Should we assume the slipper wearer was the person who fired the needle at Hackett?'

'You believe they were made this morning?'

I gave it a moment's thought, then nodded. 'Yes... No. I don't know.'

'Lennox you need to be more observant.' He turned tetchy then wrote something down.

That riled me. 'I was observant!' I protested. 'I even got into the pool.'

He muttered something under his breath.

I drummed my fingers on the table. The sun emerged from behind a cloud and suffused the room with bright sunlight.

'Lockhart had a jewelled horse from the Burmese treasure he was given as part of the prizes. It's gone missing,' I told him.

His eyes darkened under a furrowed brow. 'Is it relevant?'

'No idea.' I shrugged. 'It was tied to the Christmas tree and went missing a week ago.'

Swift thought about it some more, made a note then put down his pen. 'I questioned young Jiggens while we searched Hackett's room. He said the only people who swam were Hackett and Baroness Ginny, but she insists on Essie the housekeeper attending on the rare occasion she used the pool.'

'What about Rackham? I'd have thought swimming beneficial to him.'

'Never does, according to Jiggens, says he's too worried about slipping and falling, though it could be because he'd rather not expose his injuries,' he said, sympathy in his dark eyes.

That was a sobering thought. 'I assume Jiggens didn't see or hear anything suspicious this morning?'

'No, nor any morning,' Swift replied. 'I'd have told you if he had. None of the staff did, they were too busy lighting fires and preparing breakfast.'

'It has to be one of the Saints.' I considered. 'The killer had access to the Chamber of Curiosities, and must have listened to the lectures about Yopo and the jellyfish.'

'We've already established that, Lennox.'

'I'm just being thorough,' I countered.

'Roger Nesbit…' Swift was flicking back through his notes. 'He and Norman were dealers in rare books.'

'Yes, he said the Dickens book was worth a small fortune.'

'It's a first edition and signed by the author, I imagine it would be,' Swift continued.

'But they're all tremendously wealthy, this can't be about money,' I mused.

'So it's about love.'

We were going round in circles. 'They're doddering old folk, Swift.'

'I recall your Uncle Melrose, Lennox, and the trouble his fiancee caused. Neither were exactly spring chickens.'

I quelled the images rising to mind. 'It's affection and jealousy, not, erm…'

'Physical,' he said, laughing.

I grinned too, then turned serious. 'I was sorry to hear about what happened to your mother, Swift, and to you. It must have been difficult.'

Sorrow softened the sharp angles of his face. 'She knew the consequences, or would have learned of it shortly after starting the job. They all knew what the mercury would do to them, including the owners of the factory.' He let out a breath slowly. 'The workers were poor and desperate. I met some of them, they truly were like the characters from Dickens. Utterly impoverished lives, no money for rent, or coal, food always scarce, and if they became ill they couldn't afford a doctor or medicine. I swore I'd never work for anyone who treated people like that just for their own profit.'

'So you fight the good fight,' I replied.

'For justice, yes. It's important…to me anyway.' He glanced up. 'Lennox, Scotland Yard won't take me on as an official consultant without you. It's your understanding of this world, the toffs, the way they talk, and think and live. Billings sends us on these types of cases because of that. He said he needs both of us.'

I nodded. 'I'll be there, Swift, whenever you need me.'

'Would you sign the contract and take the retainer?' he asked.

I hesitated. It wasn't the commitment, or the work, it was the institution itself. Scotland Yard had the same lines of command, rules, regulations and procedures as the Royal Air Force. Joining any institution felt like donning a strait-jacket; even school had grated. I savoured my freedom and independence, but…I sighed.

'If you consider it necessary, Swift, of course I will.'

CHAPTER 16

He had the papers in his jacket pocket, and I had my pen still in hand. The retainer was fifteen pounds, six shillings and thruppence a month. As we used to say in the mess, that would hardly cover my bar bill.

I signed anyway and said nothing.

'We are now officially consultants to Scotland Yard!' He beamed. 'I'm back in the force, Lennox. I can't tell you what it means to me.' He jumped up and came to shake my hand. 'Thank you, and don't worry that it will change things, Billings was clear that we'd only be required when there are toffs involved.' He was almost babbling.

'Fine, fine,' I muttered and then thought I probably should have discussed it with Persi first.

'Do you think we should make a map of the house?' He changed tack.

'No.'

'But there are servants' stairs all over the place,' he replied, his jovial tone reverting to his normal tetchiness.

'Swift, how would it help? The killer could be moving

about the house, seen or unseen and it wouldn't prove anything unless he or she were caught in the act.'

'But we should be thorough. I'll call for Jiggens.' He went and tugged the bell-pull before I could stop him.

'Fine,' I said. My pen had run out of ink, so I gave up and put the lid on it. 'You didn't find any sign of a blowpipe in your search, I suppose?'

'No, although there might be one among the Curiosities. There isn't a full inventory of what's in there,' he replied.

A tap on the door was followed by Jiggens. 'Sirs, you rang?'

'We'd like a map of the house, Jiggens,' Swift told him.

Jiggens blinked twice. 'A map, sir? I'm afraid we don't have such a thing. Why would anyone have a map of a house?'

'Secret passages,' I said.

'Don't think they'd be included, sir, or they wouldn't be secret.'

'Where are they?' I persisted.

'Ah, now, there aren't any secret ones, but there's a few back stairs.' He was holding a yellow duster for some reason and tugged it between both hands as he explained. 'If you think of the hall stairs by the Christmas tree being dead centre of the house, then there's a panelled wall all around it with three doors going out – it's to stop the heat going straight upstairs, you see. Those doors open to the corridor surrounding the central hall and that leads to all the rooms on the ground floor, and the front and rear doors.' He rattled on. 'Now there's two servants' stairs behind the panelling, one goes direct to the kitchen, that's between the dining room and breakfast room, and the other goes out of the games room and down to the below stairs passage and from there to the Roman Bath–'

'Wait.' Swift held a hand up. He'd been drawing a map on a page of his notebook but the lad was talking too quickly. 'Where's the door going directly to the kitchen?'

Jiggens pointed to a spot on Swift's rough diagram, and explained, 'And that also goes straight up to the first floor where all the bedrooms are and comes out opposite the main staircase.'

'Does it go up to the third floor?' I asked.

'It does.' Jiggens grinned. 'All stone steps going up and down the house, but out of sight from the Saints. The men's bedrooms are to the west, and the ladies to the east. You've been to the Regent's office, which was General Hackett's, until, um, this morning.' His voice trailed off.

'Is there a passage or staircase going directly into the Chamber of Curiosities?' Swift asked as he turned to a fresh page.

'Nope, that area's kind of sacred,' Jiggens said seriously. 'We don't usually go in there except on order from one of the Saints, and then it's just to dust and clean where's needed.'

'Who usually supervises?' I asked.

'Mr Rackham.'

'Who went in there most frequently?' Swift was making fast notes.

'Mr Rackham, but the General was often in there too,'

Jiggens explained. 'And sometimes Captain Lockhart would go; he was supposed to be a curator with Mr Rackham, but he hardly did much.'

'Has anyone been in there recently, who you wouldn't expect?' Swift continued his rapid note-taking.

'Lady Matilda has, the day before Sir Jasper died.' Jiggens had wound the yellow duster tightly around his hands. 'I saw her come out but she didn't see me. I was coming from the servants' stairs, there was a north wind blowing and I went to shut all the shutters in the attic. It's to stop the windows rattling up there and bothering people at night.' He looked down at the duster, his young face pale and unhappy. 'Can I start cleaning the General's bedroom, now, sirs? 'Cause the closer we get to Christmas, the more busy I'm going to be and I'm run off my feet already.'

'Yes, you may,' Swift told him. 'But find Lady Matilda first and ask her to come here, please?'

'Righto, sir, but I think they might still be in their meeting. I'll take a note in to her, and then she'll come when it's finished.' Jiggens hesitated as though there was something else he was going to say, but then dashed off, evidently keen to be elsewhere.

I was contemplating coffee while Swift found a ruler and drew a tidier version of his map of the house. The door opened on a knock and the housekeeper, Essie, slid in.

'Hello, sirs.' She was almost whispering. 'Ralphie said you was here. Ralphie's young Jiggens' proper name.' She bobbed a curtsy as she came to the reading table. 'It's about the carbolic. Some'un said you was talkin' about it.'

'You're Essie Jiggens?' Swift spoke kindly to her.

'Yes'um, sir.' She bobbed another curtsy, and tried a timorous smile. Her thin face looked more lined and strained than yesterday. Her cap was tied askew, so was the bow under her chin, grey strands of hair were escaping and there was a smudge of flour on the canvas apron she wore over her drab navy frock.

'Would you like to sit down?' I asked her and stood to help.

'Oh no, no, not in front of the gentry, sir.' She backed away, arthritic hands clasped together.

'Fine,' I sat down again as I seemed to be making her more nervous. 'You'd like to tell us about the carbolic?'

'I talked with Ralphie, and he said maybe I should, but Papa didn't want 'owt said. Papa's sad now and won't come from his room. It's a blessing we have your Mr Greggs. A very fine man, he is.' She sighed then tried another smile. 'A bar of carbolic went missin' from the store cupboard under the stairs in the hall.' Her voice was very low and we had to lean forward to hear her. 'I was going to use it to clean Sir Jasper's room after he went an' died, but I couldn't, 'cause it were gone.'

'We thought carbolic was kept in the Chamber of Curiosities,' Swift said.

'A bar usually is, an' in the kitchen too, but I'd used it all up 'cause of having to clean the floor after that spill.' Her shoulders were stooped and yet below the nerves and worry it was clear she was a contented soul. The kindly smile curling her lips upwards, her brown eyes soft and placid.

'There's a spare bar kept in the under stairs cupboard, but like I said, it weren't there. Then I went to look in the Curiosities and found a bar there, which were strange. Anyhow, Ralphie had ordered six bars from the chemist which hadn't come by then, but now they have. So we've plenty.'

'Did you put the bar back in the Chamber after you used it in Sir Jasper's room?' I asked.

'No, I didn't touch it, 'cause one of the gentry must 'a moved it.' She nodded for emphasis. 'I used washing soap to clean his room instead, which in't as good, but dun't smell as bad.'

'What was spilled?' Swift turned policeman.

'I don't rightly know, but it were Baroness Finch as spilled it. She and Lady Matilda showed me. It were oil of some sort – up in the Chamber, and I had to scrub it for three days in a row before it was cleared.'

Lady Matilda hadn't told us about this – nobody had.

'Can you recall the date?' Swift persisted.

She shook her head, the cap falling sideways; she didn't seem to notice. 'I don't even know what day it is most times.' She smiled. 'But it might be a week back, maybe more. I've been fretting if'n I should tell you. Papa had to lie down, all this is worriting him so much. Ralphie's just a young 'un, but he's worrit too. Janet and me had a talk, and I said I'd tell you if Ralphie agreed I should.' She bobbed again. 'Janet's the cook, which ye might know already.'

'Let me get this straight,' I said, because her account was rather disjointed. 'You used all the carbolic to clean some oil spilt in the Chamber of Curiosities, except for the spare bar in the under stairs cupboard. And you found that it had been taken to the Chamber of Curiosities when you searched for it the day after Sir Jasper died?'

She nodded. 'That's just as it was, sir.'

Swift wrote as I paused to consider soap.

'Can I be going now then, sir?' Essie asked.

'Yes, no…wait,' I said. 'How do you use a bar of carbolic soap to scrub a floor clean?'

Swift frowned at me for some reason.

Essie giggled then put her hand over her mouth. 'Don't ye know?'

I shook my head.

'Well, ye scrub at it with a scrubbing brush and it comes all foaming.' She made a scrubbing motion with her hands. 'Then ye clean with the brush, or a cloth if it's summat delicate needs wiping.'

'Have you seen any of the residents going up to the top floor recently?' Swift had turned to a fresh page and looked up from his notebook.

'I haven't, sir, no. I don't normally go up, 'cept when asked.' She became nervous again. 'Ralphie said to be sure an' tell you that.'

'What about down to the pool?' I tried a calming tone. 'We know General Hackett used to swim most days.'

'He did, and sometimes the Baroness did, but only if I helped. She's not good on her feet. The only other I saw going down there was Mr Norman, he's the one with the wig. He's funny, makes me laugh even if he doesn't mean to.'

'Was he going swimming?' I asked.

'Don't think so, nobody said anything. The General had rules about the pool: it always had to be kept mopped, and the towels clean and folded. If any of the masters or mistresses wanted to swim, they had to tell him first, then he would tell Papa and he'd tell us to tidy up afterwards. The General was very strict, he was Regent, so, I suppose he had to be.'

'Thank you, Essie,' I said, and meant it. 'And do you know who wears slippers with rubber soles?'

'All of 'em do, sir. Most of them come down to breakfast in them. Lord Balthazar wears his all day, an' never goes outside at all.'

'What about Miss Sissinghurst, or her maid?' Swift asked.

'Now, sometimes they bring slippers if the weather's bad 'cause they'd not be wanting to wear boots all day, not in the house where it's so warm. The girl's a pretty one, in't she?' She smiled fondly. 'Just right for our Ralphie.'

'Um…yes, possibly,' I said, thinking she probably hadn't encountered the full force of Freya's personality.

The door swung open and Lady Matilda came in, then stopped and raised the lorgnette to her eyes. 'Ah, Essie, dear soul. Might we have an afternoon beverage? A pot of coffee perhaps?'

'I'll arrange a tray now, m'lady,' Essie replied instantly, and bobbed another curtsey. 'It won't be but a moment.'

'Thank you so much.' Lady Matilda waited until the timid housekeeper had rushed out, closing the door carefully behind her. 'Now, gentlemen, I believe you would like to interview me?' She stalked over, head held high, purple crepe frock rustling, the afternoon sunlight catching her coiffed white hair.

I gazed for a moment, thinking the difference in style and attitude of the two women was legion. Swift's poor mother was on my mind, how she had gone from being an Officer's wife with all that entailed, to an impoverished, untrained worker – nothing more than a pair of hands.

'We treat them well, you know.' Lady Matilda had sat down and was staring, narrow-eyed, at me.

'Yes, erm... apologies, Lady Matilda.' I had remained seated like an ill-mannered churl.

'No matter. I imagine you are both quite perplexed at the situation,' she continued. 'What may I do to be of assistance?' A smile played on her lips, her eyes suddenly gleamed with a touch of devilment.

'Are you aware of how Sir Jasper died?' Swift turned stiffly formal.

'No,' she replied.

'Yes, you are,' I called her bluff.

Her smile faded. 'Very well, I am. Gregory Hackett informed me before you arrived.'

We both sat up at that.

'Why did he tell you?' I asked.

'It was because Jasper was increasingly irritable...' She put the lorgnette on the table top. 'And Balthazar was, well, suffering his harsh tongue and it was most unfair.'

Swift's brow had furrowed. 'I'm afraid you will have to be more forthright, Lady Matilda.'

'Balthazar is going gaga,' she replied, her stiff shoulders sagging slightly. 'It can happen as one ages. Sometimes he wanders about in the night, he even came into my bedroom once, which was disconcerting. I led him back to bed, he was terribly fuddled. Pastor Peabody had to stop him climbing out of a window one day. It was on the top floor, he could have killed himself.'

'Did you give Yopo to Balthazar as a sedative?' Swift jumped in with the accusation.

'We certainly did not.' Her eyes flashed. 'That would not have helped him at all. We gave him extract of snowdrops.'

'What?' I said.

'Wilfred recommended it.' She raised her chin defiantly. 'The proper name is galantamine, it is mentioned in Homer.'

'Homer?' Swift sounded incredulous.

'Yes, *The Odyssey*. There is a copy on the shelves.' She raised a gloved hand to wave at the books surrounding us. 'When Ulysses arrives on Circe's island he is given the milk flower, "Moly", which we know as the snowdrop. This was the antidote to another drug Circe had already hidden in bowls of meal and given to Ulysses crew. According to legend it had stupefied them and allowed her to turn them into swine. The flower – or rather the extract – meant Ulysses was able to keep his wits. It clarified his mind.'

I was inclined to say 'what?' again but pulled myself together. 'There are any number of versions of *The Odyssey*.

Homer's tale was passed down by word of mouth, then written and rewritten numerous times over.'

'And we have them all, Major, and Moly is mentioned in each. We have one of the most extensive libraries in the country, and many great men of learning have resided in this house. We were assured that the extract of snowdrop allows the recipient improved clarity of thought, and we discovered that to be true,' she declared, then added, 'although one must accept it cannot reverse the effect of mental decline.'

'Is the extract of snowdrop medically approved?' Swift asked.

A light flush reddened her cheeks. 'It is not.'

'You gave him experimental drugs?' I was incredulous.

'It is a herbal remedy, Major, going back millennia,' she retorted sharply.

Swift regarded her steadily, his lean face hawklike. 'What effect did the drug have?'

'Exactly as desired.' She straightened up, determined to defend their actions. 'He is perfectly happy. He doesn't wander about in the night now and is much brighter.'

Considering how confused Balthazar had seemed to us, it was hard to imagine he could have been worse. 'Are you still giving him the extract?'

'Yes, and we have explained to him what medication he is taking. It is done with the deepest consideration for his welfare.' She tapped a gloved finger on the table top. 'And Wilfred is passing his findings on to contacts in his own field of work – he is a highly respected botanist. We hope something useful may come of this.'

A tap on the door and the dignified entrance of my butler interrupted the interview, which was a good thing because Swift and I were rather bemused.

'Coffee with cream, and a selection of Cook's biscuits,' Greggs announced in his loftiest manner, and proceeded to set down the tray and serve the goodies.

CHAPTER 17

'You won't forget our rehearsal this evening in the games room, Mr Greggs?' Lady Matilda spoke archly.

'I have been counting the hours, m'lady,' he simpered.

'Greggs…' I began.

'*Ahem*, of course, sir, your coffee.' He had already served her ladyship and Swift. He plonked the cup in front of me and picked up the silver tongs to hover over the platter of goodies. 'A coconut swirl, m'lady?' He held a pretty porcelain plate at the ready.

'Oh, one only, thank you.' She smiled gaily. 'One must retain strict control of one's intake.'

'Indeed, m'lady.' He served the cherry-topped biscuit reverentially, then straightened up. 'If I may be excused, m'lady? There are a multitude of tasks awaiting my attention.'

'Of course you may,' Lady Matilda allowed. 'Toodle-oo.' She waggled silk-gloved fingers at him.

I rolled my eyes; Swift grinned.

We finished our coffee and the biscuits, then Swift picked up his pen. 'You were in the Chamber of Curiosities the day before Sir Jasper died, and you were also there sometime before. Why?'

'As I have said, Balthazar was being treated with the extract of snowdrops. The jar was kept in there. His treatment began on December the first. Baroness Finch and I went to fetch it, and we minister two teaspoons to him every evening. We had to replenish the supply on December the fourteenth and unfortunately the Baroness knocked over a bottle of Tincture of St John's Wort.'

Swift wrote this down as though he knew what it meant.

'Is the tincture oily?' I asked.

'More of a syrup,' she replied.

'You asked Essie to clean the spilled tincture with carbolic,' Swift stated.

'I did not specify how she cleaned it, merely that she did so,' Lady Matilda replied.

'What is St John's Wort?' I asked.

'It is quite a common plant with large yellow flowers, surely you are familiar with it?' she replied.

'No.'

She let out a huff. 'It is a well-understood concoction. The flowers are steeped in alcohol and honey for six weeks and one then takes a spoonful twice a day. It lightens the mood of depressives.'

'What sort of alcohol?' I asked, thinking any sort was bound to lighten the mood with or without flowers.

'We have discovered vodka to be the most effective.' Her tone was one of distaste.

I'd only ever drunk vodka during the war; it had been passed around as a novelty. I'd thought it potent stuff with a raw bite to it.

'Did anyone here take St John's Wort for depression?' Swift was writing quickly.

She didn't answer and he stopped to look up.

'Oh, I really wish the General were here,' she said in exasperation as much as sorrow. 'Jasper took it. He was morose, it was part of his nature. He'd been taking it for months and firmly believed it helped him.' She turned her gaze to the window and winter blue sky beyond. 'The bottle that was knocked over was his reserve. He had a small amount in his room, but there was very little left. Wilfred instantly set to work making another tincture but as I said, it takes six weeks to mature, and there were no fresh flowers to be had in winter. He had dried flowers but they do not have the same efficacy.' She pursed her lips.

'Jasper took Yopo in its stead, didn't he?' I guessed.

She nodded. 'Only as a stopgap, because there wasn't very much of that either, although it is very potent and very little was required. Wilfred showed him how much to put in a cup of hot water and honey. It was ground beans. One small pinch, and then only before bed.'

'Who knew about this?' Swift recommenced note-taking.

'Very few, I believe, but I don't really know. The St John's Wort had helped him but the Yopo made a very noticeable difference. He began to emerge from his shell; he joined in more often with the games and was apparently enjoying them, and the company.'

'Did you consult a doctor about these remedies?' Swift looked up from his careful notes.

'No. Wilfred knows botanics inside out, and Cicely is very experienced, she worked in hospitals during the war. We all turn to them first if we need medication.'

'You said St John's Wort is a well-known concoction,' I reminded her. 'If so, why couldn't it simply be ordered from a pharmacy?'

'It is not a recognised medicine and the ingredients vary to a great degree. It is far better if it is made by a professional.'

'Such as Wilfred Rackham,' I said.

'Indeed. And Cicely, of course. They intend teaching Freya too, which we consider a great benefit to us all.'

I didn't reply to that.

'Was Sir Jasper's death originally assumed to be an accidental overdose?' Swift returned to questioning.

'It was, and that is what Gregory and Wilfred considered on the evening of Jasper's death. A local constable had just informed Gregory that there was something amiss,' she said. 'Then an inspector from Bath came the next morning and he insisted the death be reported as suspicious. Gregory demanded he be allowed to make use of his connections. The inspector was dubious, but then Cicely was consulted and she recommended you both. Gregory spoke to Scotland Yard to request your assistance and that satisfied the police. We thought Gregory would simply explain the situation to you, but he did not, and we couldn't understand the reason for it. I think he'd changed his mind and didn't want to cloud the investigation before it had even begun. After all, why would Jasper take too much? He was a careful man, he had been warned about the dangers–' She stopped talking suddenly.

'There was a book open on his lap, had he been reading it, do you know?' Swift asked.

She glanced at him, all light-heartedness now gone. 'He read *The Times*, nothing else. He said reading novels was frivolous. One would gain nothing by it.'

'Did General Hackett say anything more about Sir Jasper's death?' Swift asked.

'He did not.' She hesitated. 'Is it possible he discovered something and was killed for that reason?'

Swift nodded. 'It's possible.'

She gazed at him for a moment, then wiped a tear from her eye with a lace handkerchief. 'We shall miss him. *I* shall miss him very much,' she said with a catch in her voice.

'You appear to enjoy living here,' I tried to divert her.

She sniffed delicately, then put the handkerchief back into a pocket hidden among the folds of her skirt. 'I lost both my children to scarlet fever. A boy and a girl, little golden-haired angels, aged five and seven. We loved them more than life. My husband went into a decline. We were wealthy, he didn't need to work, but he had taken a career as an architect and adored it. He struggled to continue working, he couldn't see the point. A year later he shot himself.' She hung her head for a moment. 'I also struggled to find a reason to live. Pastor Peabody served at our church and he became a friend and my saviour. I was asked to help on the church committee and worked for many good causes over the decades. Some few years ago I was invited here, to Temple House, by the previous Regent. He was an old friend of my husband's. When I retired from my charities, I accepted. I did not expect poor Peabody to join me, but tragedy found him out, too.' She paused to gather her thoughts. 'Since I moved here, I have come alive again. We all have. We left the world behind and made our own safe and contented corner, but now it is not safe, nor is it contented. I implore you, gentlemen, please find this fiend and stop this before we are all destroyed by it.' She picked up the lorgnette and rose to her feet. 'I will leave you to continue with your work.'

We both stood too. I went and opened the door for her and she swept out with head held high.

Swift looked up. 'That was illuminating.'

'Sir Jasper was already taking Yopo; Hackett could have told us.' I dropped back into my chair.

'Perhaps he was trying to protect the ladies from our inquisition,' Swift replied.

'Nonsense,' I remarked. 'I think Jasper was the target and Hackett may have guessed the killer.'

'Which makes sense,' he replied, tapping his finger on an open page of his notebook.

We digested Matilda's information. A log in the fire crackled and spat, sending a plume of smoke up the chimney. I went to poke it and toss more logs on, then came back to sit down at the reading table.

'Why the hell didn't they tell us all this?' I returned to the puzzle.

'The usual reasons, Lennox. Secrets, fear, lies…you should be used to it by now.'

He was right, most people seemed to prefer a convenient lie to a complicated truth. Although in this case, Hackett more likely wanted to test us before taking us into his confidence.

I sighed. 'The needle…it's been bothering me. It can't have been used in a blowpipe, without a fletch it would just fall out.'

'I agree,' he said. 'It would need to have some sort of tassel or feather on the end to hold it in place.'

'It may have fallen off and been washed down the outlet pipe in the pool.'

'True.' He made a note.

'And curare is somehow predictable, almost a cliche, assuming it even was curare,' I continued. 'Do you think someone went down to the pool and confronted Hackett, either intending to stab him with it or threaten to kill themselves?'

'A dramatic denouement?' Swift considered it. 'Making some sort of demand from Hackett.'

'Perhaps they were trying to justify their actions and wanted the murder of Jasper covered up?'

'And he refused…' Swift mused. 'They threw the needle in the pool, or at Hackett, in anger, and then decided to kill him too.'

'There are quite a few given to dramatic gestures in this house,' I commented.

'The simplest explanation is that they killed him to save themselves,' he said.

'Or someone they loved?'

'Possibly,' he agreed.

'Hum…' I mumbled as I contemplated the new dimension. 'I'm going to call Persi, they may have returned to the hotel by now.'

He pulled his cuff back to check his watch. 'Unlikely.'

'I'll try anyway,' I decided and made for the door.

'Fine,' he said. 'I'll be here.'

It didn't take long to reach the games room and the steps leading down. Freya was coming up.

'Major,' she said, in a peremptory tone. 'I must say to you. This is causing sadness and unwelcome dismay to people here. I hope you are finding the person, who Miss Cicely calls a devil.'

'We're working on it,' I said as I stood aside to let her pass. 'I understand you are learning about herbal medicines with Wilfred Rackham?'

'And with Miss Cicely – she thinks I am a good pupil. We are to stay here now, it is decided.'

'Really? Doesn't Miss Cicely think it dangerous?'

'No more for us than others. We are not craven cowards, Major,' she said then trotted off up the stairs.

'You got another one, then?' Dottie, the operator said when I picked up the telephone. 'Because it's two now and there'll be another, mark my words.'

I bit back a sharp remark. 'We are talking about people losing their lives,' I retorted. 'It isn't amusing.'

'Never said it was, duckie, but you can't avoid fate. Now where is it you're wanting today?' she asked, entirely unperturbed.

Some ten minutes later I heard my lovely wife's voice in the earpiece.

'Persi,' I said with a warm feeling of relief. 'How did it go?'

She laughed in delight. 'Oh my love, I wish you'd been with us. It was marvellous. There were some extraordinary people in the lecture theatre, all terribly knowledgeable, and they listened to every word. When I'd finished my talk, they asked questions and it became a fascinating debate about the meaning of the burial mound and why the warrior had been interred in the way he had.'

'And what conclusion did they come to?' A stab of regret cracked my voice.

'Oh, they don't come to conclusions. Archeology is a quest, every stone unturned merely generates more questions.' Her voice was light and happy, obviously thrilled to be back among her peers and involved in something she loved. Swift had the same fervour for Scotland Yard.

She described the auditorium and how little Angus had sat in awe with Florence, watching the slides of the dig and the display of artefacts. Lunch had been tremendous fun, mingling with the great and good from auguste academia. We talked on, and after ensuring the operator had stopped listening, I told her about the latest murder and what we'd learned. And then the strange and fascinating items in the Chamber of Curiosities.

'Oh, I can't wait to see them!' she exclaimed.

'Ah...does this mean you and Florence are coming here?'

'Yes, we're catching the train in the morning.'

'I...you won't be able to stay in the house, Persi,' I warned.

'We have realised that,' she said. 'I've booked us into The George, it will be terribly cosy and you can come and collect us when you think the coast is clear.'

'Oh...I...good. What time do you think you will arrive?'

'It won't be until three at the earliest, it's a slow train and the snow will delay everything. We'll take a taxi to the hotel and call you from there.'

'Fine, fine.' I was on the verge of babbling. Were wives supposed to make their own arrangements, and their husbands just follow along? 'We can join you for dinner, or would you, erm, prefer if I ask you here?' Then I had second thoughts. 'But there's a murderer on the loose, with poison and all that.'

She laughed. 'I'll speak to you tomorrow, Lennox, and I love you.'

'Right, yes...Goodbye, and...I love you too.'

She laughed again and put the phone down; it went dead with a reverberating clunk.

Damn it, I thought, we need to catch this blighter.

CHAPTER 18

Swift came in as I was staring at the telephone.

'Lennox?' he asked, a frown of worry on his face. 'They're all fine, aren't they?'

'Yes, they're catching the train from London tomorrow morning.'

His brow cleared. 'Marvellous, I'll talk to Florence…' He reached for the phone as I edged out of his way. 'They can't stay here though,' he added.

'They've made a reservation at The George in Bath. We'll meet them for dinner tomorrow evening.' I made to exit. 'I'll find Norman Keene, we can interview him next.'

'Fine, I won't be long, and I didn't lock the library.'

'Because we don't have anything worth securing,' I finished the sentence for him.

'Yes,' he said dourly and rattled the hook on the phone.

I returned to the library in short order thinking to ring for Jiggens, but found someone already seated at the reading table.

'Baroness Finch?'

She turned to smile sweetly at me. 'Ginny, please.

Baroness sounds so formal, and it is rather antediluvian, isn't it.'

'Is it?' I sat down across from her.

'Well, we are all equal aren't we? Or at least socially, it is our contributions to the tribe that leads to our distinctions.'

'Erm...' I opened and closed my mouth and wondered what sort of medication she might be on. 'I don't quite follow?'

'You must have read Darwin. I imagine your education would have been of the best.' She pointed to a row of books on the shelf near the fireplace. '*The Origin of the Species*'. We have a signed edition. And Wallace, of course, he was very influential. Extraordinary men, both of them. They have brought enlightenment and understanding into our world.'

'Really...excellent.' I nodded. 'Actually, we're concentrating on Sir Jasper's death, and now General Hackett's.'

Her face was round with puffy cheeks, wrinkled and creased with age, blue eyes twinkling. She wore a cap over her thick hair, it was drab green, as was her dress. She didn't seem to have very good colour sense as it didn't suit her any better than the mustard-coloured garb of yesterday.

'I am quite aware of your task here, Major.' She smiled gently, her plump hands folded in her lap. 'It is the weak you must be wary of.'

'Is it?'

'Yes. You see, among any group of people, the tribe, or rather the troupe, if one wishes to equate the human with our ancient ape ancestors, it is the weak who have the most to lose. Although the weak feign passivity, they are very likely to mask rage. When the rage overspills, they strike, but because they are weak, they strike from the shadows.'

'You don't think it's because they're worried they will be hanged?' I replied.

'Oh, that too.' She gave a low laugh. 'Now, let me explain,' she began. My heart sank; I was a captive audience. 'You have an inner voice, we all have. On one level it is our internal logic at work, but there is another, deeper voice, one may call it our conscience.'

'Fine, but–'

'Please let me continue, Major.' She smiled again although I noticed the kindly warmth had worn thinner. 'Our conscience is our guiding voice, it stems from our primitive need to fit within our tribe. Without our tribe, we are vulnerable and lack protection and food, or help when we are injured or old. The voice of conscience arises from our deepest instinct; it orders us to be altruistic, to give, so that in exchange we may be protected and provided for. The strong protect and provide, they are the leaders – you and your inspector are strong and powerful hunters; leaders of your own tribe – just as General Hackett was the leader of our tribe. We, the residents, are followers – we are weaker. The followers fit within the framework required by the leaders and the tribe itself. We all give and take in relation to our position in the tribe. Are you following my meaning?'

'I…yes.' I'd opened my notebook but hadn't written a word in it yet.

'The altruistic exchange between strong and weak inevitably institutes tension. All humans are both selfish and altruistic. It is the eternal paradox. Each wants to take more than they give, but the weaker members cannot, or at least cannot do so openly. This creates tension within the self, but that subject is a little too complex for our discussion today.' She smiled again. I nodded dumbly. 'It does lead many to become morose or belligerent, Jasper was one such example. Despite his intelligence, he could not reconcile the need to give more in order to receive more and was seething with resentment.'

I considered writing that down, but didn't.

She carried on. 'When I say more, it does not necessarily mean material goods, it can mean more attention, or power, or even love. And so you must look among those who seek to take more than they give.'

I thought about that. 'I think you are talking about motive?'

'In a way, I suppose I am, but from a different viewpoint. I am writing a book; it is an investigation into how man's primitive instinct manifests itself within modern civilisation.' She became even more serious. 'Religion most closely follows our altruistic instincts, but this is sometimes pushed aside as society becomes wealthier and selfishness ascends. Those who can take more, do so, leaving the rest behind. Indeed, many purposefully prey on the weak, including those who are in commerce–'

'Like Jasper?' I cut in.

'No, no, this is not about specifics, Major.' She batted the notion away with her hand. 'It is the craving for materialistic goods, amongst others. Religion is abhorred because it challenges the desire to be selfish. Society fragments. Do you understand this?'

I decided it best to just agree. 'Yes…'

She continued, barely taking a breath. 'It can become extreme. There is quite a rage for eugenics at the moment, and I believe such people to be utterly wrong, indeed these ideas are quite dangerous. Darwin's half-cousin, Galton, used Darwin's own work to create the eugenics movement. This is dehumanising segments of society. Rather than help the stricken, they seek to remove them. It is a sinful perversion and it must be countered. It is a violation of our altruistic instincts. I feel most strongly on this matter.'

'Right, yes, quite understandable…' I wrote her name at the top of a clean page with a question mark against it. 'When you say some prey on the weak, did you have anyone in mind?'

'No.'

'If General Hackett was the leader, and the strongest of your "tribe", then everyone is weaker. So everyone is a suspect?'

'There is a hierarchy based on merit. You must be perfectly aware of this. We all have roles to play and so there are levels of strength.'

'Are you saying some are more valuable than others?'

'No, I am saying some are able to provide more and are therefore higher in the pyramid. It enables the balance of give and take, but every member from top to bottom is necessary to the success of the tribe.'

I ran fingers through my hair. 'Could you give any examples?'

'Wilfred Rackham has great medical knowledge, Olivia Arbuthnot is a diplomat, Pastor Peabody is a trusted counsellor. These are all contributing strength and utility.'

'The weakest is Lord Balthazar,' I said, hoping to pin her down.

'Yes, but he is *too* weak to act.'

'What about you?' I turned the tables.

Her eyes widened. 'Now Major, you must not take this lightly. I am making a very cogent point here,' she replied, all sweetness gone.

'Your son died on Rackham's expedition to Finland.' I switched to more solid ground. 'You were a member of the consortium financing them.'

She stared for a moment. She was far more intelligent than I'd considered and it was a warning to me not to jump too quickly to judgement. 'That has no bearing on this at all.'

'But Sir Jasper and General Hackett were both part of the consortium, as were you, and they are both dead.'

'Are you saying that you think there is a connection? Really Major Lennox, you are approaching this at a very obtuse angle.'

I was inclined to retort that was a fine one considering she was banging on about tribes and apes. 'We must consider every angle, Baroness, including the one you have just proposed.'

That mollified her a little. 'I do hope you think very carefully about what I have said to you, and I can assure you, the loss of our dear sons on Wilfred's expedition was a tragedy. But it has no relevance to the events happening in this house.'

'You knocked over a bottle of St John's Wort that Sir Jasper was taking?' I threw in an oblique question, the sort Swift specialised in.

She stared as though affronted. 'And what of it?'

'You know the consequence of your accident?'

'Of course, there was none left and Jasper was given very small doses of Yopo in place of it,' she spoke almost through gritted teeth. 'And I am quite aware of the implication you are making, Major, and it is utterly without foundation.'

There was absolutely nothing of the grandmother about her now; she was angry, her round cheeks flushed and eyes glinting dangerously.

'How was the drug administered?' I continued, not intimidated at all by her icy tone.

'In a small packet, like loose tea; he merely had to take a pinch and drop it in hot water, then add honey, or whatever he chose,' she replied.

'Did Wilfred Rackham prepare it for him?' I began writing as this was far more relevant than the rest of her meanderings.

'No, he merely suggested this remedy as an alternative. He lectured Jasper on the dosage.'

'Why were you and Lady Matilda preparing medications for residents?' I asked, then glanced up when she didn't answer.

'We did so under Cicely Sissinghurst's guidance. Cicely is very knowledgeable about such things. She ran field hospitals during the war, you know.'

'I am aware of that,' I replied while writing. She had told me at Belvedere that she'd encountered me when I was injured, although I'd no recollection of it. 'There are doctors in Bath, why not consult them?'

'We do on occasion, but there is a depth of knowledge in this house almost unparalleled in the country,' she replied, still very defensive. 'And many of the remedies are utterly unknown to our local doctors. Nor would they have access to the herbals that we possess.'

'Do you know how Sir Jasper died?'

She looked down; her shoulders sagged monetarily. 'Obviously you are aware that I do, or you wouldn't have asked about the St John's Wort or the Yopo. The evening of Jasper's death, Gregory Hackett was told the Yopo jar had been emptied. At first we considered Jasper may have done it deliberately. It's possible – he was a depressive. Gregory questioned Wilfred; he was adamant that Jasper would not do such a thing. He thought Jasper was much happier than he'd been and had less reason to kill himself than before.'

I thought back to Jasper's diary entries and silently agreed, although there had been something in there that had puzzled me. 'Sir Jasper and Lord Balthazar were at odds, I believe?'

'Oh, you were told about that?' She looked surprised. 'Well, it was after one of Jasper's outbursts. He and Balthazar disagreed about where to donate funds. Jasper was sometimes disparaging toward Balthazar, but at one meeting, he suddenly became quite vitriolic. Balthazar felt quite ill, he remained in bed, barely able to move or eat for two days afterwards. Matilda and I had to spoon-feed him.' Her face dropped, the creases deepening around her lips. She looked more as she had when I'd first encountered her, kindly and caring, which I believed she was, underneath it all. 'He recovered but was still very shaken. Jasper refused to apologise, merely saying he was a dead weight in the house and taking the place of someone more worthy.'

She stood up abruptly. 'The vicar is arriving shortly, I must find a black ribbon. Major Lennox, think on what I have told you. It is always of use to understand one's fellow man, particularly for one who must hunt them down.' And on such abstruse advice, she left.

Swift came in as she opened the door; he bowed politely and closed it behind her. He came to join me, a smile softening his sharp face. 'What did she say?'

I put my pen down on the table. 'Darwin, apes, and eugenics, amongst other things.'

I had to explain her theory about tribes and all the rest. He found this fascinating, and the more we discussed it the more I came to think that perhaps she had hit upon something, although I doubted it had much practical use.

'Aside from theorising about the weakest link, I think what she said about Balthazar was interesting,' I said.

'You suspect he may have been drugged too?' Swift asked, then grinned. 'You're turning into a detective, Lennox.'

I frowned at that. 'Well, it's possible, and Jasper may have been responsible. We know he wanted Cicely Sissinghurst to reside here, and he made no secret of his antipathy towards Balthazar.'

'Balthazar is too feeble in body and mind.'

'Agreed, but someone may have acted to protect him,' I said, although it all sounded rather unlikely given what we knew of the people here.

Jiggens knocked loudly then put his head around the door. 'They're having a service in the drawing room, sirs, if you'd like to come.'

'No,' I replied.

'Justice St John said I wasn't to come back without you.' Jiggens remained by the door.

We both stood up in no particular hurry.

'I assume the vicar is leading the show,' I said.

'He is, sir,' Jiggens said. 'It's a tradition whenever we lose one of the residents.' He lowered his voice. 'Kind of an exorcism too. There's supposed to be ghosts lurking about the place and they don't want any more joining them.'

'That's what comes of living in a terminus,' I remarked as we followed him out.

'I know, sir.' He led us along the corridor. 'But they have a nice time before they go, or most of them do anyway.'

We found Fogg and the three cats sitting outside the drawing room. They looked up as we arrived, then back at the door, making it quite clear they wanted us to open it for them. They ran in as Jiggens did the honours.

All the Saints were present, as was Cicely, and Freya, who was standing next to Greggs by the sideboard, presumably preparing to serve drinks.

'Ha!' Justice St John greeted us. 'About time. The vicar is waiting.'

The vicar nodded and offered a gentle smile as we went to stand among the Saints. Justice St John, regal in a long black cloak lined with blue silk, came to stand in front of us. Wilfred Rackham shuffled aside so we could get a view of proceedings.

'Dearly beloved, we are gathered here today…' The vicar raised his arms, his black cassock flowing wide on his thin frame. The cats settled about the fire and Fogg came to sit at my feet, his eyes round, ears cocked, taking a great interest in the proceedings.

'We'd like to talk to you later,' Swift spoke quietly to Rackham.

'Of course,' he replied, one eye sliding towards us, the other remaining fixed on the vicar. 'How about over a drink–'

'Silence!' Justice St John hissed loudly and glowered at us.

We lowered our heads as a prayer was read, ending on an unusual note.

'Thy duty is done, thy promises kept.

Throw off thy earthly chains and hasten ye to Heaven.

Go in peace to thy eternal rest, and remain within God's bounds; forever and always.

Amen.'

That was a new one on me. I half expected him to add "and don't come back" or something akin, but he merely smiled beatifically and headed to where Greggs was waiting with a jug of eggnog.

'Library,' Swift ordered Rackham.

'I'd rather sit in my chair by the fire,' he replied and indicated with his cane. 'It would be more comfortable.'

Swift appeared inclined to argue, but I went and sat down and waited for them to follow.

CHAPTER 19

'Who drugged Balthazar?' I asked when they'd both settled in their seats.

'There's no proof he was drugged,' Rackham replied calmly.

'Do you believe he was?' Swift asked.

Rackham closed his mouth in a firm line as he considered it, the puckered cheek stretched and taut. 'Given what has happened since, I think it possible,' he agreed. 'But I've no idea who may have done it, or why.'

Swift felt for his notebook, then remembered where we were and let his hand drop. 'Lady Matilda and Baroness Ginny gave him his medication.'

'Yes, they liked to help. I think it gave them something to do,' Rackham replied.

'You didn't tell me this yesterday,' I said, rather annoyed by the omission.

'I apologise, but I wasn't sure how things would go,' he said quietly.

'You were protecting them?' I continued.

'Possibly…I didn't know if you were simply looking for a scapegoat or actually carrying out a real investigation.'

'We're professionals sent by Scotland Yard,' Swift said.

'I understand, and I apologise for my mistake,' Rackham acknowledged.

'Please explain why you provide your own remedies,' I asked him.

'Certainly.' He nodded. 'If anyone is in need of treatment, the local doctor is consulted first, but there are certain circumstances where conventional medicine is ineffective. This is the case with Balthazar, he has a form of neurological disease which is affecting his memory. There is no cure. Cicely conferred with me as to what remedy may help and I suggested Galantamine. We agreed this with the Regent, and with Balthazar, of course, and began the course at the beginning of this month. I have no doubt that it has helped him.' He shifted his gaze to watch Freya, moving about the room with cocktail glasses of eggnog on a tray. I was keen for a drink myself, but she was serving the vicar and ladies first.

'And Sir Jasper?' Swift continued questioning. 'Did you advise on his condition?'

'General Hackett approached me.' Rackham turned his gaze towards Swift. 'Jasper was increasingly rancorous between bouts of melancholy. I spoke to Jasper quietly, just man to man, you know. He wouldn't admit to depression, but he agreed to a 'tonic'. I believe he hoped it would help him relax and overcome his shyness. Beneath the cantankerous exterior, he was really quite insecure. I think he'd spent a lifetime building a wall between himself and the world.'

He was perceptive, if nothing else.

'What happened in Finland?' I asked.

'You want drinks also?' Freya arrived at that moment. 'I have only three glasses, one for each.'

'Yes, please!' We all sat up as she served, her movements graceful and controlled.

'There, now do not drink too fast as Mr Justice is taking it in big mouthfuls and Mr Greegs cannot mix up fast enough,' she told us in her direct manner.

Foggy had settled at my feet, his nose pointing towards the fire.

'Finland?' Swift reminded Rackham as I took a sip of eggnog.

He held the cocktail glass in his good hand. 'It began with high hopes and ended in tragedy,' he replied calmly, although I heard the tremor in his voice. 'We were searching for a specific source of lichen. They're symbiotic, you see, they'll grow on rocks, tree bark, all manner of things. The lichens combine with metabolites and each symbiosis can produce unique compounds. There had been talk of a boreal forest in Finland where the lichen has powerful antiseptic qualities due to the trees they grow on. We'd planned to find it and bring home enough samples to analyse and study. You'll be quite aware of the need to find a cure for sepsis, and it was clear at the time war was on the horizon, making it all the more vital. Septicaemia kills more men than the enemy.' He took a slow sip of his drink. 'We had worked out on a map roughly whereabouts we wanted to search and had planned the expedition to commence early the following year.' He hesitated, his good eye moving toward the bright flames of the fire. 'We brought it forward to autumn instead. It was my fault. I...I had meant to be getting married, but my fiancee was having second thoughts, and then she cried off.' A crack in his voice caused him to clear his throat. 'I suggested to the team we search for the lichen before winter arrived. They all agreed; they were eager to go and we all knew how important the find could be. The site was quite far north but we were well equipped and had already experienced frozen terrains in Alaska.'

'You were caught in the open,' I stated.

He nodded. 'It was the end of October. We'd found the forest, and the lichen, and were on our way back to base. We had to cross a wide plain. It was cold but there wasn't any snow, and then in the night the wind picked up and blew itself into a howling gale. It caught the tent and ripped it to shreds, and then the blizzard arrived.' He paused for another drink, then continued. 'We huddled together, waiting for it to abate. By next morning it hadn't and we were all developing frostbite. We couldn't remain there and so walked into the teeth of it, following our compass. A stream crossed our path. We didn't know it was there, it was frozen over and hidden beneath snow. Peabody stepped onto it; he slid on the icy surface and broke his ankle. He was a good man, as kind and Christian as his father. We carried him, but it slowed us down even further. The blizzard didn't let up, and we stopped among some rocks, trying to shelter. The snow piled up around us and then began to cover us. We kept a hole clear, punching it out as it formed a tomb above our heads.' He dropped his voice. 'It helped in a way, we were a little warmer, but trying to keep the hole open was exhausting. During the night we fell asleep, one by one. When I woke up I was being pulled on a sled – someone had wrapped me in fur and strapped me in. I couldn't speak and felt nothing, I wasn't even sure I was alive. Reindeer pulled the sled, and a group of Sami – they're the local natives – were talking among themselves. It had stopped snowing, the sky was clear blue. I could see the others, the boys, I mean, all on sleds and swaddled, just as I was. We reached a settlement, about a dozen tents made of hide. The Sami treated me with hot drinks and their own medicines, but nothing helped, the frostbite was too extensive and gangrene set in. Some days later they strapped me back on the sled, I was barely conscious by this time. Eventually we arrived at a town and they left me there, along with the other three.'

'They were dead,' Swift said.

'Yes, none of them had survived the snow tomb. A hunter had found us, dug us out by all accounts. The hunter fetched the tribe and they rescued us. You know the rest,' he said and finished his drink.

'All rise,' Justice St John suddenly bellowed.

'What?' Various mutterings ran about the room.

'There is an announcement,' he continued as we all rose to our feet. 'Miss Cicely Sissinghurst is to formally join our

Order and will reside in Temple House from the beginning of the new year. Until this time, she will remain here so we may conclude our list of donations. Tomorrow we must deliberate, ladies and gentlemen. We commence at ten. And now to the dining room.' He raised an arm ready to lead off, his cloak flowing about him.

'Am I Regent now?' Balthazar asked in a tremulous voice.

St John stopped to frown down at him. 'No, I am.'

'Oh, I am so pleased.' Balthazar smiled up at him. 'It has worked out for the best. Such a shame that Jasper will miss it.'

'Miss what?' Olivia asked.

'The new regime.' He was speaking quite lucidly. 'He objected to the General, although I found him most proper.'

'Why did he object to the General?' Swift had moved closer to Balthazar.

'I…erm…I think it was Miss Cicely.' His lips trembled and confusion crumpled his face again.

Lady Matilda suddenly stepped forward to take his arm. 'Now Balthazar you mustn't worry about Jasper, he is at rest now, and cannot disrupt our peace any further. Come along. It is time for dinner.'

Jiggens was standing at the door to the dining room, ready to show the vicar to his seat. We waited as the chap was settled with due reverence and a pristine napkin. St John took the chair at the head of the table, we were shown to the far end along with Balthazar and Peabody. The food was excellent and I left it to Swift to make conversation, my head full of questions. The girls were arriving tomorrow and Christmas was now only days away.

My suspicions had moved from one of the Saints to another and yet I still couldn't pinpoint a motive, never mind the killer.

'And I believe this was told to you, Major?' Peabody was eyeing me quizzically under white brows.

'Erm…' I said. 'Apologies, Pastor, my mind was elsewhere.'

'Oh, that happens to me quite often,' Balthazar said. 'It comes and goes – sometimes, I don't know where I am at all.'

'But does it matter?' Pastor Peabody turned to him, fork in hand. We were eating roast beef, Yorkshire puddings and all the usual including a particularly excellent gravy. 'We are most comfortable, and among good company under the blessing of the Lord,' Peabody said, then speared a potato.

'It matters when there is something to say,' Balthazar replied, his eyes round and a little unfocused. 'Jasper was quite angry, and he said it was me, but it wasn't.'

'What did he say was you?' Swift fixed his gaze on the fuddled old man.

'She wasn't able to come, and it was my fault. He'd never spoken about it before, but now after they'd discussed it, he said it all became clear. Too many old men, but he was an old man. Why did he suddenly want her here?'

'Who?' Peabody asked.

'Her!' Balthazar whispered, indicating Cicely with a shaking finger. 'He had been needled, you know. I'm sure of it. Someone set him off.'

'Do you mean someone provoked Jasper into blaming you for Miss Sissinghurst not being admitted to the Order?' Swift tried to clarify.

'I do, yes, yes. And he did blame me.' Balthazar nodded enthusiastically.

'Who?' Swift asked.

'I don't know.' Balthazar turned to Peabody. 'Do you know?'

'No.' Peabody cut a carrot in half. 'But there has been a stirring in the house. I have felt it.'

'The ghost, do you mean?' Balthazar said, then looked behind him. 'Twice now. I suppose it will come again. It was in the book.'

'Which book?' I asked.

'Dickens,' Balthazar said. 'Everybody knows the book.'

'Have you seen ghosts?' Swift asked.

'Oh yes, they woke me. Then they vanished.' Balthazar's eyes widened. 'I went to look for them, but they had gone. The past and the present, now there is only the future left.'

'When did you last see the Dickens book?' I asked.

'I told you.' Balthazar gazed at me in surprise. 'Jasper had it on his lap.'

'Yes, sorry, I recall now.' I cursed myself for stupidity.

'Ha, so your mind wanders too, Major.' Balthazar giggled suddenly.

'Balthazar I believe you have hit upon something, there has been an atmosphere here,' Peabody returned to the subject. He leaned forward to address Lockhart. 'Captain, have you detected unease in the house?'

Lockhart had been gaily jousting with the ladies but turned toward us. 'Unease? Yes I believe so, but Jasper was always disruptive. I think he'd got a bee in his bonnet about something and was just kicking up his usual fuss. I never took much notice of his tantrums, myself. Better things to do.' He grinned and turned back to josh Olivia.

The ladies were seated near Justice St John, who was holding court with obvious enjoyment. Most of his attention had been on Baroness Ginny while Roger and Norman had been quizzing Cicely Sissinghurst, making her laugh on a number of occasions. Despite the terrible death of General Hackett only this morning, there already seemed to be a lighter atmosphere in the place.

Pudding was honey and almond sponge with custard, it was utterly delicious. The vicar declared he had to depart just afterwards; he'd spent most of the meal in close conversation with Wilfred Rackham, who now appeared as relaxed as the other Saints.

'Lennox!' Captain Lockhart came to my side after we'd all hailed farewell to the Reverend. 'Come on. I'm challenging you to a duel. Three different games, a guinea apiece, winner takes all.'

'Not bridge,' I stated quite clearly.

'No, no. Fox and Geese, Chequers, and Backgammon.' He grinned in rakish fashion at the ladies walking alongside us. 'And I'll ask the beguiling Baroness Ginny to keep score.'

'Captain you are nothing but an apple-polisher,' Ginny replied archly. 'And I have a challenge of my own. Pastor

Peabody is going to try to beat me at mancala, and is foolhardy enough to have wagered a crown on the outcome.'

'There is no better game than bridge for sharpening the wits,' Justice St John proclaimed loudly. 'Swift, you will be my partner.'

Swift hesitated. 'I–'

'No backing out.' St John slapped him on the back. 'Just make sure we win.'

'And afterwards, we will run through our rehearsal,' Lady Matilda said loudly.

'I'm game,' Roger called out, then giggled.

'We all know that!' Norman replied and a few others laughed.

We crowded into the games room, including Foggy and the cats, and despite it all, had a thoroughly jolly evening.

CHAPTER 20

The thud of a cat jumping off the bed and onto the floor woke me. I muttered to myself about soft-footed felines and turned over. Another thud followed, then another. All three cats, who had been snoozing in various positions around me, had now woken and were up to something. Foggy clambered on top of me, sniffing loudly. *Damn it,* I swore, then sat up to squint into the darkness.

A haze of something white – smoke, perhaps? I could smell smoke from the remnants of the fire, now merely glowing embers dying in the hearth. The haze was in the middle of the room; it grew in size, then shifted and swirled. I watched, mesmerised, as it moved very slowly not ten feet from me. Fogg had been lying across my chest staring at the apparition, then suddenly threw back his head and let out a mournful howl.

'What?' Swift sat up. 'Lennox, what the hell was that?'

I could barely see him in the dark, so I dug under my pillow for my torch and switched it on.

'Somebody's playing games with us,' I said and shone the beam at the source of the "ghost".

Swift clambered out of bed, reaching for his dressing gown to pull over striped pyjamas. 'There's something on fire in here.'

I tossed covers aside and stood up. 'Look, it's a bauble from the Christmas tree. There's smoke coming from it.'

All three cats were sitting in a semicircle around a red and gold glass bauble. The brass cap had been removed and smoke was streaming from the opening.

Swift touched it with a fingertip. 'It's too hot to pick up.' He tapped it lightly making it spin round, then tried to peer into it. 'There's a flame. I can't see what's burning.' He sniffed. 'Lavender, and something else…petroleum, I think.'

'Has someone put lavender oil into the bauble?'

'Possibly, give me your torch.' He aimed the light at the smoke seeping from the funnelled opening. 'It's been stuffed with something, a piece of fabric.'

'It might be cotton wool,' I guessed, suddenly recalling the smell from survival camp at school. 'Balls of cotton wool stuffed with vaseline. We used them to light fires; they're remarkably effective. We always kept a handful wrapped in wax paper in case we couldn't find dry tinder.'

'You're right. The smell of petroleum jelly's masked by the lavender.' He knelt down for a better look.

One of the cats raised a black paw to strike at the bauble. I quickly grabbed the animal before it burned itself. 'Nox, no.'

'I'll put it outside,' Swift said and pulled a pencil from the pocket of his dressing gown. He slid the sharp end into the opening to hook the smoking bauble and made a dash for the window. 'Lennox, can you open it?'

I held Nox under one arm and pushed the curtain aside, then threw the window wide. He dropped the bauble, still smouldering, into the thick snow covering the ledge.

'Balthazar's ghost.' I could hear it fizzle as the cotton wool cooled, then shut the window because it was freezing.

'Somebody's playing games,' Swift said as he watched through the glass.

'Hmm.' I put the cat down with the others; they all instantly hopped up onto the sill to stare out. 'What time is it?'

'Just after three.'

'Right, we'll take a look in the morning.' I climbed back into bed and pulled the covers round my ears.

Swift muttered something but switched the torch off and settled down.

Grumpy *harrumphing* woke me next morning, followed by muttered grumbling about the mess.

'Greggs.' I sat up. 'It was a smoke bomb.'

His brows shot up. 'A bomb, sir? Where?'

'Window ledge.' I got up for the second time and reached for my dressing gown.

'On the window ledge, sir! How did a bomb get on the window ledge?' He went to peer through the frost-glazed panes, smeared with a film of grey smoke.

I explained in short order then opened the window and picked up the singed bauble.

'Lennox, fingerprints!' Swift awoke and leapt out of bed to stride over in bare feet.

'Ah, sorry old chap. Forgot. But I doubt there would be any.'

He sighed. 'Has it burned out?'

'Yes.' I turned it over in my fingers.

'I'll get my tweezers and magnifying glass.' Swift reached for his satchel lying on the desk.

'Petroleum jelly and cotton wool, sir,' Greggs said. 'An old-fashioned fire lighter.'

'I know,' I mumbled. 'Who did it though?'

'The killer, sir?' he suggested, helpfully.

The glass bauble was blackened around the opening, the red and gold colouring dulled. Strands of charred cotton were clearly visible inside it. It was clever, and devious, and although anyone in the house could have made it, the number who were likely to have done so was fewer than the whole.

'Could you put it onto the blotter without breaking it?' Swift was ready with his tweezers.

'Fine.' I did as asked, then Greggs and I watched as he quietly delved about, picking out blackened strands of cotton wool.

It was tedious so I decided to get dressed. Greggs set about tidying up and I was just in the middle of shaving when a sharp rap on the door was followed by Freya.

Greggs gasped. I stopped, razor poised on cheek. Swift, who was still in his striped pyjamas, grabbed a cat for some reason.

'Miss Freya.' Greggs drew himself up and spoke sternly. 'This is the men's quarters! We require privacy.'

'Pah! I have five brothers, you have nothing I have not seen. Justice St John wants to speak with the detectives, and says you must go to him.'

'Jiggens should have brought the message.' Greggs was still on his high horse.

'Old Jiggens is staying in his bed till no more peoples die, and young Jiggens is lighting fires for breakfast,' she declared. 'You must come now.'

'Five minutes,' I said. 'Wait outside.'

'I must–' she began.

I straightened up. 'Out. Now.' I pointed at the door with my razor.

She huffed but went.

'Young people today, sir.' Greggs had gone quite pink. 'They do not know their place.'

Swift decided he should dress, and reached for his shirt. 'And nor should they,' he declared. 'The world is turning, Greggs.'

'Not in terms of privacy, and respect, sir!'

'No, but they no longer need to "know their place",' Swift continued.

That didn't placate my old butler, we left him muttering to himself and went to find Freya waiting in the corridor. She led us to Justice St John. Swift brought the burnt bauble with him.

'Well, who was it? Have you a name for me?' St John was sitting in a royal-blue velvet dressing gown with a matching cap on his head. Even his slippers matched. His bedroom was twice the size of ours and sumptuously furnished with a magnificent walnut four-poster, dressing table, desk, sideboard and whatnots. The fire, in a carved fireplace, burned with black coals amid bright orange flames. The Judge sat next to it, his cheeks rosy with warmth. He waved at us to sit across from him.

'We believe it was a man,' I said as I sank into a deeply cushioned chair in ruby red chenille.

'Why?' the Judge demanded.

'This.' Swift gave him the bauble. 'Among other things.'

'Explain.' The Judge held it between chunky fingers to gaze at it, a frown between bristling brows.

'Vaseline,' Swift said. 'Or scented petroleum jelly, if you prefer, stuffed into cotton wool and pushed into the bauble. It was set alight and rolled into our bedroom in the early hours this morning.'

The Judge closed one eye and peered into the blackened opening. 'Smouldered rather than burned. Not enough oxygen. Were they trying to smoke you out?'

'I think it was to create a ghostly vision,' I said. 'Perhaps they sought to scare us.'

'Ha! Doubt you'd scare that easily. What's in their minds, eh? Kill two good people, what do they gain by it? Not money, we've all got plenty of that,' he rambled on. 'Power, d'you think, or influence? After the Regent's job? Foolish if that's their game. It's not the Regent who holds power, it's the Dead Reckoner.' He glanced over at us, one eye still shut. 'Keeper of the Books, I mean. Miss Sissinghurst.'

'When was she nominated a Saint?' Swift asked.

The Judge handed the bauble back. 'Oh… now it could be two months back, I believe. Hackett was the final arbiter, he would have known. Although the rumour's been running about ever since her nephew died at Belvedere.'

He frowned again. 'You were there weren't you? One of your cases, according to my pals on the circuit.'

'Yes, it was,' Swift confirmed. 'Last July. He died at the summer ball.'

I assumed his "pals on the circuit" were High Court Judges. It was interesting to hear they knew of us.

'Were you one of the "wise men"?' I asked.

He nodded. 'I was once, yes. Never married, the job came first.' He folded his hands in his lap. 'When I started in chambers, times were much hasher. Deprivation, starvation, children forced into labour, slums, workhouses. Terrible, terrible hardships and people suffered for it. They were still transporting convicts to Australia – those they didn't hang, and they were keen enough on that. If you don't remember how bad it was just read Dickens; he saw it all and wasn't prepared to whitewash it. Excellent man, we were members of the same club. I worked to reform the justice system – dedicated my life to it – I even managed to make a few changes for the better. People like Lady Matilda, Pastor Peabody, Olivia Arbuthnot and Cicely Sissinghurst, we were of the same mind and the same mould.'

'So you all knew each other?' Swift asked in his pedantic way.

'We knew of each other, helped the same charities, held the same goals. We belonged to what people would refer to as the "establishment". An amorphous group, with many pretenders creeping about the periphery.'

'You were involved in selecting the Saints,' Swift said.

'I was, before I retired and came here.'

'Which of the Saints did you select?' I asked.

'Hackett, Jasper, Lady Matilda. None of the rest.'

'Who's been here the longest?' I asked out of curiosity.

'Balthazar, since '09 I believe. After his mother died.'

'He never married, or had a career?' I continued.

St John shook his head. 'Fond of learning, that was all. Never cut the apron strings from what I understand, just read books. Shame he's forgotten it all.'

We nodded at that but made no remark.

'The last Saint I wanted to nominate was Cicely,' he rumbled on. 'But there was that damned awful nephew. We hoped she'd disinherit the devil, but she refused.' St John's voice mellowed. 'She saved many lives by her work during the war, and she's a formidable administrator. Made our money work for us; the Order's better off now than it has been in decades, even centuries.'

'We found Sir Jasper's diary,' Swift told him. 'Once he heard she was to join the Order, he was keen for her to move in. He was irritated that there wasn't a vacancy and considered Lord Balthazar an obstruction.'

'You're saying he wanted him dead?' St John quizzed.

'We thought it was more wishful thinking than a murder plot,' I remarked wryly.

'But Balthazar informed us he had seen two ghosts,' Swift said. 'Someone may have put a smouldering bauble in his room too.'

'*Humph*,' St John spluttered. 'Lucky it wasn't filled with poison, the gas might have finished you off – or him.'

We both looked up sharply at that. It hadn't occurred to either of us.

'He was ill, shortly after he had a row with Sir Jasper,' I said.

'Oh, he was merely confounded.' St John was dismissive.

'Now that Miss Sissinghurst is in residence,' I said, 'the killer may have achieved what they wanted, and were merely attempting to scare us off.'

'Next time he may not simply try to scare you off, gentlemen,' St John warned. 'I suggest you nab the blighter before he decides you're too much of a nuisance.'

'We're working on it, sir,' Swift said, then stood up. 'If you will excuse us, we'll get back to it.'

'As you should.' St John nodded, his velvet cap slipping forward.

I made polite noises then followed Swift out.

'Breakfast.' I clapped my hands, looking forward to my favourite meal of the day.

'Lennox, we're supposed to...' He frowned, then muttered, 'Fine.'

Foggy had beaten us to it, he was sitting by the blazing fire. He *woofed* and came to greet us, tail wagging happily. I assume he must have come down with Greggs; the cats were nowhere to be seen.

'Morning, sirs.' Jiggens was remarkably chirpy. 'I've set out platters. Cook and Auntie Essie have been cooking fit to bust, and now we're almost overflowing with provender.' He was standing next to the refectory table and lifted the lid of the nearest silver domed dish. 'Bacon.' He grinned.

There was a large stack of rashers arranged in layers on the plate. 'There's loads of sausages, black pudding, mushrooms, eggs and whatever else you'd like.'

'I'll have some of everything,' I told Jiggens.

'So will I,' Swift said.

We took the table by the window, the pale dawn filtering through frost-glazed panes. Foggy sat at my feet to wait in hope and anticipation.

'Freya's gone to fetch the tea.' Jiggens chatted away while piling the goodies onto two plates. 'She's stopping here now, might even be here for always. It's going to make it all abuzz, she's just that type. Bossy and interfering. I reckon the best thing would be for her to marry the doctor and clear off, 'cos we'll never have a moment's peace otherwise.'

'She's a hard worker,' I said. 'Surely she'll make your life easier.'

'She will and she won't.' He came over with the plates, steam rising from the hot food. 'She'll make as much work as she'll mend.'

'Do you think the doctor was keen on her?' Swift asked as he picked up knife and fork.

'Course he was, couldn't take his eyes off her. Not that she took no notice–'

'Jiggens, what is it you are saying?' Freya came in with a tray of tea, milk jug and sugar pot. The cups and saucers were already on the table.

'That the doctor was sweet on you and I hope you run off with him and leave us in peace,' Jiggens didn't hesitate to reply.

Freya stopped and stared at him. 'That is very silly of you. I would not leave Madam, not for a doctor nor anyone.'

Captain Lockhart had come in behind her, but she hadn't noticed.

'Well, that is excellent news!' He grinned. 'We wouldn't want to lose our lovely young lady.'

'Pah.' Freya plonked the tea on the refectory table for Jiggens to pour. 'All men are silly.' She flounced out.

Lockhart grinned in piratical fashion. 'Great girl, that,' he said and came to sit with us.

CHAPTER 21

'Did you ever marry, Captain?' Swift asked him as he cut into a rasher, then slipped some to Foggy.

'Once,' Lockhart replied. 'She was as fiery as that lass, and from the same Viking stock. Hildebrand. I met her in Norway when I was delivering a yacht. We had eight marvellous years together, full of adventure and joy. Then she died giving birth to our son. He didn't last long afterwards, too weak…' The lines on his handsome face cut deeper around his eyes and lips. 'I've never stopped missing her. It will be rather pleasant, in my old age, to have young Freya around to remind me of her.'

Jiggens had loaded another plate and brought it to him, then poured tea for us all before bustling off.

'Did you hear anyone moving about last night?' Swift asked him as we all ate the sumptuous feast.

'No,' Lockhart replied and tossed Foggy a half sausage. 'I sleep like a dog.' He eyed us. 'You men are married.' It wasn't a question.

'Yes,' Swift answered. 'How did you know?'

'You have the look about you.' Lockhart grinned.

I raised a brow.

'Content. Settled,' he replied. 'At peace with yourselves. That's something we all miss here.'

'There's plenty of close friendships,' I remarked, cutting up a black pudding.

'Agreed,' Lockhart said. 'It's a fair compromise if one can't have the real thing.'

'Would anyone here kill for love?' Swift had finished his meal and placed the knife and fork neatly on his plate.

Lockhart's eyes slid in his direction. 'It would seem rather bizarre, Inspector; as we are all living under the same roof. And what would be the point? We're none of us kitted out for a honeymoon, now, are we?' He loaded his fork. 'If creating a vacancy for Miss Sissinghurst was the objective, then the question is why? Is it because the culprit wants to be near her, or is it because they want to kill her?'

'We think they simply want her to reside here,' Swift replied.

Lockhart chewed it over. 'I hope you're right, but there are two vacancies now. What if it's whoever is nominated to fill the General's vacancy?'

'Do you know who it will be?' I asked, thinking we should have asked Justice St John that question.

'Haven't a clue,' he replied.

'Major Lennox, Inspector Swift.' Cicely Sissinghurst entered the breakfast room. 'I would like a moment of your time, please. We can talk in the library.' She turned around and marched back out again.

That didn't leave us much choice but to follow, although

we both gulped down our tea first. Lockhart grinned as we trooped out. Foggy stayed with him in the certainty of more tidbits tossed his way.

'Miss Sissinghurst.' Swift helped her be seated at the reading table before taking his usual chair and opening his notebook on a fresh page.

I sat down, considered taking notes, and decided against. 'Before you say a word, who is nominated to take General Hackett's place?'

'As a Saint or Regent?' she demanded.

'Either.'

She frowned. 'I do not know about the Regency, although St John seems determined to have it. As for the Saint, there is always a short list, but no-one has actually been nominated yet. We usually have more time to consider new Saints.'

Well, that answered that question. Swift made a quick note, then looked at Cicely. 'You have something to tell us?'

'I found this in Freya's room.' She put an extraordinary jewelled ornament on the polished table top.

'Lockhart's horse, part of the Burmese crown jewels,' I said and picked it up. 'He described it to me.'

Swift watched as I turned it over in my hands. A prancing horse about four inches high, expertly executed in solid gold with inlaid rubies, sapphires and lapis lazuli. The early morning sunlight caught the gems as I held it up.

'I am quite aware what it is and who it belongs to,' Cicely said. 'But I do not know how it came to be in Freya's possession.'

A red ribbon was tied around the horse's middle, neatly cut just above the knot. 'Lockhart told us it had gone missing, he'd tied it to the Christmas tree in the hall.'

'He does so every year,' Cicely replied. 'The horse is fixed just below the angel, he says it's her ride when her wings grow weary.'

I hid a smile; the captain had a nice sense of humour. 'If you'll excuse me a moment.' I stood up. Swift frowned. 'I'll be right back,' I promised.

The cats had been playing with a ribbon and I'd seen the ragged remains in the log basket next to the fire. I strode along the corridor and straight to the lidded hamper. All three cats were curled up inside with Tubbs in the middle. He opened an eye, stretched when he saw me, then snuggled down again. The ribbon was still caught on the wicker rim; I plucked it out to examine it. The ends had been cut neatly through although the cats had mangled it since.

'Oh, that's another one they've stolen, the little minxes,' Jiggens remarked as he came in with an armful of logs. 'That's the third or fourth I've found since we put the tree up.'

'Really, were they all cut?'

He raised his brows. 'No, the cats knock the baubles off the tree and bat them around, then chew up the ribbons.' He leaned over to stack the logs with the rest of the pile. 'It's a game, they do it every year.'

'This has been cut.' I showed it to him.

He finished with the logs then stood up to peer at it. 'Gosh, you're right. Now who did that, I wonder?'

I raised a brow, but didn't reply.

'Not the killer, ooohhh,' he drew a horrified breath then fingered the mangled ribbon. 'To think this is part of a murder…' His pleasant face suddenly dropped and he looked close to tears. 'It's horrible sir. In a place like this where only good people come. They're really serious about helping poor folk. It's terrible to think one of them's a heartless killer.'

'I don't think they're heartless, but they certainly don't object to killing,' I said, then thought I'd better go. 'If you see any more baubles on the ground, will you save them for me, please?'

'I'll do that, sir,' he said and sniffed sadly.

I returned to the library in quick strides. Swift and Cicely were in comfortable conversation about Scotland.

'You came back,' Swift remarked, seemingly surprised.

'I said I would. Here.' I held the ribbon out.

He took his magnifying glass from the inside pocket of his jacket and stared at the ragged ends, then at the ribbon tied around the horse.

Cicely leaned in too. 'I'd say they match.'

'I agree,' Swift said, then put the magnifying glass down. 'Could Freya have taken it?' He asked the direct question.

Cicely's thin face paled, then she nodded. 'She's somewhat of an enigma; kind, helpful, determined and an indefatigable worker. But she doesn't entirely understand about private property. She will "borrow" something for a while and then return it without a word. She comes from a large family, and I really don't know much about Norwegian culture, so perhaps it is normal for her.'

'How did you find this?' I indicated the jewelled horse.

'In her room, she has been allocated one next to mine,' she explained. 'There are more vacant women's rooms than men's, so she has been granted one of her own. I could not find my tortoiseshell comb this morning and went to her room. It was on her dressing table, next to the horse.'

'Will she be upset that you've taken the horse?' I asked.

'Not at all,' Cicely said. 'As I explained, she doesn't understand ownership, everything is something to be used and shared as required.'

I had no idea about Norwegian habits, and I doubted Swift had either.

'Freya is being taught about medicines by Wilfred Rackham,' I began.

'They are herbal remedies, Major,' Cicely corrected me. 'Although in most cases they are one and the same. And you are quite right, Wilfred is passing as much knowledge as he can to me and Freya before he loses his sight. Lady Matilda takes a great interest too, and she has tended to Balthazar and Jasper in recent weeks.'

'And Baroness Ginny has involved herself too,' Swift remarked.

'To a degree,' Cicely replied. 'Virginia studies the human psyche, and is most interested in the effect the physical world has upon it.'

'Including drugs,' I said.

'Of course.' Cicely nodded.

'It seemed to me, the Baroness regards people as subjects to be analysed and observed,' I remarked.

Cicely narrowed her eyes. 'She is not cold hearted, Major, merely analytical.'

I nodded, and said nothing more.

'Freya knew about the Yopo.' Swift turned policeman.

Cicely sighed. 'She did, and the snowdrop extract given to Balthazar.'

'What about the blue powder?' I asked.

She shook her head. 'Not to my knowledge.'

'Were you and she here the day of Sir Jasper's death?' Swift asked, although he knew she was.

'Yes,' she replied.

'And you were here the morning General Hackett died too.' Swift had been writing rapid notes and paused to wait for her answer.

'You are quite aware we were,' Cicely spoke sharply. 'But please do not imagine that Freya is involved in these terrible incidents, she has no reason whatsoever to harm anyone here – or indeed anywhere.'

'Where did you find her?' I decided to try a different tack.

'She found me,' Cicely replied. 'Last year my maid married a man who worked in insurance and they moved to Surrey. It proved quite difficult to find anyone to replace her; girls don't want to work in service any more. I asked around my friends, which didn't help, and then put a notice in the Post Office. Freya found it and came and knocked on my door. She's very intelligent, but stubborn and does only as much as she chooses.'

'She's capable of learning about herbal remedies though,' I remarked.

'Indeed, and she finds that very interesting,' Cicely replied, her long face still quite serious. 'She listens carefully to Wilfred, they seem to have sparked an accord.'

'Is there any romance between them?' Swift asked.

'My understanding is that his injuries preclude any physical "romance",' she spoke carefully. 'When Wilfred was proposed as a potential Saint, the Wise Men made enquiries and his physician confirmed he had been badly affected by frostbite. I have not personally checked, you understand,' she added acerbically.

I thought about that, or rather tried not to.

'Is he very wealthy?' I asked.

'Oh yes, his family always were,' she replied. 'He inherited everything. They lived quite close to Bath, Harcourt Manor, you may have heard of it.'

'Yes, I have. I assume it was his mother's side of the family,' I said, given his name of Rackham. I'd heard of the Harcourt family, everyone in the upper echelons had, they'd started as old-fashioned merchants in the long-ago past and had since worked their way up to the highest ranks of political power.

'It was his mother's side, yes, and the Harcourt assets are now liquidated and awaiting transfer upon his demise,' Cicely said matter-of-factly.

'But he can back out, if he wants to,' Swift said.

'Yes, he can, but I cannot imagine he will.' She rose to her feet. 'I think I have given you sufficient food for thought, gentlemen. Are you close to solving this appalling violation?'

'If you mean the murders, no,' I replied.

She pursed her lips. 'Then you must amplify your efforts. This cannot be tolerated, and I must warn you, I have the ear of the Police Commissioner. Do not fail me.' She rapped her knuckles on the desk and marched out, reminding me of a head teacher telling a couple of duffers to pull their socks up.

Swift sighed. 'Lennox, do you have any clue at all who is behind all this, because I have no damned idea whatsoever.'

CHAPTER 22

'No,' was my answer.

He raked his hand through his hair. 'I can't pin down the motive. Nothing makes sense.'

'Should we talk to Norman?'

He frowned. 'Interview him, you mean?'

'Yes, Swift, *interview* him.' I laboured the word.

'Of course we should. Process and procedure, Lennox.' He leafed through his notebook, back to the list of suspects. Then he shuffled through the statements the Saints had made the day before yesterday. 'And Balthazar, we've barely spoken to him.'

There was a good reason for that, I thought but didn't say. 'I'll go and find one of them,' I said and made an exit, thinking that I'd prefer a walk in the snow with my dog.

Swift was right, none of it made sense. There was no apparent motive, and without it, there was nothing to point the way. Why? Why had the two men been murdered? The puzzle kept spinning around in my head.

Balthazar was emerging from the breakfast room as I approached. He was leaning heavily on a smart ebony cane with a gold handle and seemed rather more doddery today.

'Hello, how nice to see you.' He smiled vaguely, I don't think he remembered who I was.

'Greetings, Lord Balthazar. Would you like to join us in the library?'

His smile widened. 'Is there a recitation? I am most fond of recitations. Jasper will interrupt, you know. Perhaps it's better not to mention it to him.'

'I don't think he will be joining us today,' I said and steered him towards the library.

'I have medicine, it is most efficacious,' he said as we made slow progress along the passage. 'The Baroness gives it to me, she is quite knowledgeable about such things. It is in a bottle. Jasper has his in his tea and brandy in the morning. Really, it is most injudicious to drink tea with brandy, one cannot taste either the tea or the brandy.'

'Yes,' I agreed and opened the door to the library. 'Here we are.'

Swift stood up and waited while I seated the old fellow.

'Good morning Lord Balthazar,' Swift began in formal tone. 'Do you know why you are here?'

'I do,' Balthazar replied. 'Are you going to sing?'

Swift blinked. 'No. We have some questions for you… didn't Major Lennox explain?'

'Oh, yes, haha, a most excellent recitation,' he chortled happily.

Swift glanced at me. I gave a shrug and sat down.

'What do you recall of the day Sir Jasper died?' Swift had his pen poised over his open notebook.

Balthazar's eyes widened, his mouth fell open and his chin trembled. 'Died? Jasper is dead? But why, when?'

Swift looked at me again.

'The medicine may not have taken effect yet,' I said.

'Oh dear, this is awful.' Balthazar was trying to pull a handkerchief from the pocket of his velvet smoking jacket. 'Poor Jasper, my old friend. The cause…what was the cause?' Tears were filling his eyes and he sniffed loudly.

'I'm afraid he was murdered.' Swift's stern police front evaporated. 'I'm sorry, we have mentioned it to you before.'

'Perhaps you forgot.' I tried to think of words of comfort. 'He probably didn't feel anything.'

'His medicine?' Balthazar's voice trembled. 'That was it wasn't it? Too much, it is too much.' He wobbled to his feet. 'I must consider the consequences,' he mumbled half to himself. 'Oh Jasper, what has become of you? And of me?'

There was nothing to be done other than escort him out again. I helped him to the centre hall where I found Freya rearranging the baubles on the tree.

'Those bad cats have been playing, I am hanging the balls higher,' she explained, then noticed Balthazar's distress. 'Major. What have you done to this poor man?'

'Nothing, we were trying to question him–'

'Pah. Like some bad politiet, always with shouting, and sticks. This is not correct. You will not persecute him like this, nor no-one.'

I was surprised she knew the word persecute. 'He'd forgotten that Sir Jasper had died and we mentioned it–' I tried again.

'It is necessary to be gentle.' She took Balthazar by the arm. 'Come, you will return to your bed, I will show you, and you will not think on what these bad politiet have said.'

'But I must, I must,' Balthazar said. 'It cannot be forgotten.' He whispered loudly to her: 'Murdered.'

She scowled at me as though it were somehow my fault, then led him towards the stairs.

A black paw pushed its way from under the lid of the wicker hamper, followed by a nose, whiskers and then the cat. It was Nox, he slid out in one silky movement. Furz slinked out behind him. Tubbs shoved his head between the lid and hamper, then wiggled until his fat little tummy cleared the edge and he tumbled to the floor. He never had been the most graceful of felines.

Nox had already trotted over to the tree and sat staring at the shiny red and gold baubles, now tied to the higher branches. He reached up on back feet to bat one with a black paw. It had been tied tightly to the needle-spiked branch and didn't fall. Furz joined him and struck it harder. It spun over but remained firmly tied by its red ribbon. Tubbs went straight for the thick trunk and clambered up it – and kept going until he was halfway. Nox gazed at him with green eyes, then followed suit. Furz did the same and the tree swayed alarmingly.

I told them very firmly to get down, which they ignored. I grabbed the tree, then tried to prise a cat off. That didn't work, it just climbed higher. The tree began toppling. It was taller than me by a good three feet. Damn. I tried to grab another cat; they thought it a great game. I stood back, Tubbs was now near the very top causing the branch to arc precipitously.

I untied one of the baubles and rolled it across the chequered floor. The cats instantly shimmied down and raced about chasing it.

'Major Lennox.' Norman had come in without my realising. 'I really must protest, you have not interviewed me and yet you find time to play with cats.'

'I wasn't–'

'I saw you.' He turned dramatic. 'Really, there are two people dead – murdered, no less – by some terrible brute and you apparently have nothing better to do than amuse yourself with animals. And I might remind you that the tree and decorations–'

It was my turn to interrupt. 'Right, fine, come on,' I retorted then marched off.

He complained all the way, which fortunately wasn't very far. Swift looked relieved to see him, but reverted to police mode almost immediately.

'Please be seated, Mr Keene.' He waved at the chair just vacated by Balthazar.

'It's Sir Norman, actually,' he retorted, then sat down and crossed his legs.

I refrained from asking if Roger was a Lady.

Swift had the statements in front of him. He took the top one and read it silently, making Norman wait with increasing and obvious impatience.

'What do you know of these murders?' Swift threw at him.

He didn't bat an eyelid. 'Nothing, and I believe it is your job to solve them, not mine.'

'We're not asking you to solve them,' I said.

'Answer the question,' Swift snapped.

'I have an impediment, you know. You shouldn't upset me,' he objected in petulant tone, his brown eyes sharp with irritation.

'You have fits,' I said.

'I do. Everyone knows, and they have to help save me if I start twitching.' Colour rose in his perfectly smooth cheeks. He was mildly overweight, a sign of comfortable living rather than serious overindulgence. The years had been kind, he remained almost wrinkle-free, a soft chin and plumpish cheeks, fair brows at odds with the brown wig, and a superbly tailored cream jacket over a pink shirt and dark red v-neck sweater.

Swift eyed him, then sighed. 'We don't want to cause you any difficulty, Sir Norman. But this is a very serious matter.'

Norman nodded to acknowledge the offer of peace. 'I really don't know anything of help. Roger and I weren't told what happened to Jasper other than he died.' He raised a hand to carefully pat the brown hair, it seemed fairly firmly fixed. 'And General Hackett's death was a dreadful shock. I had to take a valerian bath.'

'A what?' I said.

'An infusion of herbs,' he replied. 'Wilfred says there's nothing that can help my epilepsy, but herbal baths are calming. Valerian, camomile, ginger and a hint of acanthus. I take one most mornings.'

That would explain the flowery scent wafting about him.

'Do you suspect anyone in the house?' Swift asked, pen poised over his notebook.

'I do not, but…' he paused, a finger raised to his soft chin, '…if it were a question of personality, I'd have to point at Cicely.'

'What?' We both spoke at once.

'She's very hard-hearted, you know, and absolutely rules the roost here.' He fidgeted. 'If she decided it's time for one to go, just to boost the funds you understand, then I think she wouldn't hesitate to do the deed.'

'Utter nonsense,' I snapped back. 'She cared for the sick and injured during the war. Including me, apparently.'

'And what of those who were too far gone to be cared for? We've all heard it went on, there were rumours,' Norman retorted.

'Scurrilous rumours without an ounce of truth in them,' Swift replied, the anger clear in his face.

'Oh, if you say so.' Norman waved a hand. 'I haven't come here to argue with you.'

I took a breath to calm down. The damned man had hit a nerve; we'd all heard rumours, and some of them were probably true. 'Did anyone from here purchase books from you?' I turned policeman, or tried to.

'Oh, almost everybody.' Norman shifted to straighten his back. 'Some of our books were virtually priceless. Now, the Baroness is keen on psychology and anthropology

– have you spoken to her about her theories? I find them quite fascinating, although she is rather inclined to view mankind in…ah…experimental terms.' He smiled while dropping another piece of invective into our laps.

'We have spoken to her,' I said dryly, and leaned back to regard him.

He fidgeted again. 'Hum, as I said, we supplied almost everyone. General Hackett wasn't a great reader – he liked biographies; Wellington, Napoleon, that sort. Captain Lockhart mostly reads Conrad, Balthazar was a great collector of history and encyclopaedias before he…ah… rather lost his way. He was extraordinarily knowledgeable, particularly about this house. Such a shame, and his mother went the same way, her memory gone. She'd been very fond of the classics. Well, Jane Austen, if you consider her a classic, and the Brontës, George Elliot, Thomas Hardy…oh, and Dickens, of course, although she found him quite unsettling. Olivia and Matilda share similar romantic tastes, and the dear Pastor is keen on Trollope, and who isn't!'

None of that enlightened us one iota. Swift wrote it down anyway.

'What about you?' Swift asked without looking up.

'Oh,' he simpered. 'Murder! Killing people off in the most ingenious ways possible…but you mustn't take that literally,' he quickly added. 'Martin Hewitt is my hero!'

'You went down to the pool recently.' I returned to questioning.

His cheeks suffused with colour. 'Who told you that?'

Swift stopped writing. 'Never mind. Why did you go down there?'

He turned sulky. 'It was a private matter.'

'You're not leaving this room until you tell us,' I threatened, although it was an empty one because we could hardly force him.

'You're really quite the brute,' he prevaricated, then picked at the sharp crease in his cream trousers. 'It was about Justice St John…' he began and stopped again. His discomfort at spilling the beans appeared genuine. 'There's someone he wants brought in – another Saint. St John is quite domineering, he's used to getting his own way, and I know we all are really. Too much money.' He waved a hand. 'It does make one rather self-centred. But St John has such an opinion of himself that he thinks he can do no wrong. I went down to the pool to discuss it with General Hackett, where I thought I wouldn't be observed.' His cheeks still showed red, but the colour was fading.

'When did you have this conversation?' I asked.

'A week ago,' he replied.

Swift wrote that down. 'Could you tell us what was said, please?'

'I informed Hackett that he was in danger of being ousted by St John and his fellow justice. St John believed that the donations should be directed towards social issues, which means dabbling in politics. We already allocate a proportion to legal lobbying, but most of us would rather stick with the balance we have. St John was very angry about Jasper's request for the horse sanctuary, he said humanity's problems take precedence over animals. Hackett disagreed.'

'Did they argue?' Swift's lean face had sharpened.

'No,' Norman sighed. 'St John doesn't believe in open confrontation, he thinks matters should be arranged surreptitiously. He spoke to some of us quietly, sounding us out, asking if we would support an overthrow of the Regent so he could take his place.'

'How many votes did he need?' I asked.

'Six, plus his own, but he would never get them. Nobody wants the Order to become involved in politics, not even for a good cause.'

'What did Hackett say when you discussed this with him?' Swift started writing again.

Norman shrugged. 'He was entirely unconcerned. He said he'd always admired St John's dedication to fighting social injustice, but he'd have to do it through his own judicial network. The Order of Saints would never change, and nobody here would support him.'

'Do you think that's true?' I asked because I wasn't so sure.

'Well, Olivia is very keen on social legislation, and so is the Baroness. I think Rackham might be too. Anyway, I felt reassured by Hackett's reply and put it aside...until he was murdered.'

'You should have told us earlier,' Swift said.

'I thought as detectives, you would have found out yourselves,' he riposted. 'Anyway, some of the others knew, they could have said.'

'Do you know Cicely Sissinghurst's opinion of this?' I asked him.

'No, but she would be adamantly against it,' he spoke quite forcefully. 'She's a traditionalist and I'm certain would strongly oppose any such change.'

I'd have judged Cicely the same way too.

He looked at his watch. 'It's almost time for our big meeting. It's the last day to decide where our donations are given. I do hope St John won't try to browbeat us, I find such pressure quite unbearable.' He made to rise but stopped suddenly. 'You won't repeat anything I said, will you?'

People seem to have no idea what a police investigation is actually for.

'No,' I lied. 'Won't mention a word.'

CHAPTER 23

'I don't believe St John would kill for a good cause,' I said as the door closed behind Norman Keene.

'Neither do I,' Swift replied. Then wrote it down anyway.

'The Saints will be at their meeting all morning.' I leaned back in my chair, gaze drifting towards the window and sparkling sunshine beyond.

'All day, probably,' he muttered, his focus still on his notebook.

'How about a change of scene?'

'What?' He looked up.

'Bath. It's full of shops and I haven't bought anything for Persi, yet.' Or anyone, actually.

'I thought you were going to buy her a car.'

'So did I but the bank manager said otherwise.'

'We can't go Christmas shopping in the middle of an investigation, Lennox.'

'It might give us perspective.'

'What sort of perspective?'

I didn't have an answer to that.

'And we should search their rooms…' He was prevaricating.

'They'll have a fit if we do,' I objected.

'We're conducting a police investigation.' He put his pen down and turned to the window. 'We could go to the station and talk to the local coppers,' he suggested.

'Right, come on then!' I was on my feet and heading for the door before he had a chance to change his mind.

Greggs was pootling along the corridor, his mood now benign. I gave him the jewelled horse. 'Tie that back on the tree would you old chap? And not a word said about it.'

He raised his brows but didn't demure. 'Very well, sir.' He peered at it. 'This is no mere bauble, sir.'

'No, but this house is full of hidden treasures,' I said. 'We're off to Bath…erm, to interview the local constabulary,' I added. 'See you later.' I cleared off before he had time to quibble.

Swift must have been locking the library door or something because he didn't arrive outside until I'd retrieved the Bentley from the coach house, coaxed her into spluttering life and motored the short distance to the front.

'Lennox, we really shouldn't–' he began as he settled in the front passenger seat. I couldn't hear the rest because I revved the engine, spun the wheels through a drift to send a spray of snow flying, and roared out of the open gates.

Fifteen minutes of winding lanes later I drew to a halt outside a likely looking tavern.

'The police station is down there.' Swift pointed to a smart stone building with the usual blue lamp above the front entrance.

'Fine,' I said and climbed out of the car.

'Aren't you coming?'

'Swift,' I said, 'I'm going shopping.'

He looked beyond the station to the bustling town square. Garlands were strung above shop windows, a Christmas tree stood tall on snow-trampled cobbles and the scent of roasting chestnuts, ginger cake and mulled wine drifted from market stalls set around the periphery. He hesitated. 'Right, but we'll go to the station before lunch.'

I grinned and strode towards the crowded city centre and all the delights it had to offer.

'Perfume?' I hesitated at the large bow window of a pharmacy.

'As part of her gift set.' He was gazing at the tempting display of fancy bottles, some with diamanté-encrusted tops.

'What? You mean I have to buy more than one present?'

'Yes, Lennox.'

I stuck my hands in the pockets of my greatcoat. 'Well, what else should I get?'

'You'll have to work that out for yourself.'

Damn. I should have asked Greggs. I wondered if I should telephone him. 'What are you going to buy Florence?'

'A portfolio of music scores. She's very fond of Bach's harpsichord concertos. She's been practising at home and I know she'd like to show Angus the keys.'

'He's barely three.'

'He likes to listen to music, it puts him to sleep.'

It would probably put anyone to sleep. 'What else?'

'Knitting patterns, and as much Aran wool as I can find. She's also just started spinning so I've arranged for a fleece to be delivered when they next shear the flock.'

I gave him a sideways look; he seemed quite serious.

'Persi doesn't knit.'

'How about a magnifying glass?' He headed for the shop door.

I followed. We both paused on the coconut mat to stamp snow from our boots.

How many presents were in a "gift set"?

I bought scented talc – apparently this is a perfectly acceptable present if suitably wrapped and ribboned. Also a very small bottle of Guerlain perfume called "Shalimar". Some soap, also scented, and a glass jar full of coloured cotton wool balls. The lady behind the counter assured me that my wife would be delighted with such feminine fripperies. I remarked she didn't know my wife, which seemed to upset her.

'Vaseline,' I said.

Swift brightened at that.

'Good thinking, Lennox,' he said then turned to the lady serving us from behind the glass-topped counter. 'Does anyone from Temple House come in here?'

'Why would you want to know that?' She bristled.

His mouth opened and closed.

'One of the ladies recommended you,' I said.

She smiled. 'Now, that's very nice of them, but they don't come down to the city very much in this weather. Haven't seen any of them since harvest festival.'

'Actually it was Miss Sissinghurst,' I fabricated.

'Ah, her maid's in here most weeks,' she replied, a stocky lady with grey curls and a rather severe expression.

'Freya,' Swift said. 'She's fond of, erm…'

'Carbolic soap,' I said.

She looked from one to the other of us. 'Well, she did buy some only last week, but I can't imagine anyone being fond of it.'

'Fond might not be the exact word. Anyway, I'd like a bar, please,' I said.

'Very well.' She added one to my bag of purchases.

'Thank you, madam.' I picked up the bag. 'Wait.' I held up a hand. 'You don't have a spade do you?' I'd suddenly been struck with an excellent idea.

She stared at me. 'We do not stock spades, sir. We are a chemist.'

'What about a trowel?'

'I think you will need the ironmonger, sir,' she said then pursed her lips.

I decided against asking for directions.

'Surely Persi must have a spade,' Swift said as we exited out into the square.

'She has quite a few, but she might like another one.' I noticed one of the stalls was selling mulled wine.

'There's a jeweller on the corner.' Swift pointed to an elegant building with understated decorations surrounding the large front window. The interior glittered with finely wrought jewellery under a string of sparkling festive lights.

'No,' I said, having made the mistake of entering

a jewellery store in London and coming out virtually impoverished.

'Does she like art or crafts?' Swift suggested.

I stopped walking. 'She might. When she digs things up, she makes drawings of the finds... she could take photographs. Should we look at cameras?'

'Drawing is probably better,' he said. 'We can go to the stationers.'

'Yes,' I agreed, then veered off toward the stalls surrounding the market square.

'Lennox?' Swift called after me.

'Two glasses of mulled wine, and, um...a slice of Dundee cake please.' The nearest booth had a full range of Christmas goodies.

Swift didn't say a word although his face said it for him. The mulled wine was excellent, so was the cake. We watched the colourful crowds browsing shop windows. Stiff gentlemen with rolled umbrellas, ladies in winter bonnets and fur-trimmed coats, children running about in felt hats, scarves, thick wool jackets and button-up boots.

'I'm going to the police station, Lennox,' Swift declared.

'Fine, I'll find some drawing paper and whatnots, and meet you back at the car.'

He went off; so did I. We met at the Bentley almost an hour later. As the car was parked outside the tavern, I insisted we have lunch. At two o'clock we drove back to Temple House. When we returned we discovered nothing at all had happened, so we headed for the library to spend the afternoon in debate about who may, or may not, have murdered two of the Saints. We hadn't made an iota of progress by the time we left for The George to meet our lovely wives.

'They were so sweet. They asked questions in the most courteous and roundabout manner,' Florence said. 'It was quite funny, but Persi kept a straight face all the way through.'

'They're just not used to having women in the lectures, least of all actually speaking.' Persi smiled, fork in hand.

'I thought there were quite a few women in the archeological world,' Swift said, ever ready to champion the underdog.

'There are,' Persi replied. 'But they aren't often invited to the lectern.'

'One chap fell asleep,' Florence told us. 'And Angus asked me loudly if the man was dead. He woke up when everyone laughed.'

'At least he didn't snore through my talk.' Persi smiled. 'He wouldn't have been the first one.'

'Everyone else was hanging on your words, especially when you showed them the sword,' Florence said.

'Yes.' Persi became solemn. 'A warrior's weapon designed for a boy…rather sad really.'

We were midway through roast beef and dumplings with mash in the snug comfort of The George's best restaurant. Dark red walls, blackened beams, stone-flagged floor and a roaring fire. They'd told us all about the British Museum and the lectures. We'd listened and chatted, then we explained what we'd learned at Temple House, or rather Swift did; I ate my food and enjoyed the excellent wine.

'Were there many from Oxford?' Swift returned to the subject of the dig.

'Yes, three.' Persi's face lit up. 'They were the chaps we gave the Viking stone to. They dated it to around 800 AD, and believed the tribe to be from Gotland, a Norwegian island. It's probably a commemoration to their dead warriors sailing to Valhalla.'

'Wasn't there a crow, or something?' I slid some mashed potato into my gravy.

'Yes, and there was also a woman depicted, the Goddess, Freya.' Persi gave a throaty laugh. 'Which is quite a coincidence.'

Swift and I both looked up. 'Freya?'

'The most powerful woman in Norse mythology,' Persi replied. 'Her name means "Lady". She was primarily the Goddess of fertility, but she also hand-picked half the fallen warriors to go to Valhalla. Odin chose the other half.'

'And that's why she was on the stone carving?' Swift asked.

'Yes, and she had a chariot drawn by cats,' Persi replied. 'I've always rather liked the idea.'

'That wasn't on the stone,' I said.

That made both girls laugh.

'No, it wasn't,' Florence said.

'But she was at the centre of things?' Swift said.

'One of those at the centre, and a sorceress, of course, as most alluring women in myth are depicted,' Persi said dryly.

'You would have been one of them,' I said quietly to her.

That made her eyes glow and she smiled softly.

'Remarkable coincidence,' Swift mused. 'The stone you uncovered depicting Freya – a dazzling young woman among the dead and dying.'

'Just like Temple House,' I said.

Persi laughed. 'Hardly a Viking ship.'

'But still a terminus,' I said.

'And their exit is designed to be in great comfort,' Florence replied. 'By the usual course of nature.' She sighed. 'Do you have any idea who it may be?'

'Without a motive, we're stumbling in the dark.' Swift tried to keep his voice light but I think we all heard the anxious note.

'Would Wilfred Rackham be able to manage the steps down to the Roman bath?' Persi asked.

'I think so,' I replied. 'He can go up and down the main stairs without any problem.'

'But stone steps would be quite difficult, particularly if they were damp and slippery,' Florence said.

I nodded, we'd already considered that. 'The footsteps were from rubber soles, it would help him maintain a grip.'

'The motive isn't money,' Persi began. 'They have no need of it.'

'Unless the coffers aren't as full as they're purported to be,' Swift said.

Nobody spoke for a moment.

'That would implicate Cicely Sissinghurst,' I said.

We'd all finished eating and the waitress came to clear our plates.

'And your little tot is sound asleep upstairs in your

chamber, and the maid's sitting in there with him,' she told Florence. 'He's full of beans, isn't he! And really good at imitating trains and aeroplanes. Loud as can be too. Made everyone smile, he did.'

'He's just come with us on the train from London and was terribly excited,' Florence explained. 'I do hope we haven't disturbed anyone.'

'Not in the slightest.' The waitress leaned a little closer. 'And if you have, they can jolly well lump it because nobody should grouch about children, 'specially at Christmas.' She took the plates away, a smile lighting her plain face.

'Jasper was in business,' I said. 'He could have discovered any discrepancy, but I think he'd have made a note in his diary if he had.'

Swift took out his notebook and pen.

'But if it were Cicely,' he turned to an empty page, 'would he have covered for her?'

'Even if he would do such a thing,' Florence answered, 'it would surely have destroyed his adoration of her.'

'Yes,' Swift agreed and wrote it down. 'General Hackett was keen on her too.'

'He said she had good ankles, Swift,' I replied. 'That hardly constitutes undying devotion.'

'You said Captain Lockhart might be hiding a dishonourable debt.' Persi looked at me, her blue eyes glowing in the candlelight.

I reached a hand to take hers. 'It would have been discovered by the Wise Men before he was even invited to join the Saints.'

'I agree,' Swift said. 'The Burma campaign was decades ago, any debt would have been uncovered by now.'

'And that rules out love and money,' I said.

'I'm not sure I agree, I think it could be love.' Florence finished her food and wiped her lips with a napkin. 'Jasper wanted to make space for Cicely, and he was quite old. He might have thought she wouldn't come to live in the house in his lifetime unless a vacancy were created.'

'That would make Balthazar the most likely culprit,' Persi said. 'Because he'd have believed his life to be in danger.'

'You wouldn't think so if you'd met him,' Swift said dryly.

'The snowdrop essence spoken of in Homer is fascinating,' Persi said. 'I've never heard anyone make that interpretation before.'

'And it makes one wonder how much more the Greeks knew, and has been lost to history,' Florence added.

'If it's not love, or money, then it can only be power,' Swift stated.

'Justice St John,' I said.

'Killing in a good cause?' Persi said with a lift of her brow.

'His reputation was one of meting out tough justice,' Swift said. 'But he was always fair. Everyone held absolute respect for him, including me. I can't see him killing for any reason.'

'As you've told me in the past, Swift,' I reminded him, 'it's not a popularity contest.'

He'd frowned and made a point of writing this in his notebook.

'You mentioned there were two military men among them, General Hackett and Captain Lockhart,' Florence spoke carefully in her soft Scottish accent. 'Such men kill for good causes, it's their job, and I think, part of their nature. Either one of them may have done so if they thought it important enough.' Her father, the Laird of Braeburn Castle, had been an army man.

'Especially if it were on someone's orders,' Persi added.

They were astute, I thought. I knew it already, but they still surprised me.

I looked at Swift.

'You're assuming Justice St John ordered Hackett to kill Jasper, and he then killed Hackett in turn?' he said calmly.

'It didn't necessarily have to be the Judge,' Florence spoke slowly. 'Someone else may have persuaded them it was necessary.'

'It may have been one of the ladies,' Persi said.

'Does that seem logical to you?' I asked.

Persi and Florence sat in a moment's silence, apart from the other diners making a racket, of course.

'I suppose it isn't, because the Judge, or anyone, could have simply killed Jasper themselves without involving the General,' Persi rationalised.

'Which also would have avoided risking the reputation of the Order,' I added, and then squeezed her hand in case she was annoyed at me.

'So that only leaves tragedy,' Persi said. 'Wilfred Rackham's expedition.'

That had been playing on my mind. What if it wasn't as

Rackham had relayed? Who would know? And then there was Freya, where did she fit into all this?

'If it were, why wasn't Rackham the victim?' Swift said.

That brought about another debate, which equally went nowhere.

We finished the evening with marmalade bread pudding and custard, a couple of glasses of dessert wine – well I had two anyway – and a fond farewell outside in the snow.

'It's the recital tomorrow evening,' Swift said once we were back in the Bentley and on our way.

'Is that a hint, Swift?' I steered the car toward the lane climbing up the icy hill to Temple House.

He sighed. 'Possibly. Did any of that shed light?'

I didn't reply for a while, my eyes on the road, snowflakes sticking to the windscreen and the underpowered wipers feebly trying to sweep them aside.

'I have an idea.'

He turned to me, his face sharp angles in the shadows of the car interior.

'Truly?'

'Tomorrow morning we will gather them together and force it out of them.'

'You can't use force, Lennox.'

'The force of logic, Swift, because that's all we've got.'

CHAPTER 24

Justice St John was waiting for us in our room when we arrived back at Temple House. We were merry from a night out and a tipple or two with our lovely wives. Fogg was with him – he gave us an ecstatic welcome, whereas the Judge was glaring from beneath bristling brows.

'This will not do,' he growled in ringing tone. 'Dereliction of duty. Absent without leave. Tomorrow I am calling the Yard.'

Swift paled.

'No need old man,' I said affably. 'We've been conferring, and the name of your killer will be revealed in the morning. Instruct everyone to gather in the library, including old Jiggens and Essie, the housekeeper.'

He wasn't used to taking orders and his jaw dropped for a moment. 'What, what…?' he spluttered then recovered. 'The name, man. Give me the name.'

'Tomorrow, Your Honour.' I steered him gently by the arm. 'We all need a good night's rest.'

'But you…' he was still spluttering when I closed the door behind him.

Swift slumped down in the chair by the dying fire. 'Damn it, Lennox, are you sure you can do this?'

I considered saying no, but prevaricated instead. 'The killer will need to maintain the lie in the face of the crowd; it will cause them to stumble, Swift.'

'Not necessarily,' he grumbled. 'Some people love being centre stage; keeping up a deception is an act, and there are plenty of people given to drama here.'

That gave me pause, he was right. 'Nil desperandum, Swift. I'm going to bed.'

'Fine,' he muttered, and went to the desk to write more notes in his book.

Dawn crept in with soft rays of pale pink and yellow sliding between the drawn curtains. Swift was already up and dressed. All three cats were curled around me with Foggy snoring beside them.

Who was the killer? The night had brought ideas tumbling in the dark. I was pretty sure who it wasn't...well, fairly sure. And as for those who were left...their faces would tell me, unless they were better than I thought. And if not, someone would surely catch a lie...

'Lennox, are you going to get dressed?'

'What?' *Damn.* 'Right.' I threw back the covers and made a start to the day.

* * *

'It doesn't matter where you sit,' I said, trying to keep the exasperation out of my voice.

'Of course it does.' Lady Matilda raised her lorgnette to glare at me. 'Although I remain unconvinced of the need for this, Major Lennox. It is a further disruption and our nerves are already jangling.'

Lady Matilda was putting up a resistance consisting of quibbling and fuss. It caused agitation amongst the rest of the Saints, who were now milling about the library rather than sitting in the cushioned armchairs grouped in two rows of a semicircle in front of the fire. We'd set Jiggens to work after breakfast and the clock on the mantelpiece was now striking ten.

Wilfred Rackham remained one of the few level-headed ones among them and walked calmly to the front and sat in his usual chair. Jiggens had brought it in earlier at our request.

'I should sit closest to him,' Roger was saying as they both stood among the chairs.

'The Major?'

'Of course!'

'Why do you want to be close to him?' Norman demanded.

'So that I can hear him,' Roger retorted.

'There's nothing wrong with your hearing, it's my hearing that's the problem,' Norman said.

'Well, if you weren't wearing that ridiculous rug you'd be able to hear perfectly well!' Roger riposted.

Norman was outraged. 'Oh, you absolute hussy, I do not–'

'All of you, sit down,' Swift suddenly yelled, his patience worn thin.

'But why?' Balthazar asked for the fifth or sixth time.

'Come and sit next to me,' Olivia Arbuthnot said and patted an armchair beside her.

His face brightened. 'Oh, how kind of you, my dear. I will be honoured to do so.' He sat down, fidgeted, then clasped his hands together on his lap like an attentive schoolboy.

Baroness Ginny was already seated on the other side of him. She had dressed in a dull brown frock, the colour of dried clay. 'I find this quite fascinating. It is a unique opportunity to observe the modern hunter at work,' she said, although she didn't seem to be talking to anyone in particular.

'Hunting what?' Balthazar asked.

'The culprit, of course,' Ginny replied.

'The culprit?' Balthazar quavered. 'Have we been robbed?'

'Has he had his medicine today?' Olivia hissed to Ginny. She'd dressed in dusky red silk. No-one seemed to have donned mourning gear for the recently dead.

'Yes, the usual dose,' Ginny whispered back.

I was inclined to say it wasn't enough but didn't.

Pastor Peabody wandered my way, peering through round glasses and looking more like Santa Claus than unusual, in a red sweater. 'Are you truly certain this is absolutely necessary, Major?'

'I'm afraid it is,' I said with as much patience as I could muster.

'It will add to our troubles,' he said, with a sorrowful shake of the head.

'I'll find you a comfortable spot, shall I Pastor?' Young Jiggens offered. He steered him toward the second row and plumped a cushion to place at his back.

Cicely Sissinghurst had been the first to sit down. She began drumming fingers in irritation on the arm of her chair. 'Major Lennox, do not make this into something tortuous,' she spoke sharply.

I didn't respond.

Old Jiggens was standing at the further end of the room, dressed in crumpled butlering togs and patently unhappy. Essie the housekeeper was with him, she was wringing her hands and looked equally upset. Greggs was wandering about, settling people down and plumping up cushions with a simpering smile as though it were a theatre show.

I went over to Swift. He was arranging a small side table with items of evidence. It looked more like a bric-a-brac stall. I'd already added the golden horse from the tree and the mangled ribbon.

Lockhart had stopped when he saw it. 'Where was it?' He turned the horse over with strong fingers, the gold and jewels dazzling under the chandelier.

'Freya had it.' I decided on honesty. 'Did you give it to her?'

'What on earth for?' Lockhart was bemused.

'She reminded you of your wife.' I plucked an idea from the air.

He frowned. 'My wife was a hot-blooded woman. Strong and worldly. I called her my Viking. Freya is a naive young girl, despite her temperament.' He went and sat down, arms crossed and looking rather sad.

Swift was still lining up the evidence. 'Empty jar of Yopo,' he muttered as he ticked them off. 'Empty jar of Chironex fleckeri, *A Christmas Carol*, bar of carbolic soap, burnt bauble, vaseline, cotton wool balls, one bone needle–'

'Swift?'

'What?'

'That's not the same needle.'

'I know. There's a box of them in the Chamber, I took one as a substitute.'

'What time will the police have the results of the poison?'

He pulled his cuff back to check his watch. 'I could telephone again?'

'Yes, please, before we start.'

He made for the door almost before I'd finished the sentence. I surveyed the table. The evidence was pitiful; no gun, dagger, or weapon of any sort. We had added Jasper's diary, which I'd felt uncomfortable with, but Swift had insisted.

Freya arrived; the cats raced in after her in a jumble of black whiskers, legs, and tails.

An image of Freya as a Norse Goddess riding a chariot pulled by cats sprang to mind. She wouldn't have got very far, cats never did a damn thing they're supposed to. And there was something amiss with the Norse Goddess idea too, something that didn't sit right…

Foggy wandered in and was greeted with cooing and kind words before finally coming to my side. He flopped down, his tongue hanging out and gazed around, probably with the hope of tidbits in mind.

'All be seated.' St John marched in wearing the black cloak with blue silk lining. He made his way noisily to the front and sat in the chair closest to the evidence table.

'Is that it?' He demanded.

'Apparently,' I replied, not prepared to be drawn.

'Where's Swift?'

'He's–' I began but stopped as he raced in.

'Lennox.' He beckoned and I went to listen as he spoke quietly to me. 'Honey mixed with ricin.'

'With what?' I whispered back.

'Ricin. It's from the castor oil plant. It wasn't curare.'

It still didn't make any sense to me. 'Well, what effect does it have?'

'It causes haemorrhaging, then organ failure. It's not instant, it would have taken a few hours,' he continued.

'I assume it was from the Chamber of Curiosities?'

'Yes, I've brought the jar down with me.' He withdrew it from his satchel, which explained why he was carrying it. 'It's been cleaned with carbolic, here, smell it.' He stuck it under my nose.

I recoiled. 'Yes, fine Swift. Put it on the table–'

'Are we going to be here all day?' Justice St John barked.

'We're just completing the evidence, Your Honour,' Swift said and rushed to place the blue and white ceramic jar with the others, then moved aside as I stepped forward.

'Ladies and gentlemen…' I raised my voice above the chatter. They didn't shut up.

'Order in court,' St John bellowed, which did the trick; they all sat up and peered toward the front.

'Sir Jasper Crawford died in the hospital five nights ago of hypothermia,' I stated.

That brought some confused muttering.

'Are you sure?' Pastor Peabody asked. 'I thought he died in his chair.'

'I'll explain. Yopo,' I said, and picked up the ceramic jar to show it, then put it down again. 'Someone threw the contents of this jar onto Jasper's fire. He didn't realise it, he was probably asleep at the time. The fumes would have put him into a sleep so deep he was assumed dead.'

'Comatose,' St John interrupted.

'Precisely, Your Honour,' I agreed.

'But what happened?' Pastor Peabody said. 'Why were we told he had died sitting beside his fire?'

'At first, that is what was believed,' I replied and then explained about the unfortunate events at the morgue and the hypothermia.

'You should have been clear from the start, Major Lennox.' Lady Matilda lowered her lorgnette to castigate me. 'I had offered to help, but was refused. Did you assume I was a suspect? Am I still?' she demanded in a haughty tone.

'I apologise, but we had barely begun to gather the facts.' I gave the only excuse I had without actually answering her questions.

Swift added a policeman's explanation. 'The Regent initially thought Sir Jasper had a heart attack, and when the truth was discovered he decided to restrict details during the investigation.'

I distracted them by waving the book in the air. 'This book was left upon his lap.' I held up Dickens' *Christmas Carol*. 'Jasper didn't usually read novels, did he?'

'No,' Olivia said. 'He was as careful about spending his time as he was about spending his money.'

Murmurs of agreement were made until the Judge *harrumphed* again, which quietened them down.

'Presumably this was left with him as some kind of excuse,' I continued. 'An indication of why he'd been murdered…but was it? The person who threw the Yopo into the fire couldn't have known Sir Jasper would die, and certainly not in the way that he did. It was perfectly possible he could have recovered his senses later in the day and been little the worse for the experience. He would have woken with the book on his lap, and perhaps wondered what it meant.'

'You are saying his death truly was an accident,' Baroness Ginny stated.

Wilfred Rackham answered her. 'I've been thinking that it is feasible. The Yopo would have made him hallucinate, he would have been in a dreamlike state,' he explained. 'Someone may have spoken to him while he was under the influence of the drug, trying to make him change his ways. It may have been the motive, and while reprehensible, it was not necessarily murderous.'

'He was drugged to persuade him to give up his miserly ways, you mean?' I said.

'Yes, I do,' Rackham replied.

'But was that truly the message of *A Christmas Carol*?'

I asked. 'Wasn't it about redemption; those who were well provided for, helping those less able to help themselves. Caring for one's fellow man…'

'And the children,' Pastor Peabody called out. 'Don't forget those poor little children under the ghost's cloak.'

'They were called Ignorance and Want,' Roger added. 'Jasper had no thought for them.'

'Yes, thank you.' I held up my hand. 'Jasper wasn't simply mean with money, he was mean with people. What if the person who killed him had merely wished for him to be kind to his fellow man. That's why each of you were chosen to be Saints isn't it? To help your fellow man have a better life.'

'It was,' Olivia spoke up. 'But Jasper wasn't the usual sort that was recruited. He was chosen for his immense wealth.'

'Is that true, Miss Sissinghurst?' I turned to her.

She looked away, her lips pursed.

'You have it right,' St John rumbled. 'Jasper was richer than all of us put together. Made most Saints look like paupers. Inherited a huge fortune from his grandfather, and he'd made it from plantations in the Far East and the Caribbean. Jasper sold the lot, then began investing in new enterprises in Britain. He ended up bankrolling some of the biggest industries in the country; steel, coal, manufacturing. He gave us permission to liquidate it all when he came here, and we didn't need to hold the funds until his demise; he put the money straight into our coffers. Said he wouldn't go back on his word, the money was ours to spend provided we agreed with him where it went.'

'We should have been informed of this,' Swift said.

'You should have found out,' St John countered, which brought colour to Swift's lean cheeks.

'Was that true?' Wilfred Rackham leaned forward to ask Cicely Sissinghurst.

'Yes,' she replied tersely. 'We, he asked that it be kept private.'

'So our debates over donations were irrelevant?' Baroness Ginny spoke angrily.

'No, we merely agreed that a portion would go towards charities close to his heart,' Cicely replied.

'Well, the secrets are certainly falling out of the woodwork today,' Captain Lockhart said loudly.

'And yet he did threaten to withdraw his funds,' I reminded the Judge.

'It was bluster,' St John rejoined. 'And he knew it.'

'Did everyone believe it to be bluster?' I asked and looked around the room. 'What would it have meant if he really had gone ahead with his threat? The Order itself would be at risk. And how many projects would have had to be put aside?' I swept my gaze over their faces, all watching me intently. 'Was that why he was given the Yopo, to make him see reason? Or was it to kill him?' I added.

'I would prefer to believe it was an accident,' Olivia said. She was looking strained, her cheeks hollowed, her bright eyes dimmed.

'Then why did General Hackett have to die?' I said, to which no-one gave an answer.

CHAPTER 25

'General Hackett died from coming into contact with a poisonous powder,' I began. 'It was in his socks–'

'Poison in his socks?' Lady Matilda said in a tone worthy of Lady Bracknell. 'How can one have poisoned socks?'

'Is this true?' Pastor Peabody asked, his white brows drawn. 'Because it doesn't sound true.'

'It sounds utterly ridiculous,' Norman said.

'Why?' Roger cut in. 'I think it's clever. Who would imagine one's socks were poisoned?'

'Anyone would notice powder in one's socks,' Norman replied. 'I am extremely particular about socks, I would have noticed immediately.'

'Will you please–' I tried, then Swift stepped forward. 'Quiet! Someone poured the desiccated remains of box jellyfish into his socks. We've had the results of the analysis back from Scotland Yard this morning. There is no doubt.'

'Precisely,' I said. 'Chironex fleckeri.' I read the name from the label on the jar I had picked up. 'One of the most powerful toxins known to man.'

A few gasps went around on hearing that.

'Should we applaud?' Balthazar asked, looking about owlishly.

'No, it's not a show,' Olivia told him in a loud whisper.

'Captain Lockhart presented a lecture about that.' Baroness Ginny pointed at the jar, then turned to look at him, her expression almost accusatory.

'And now I wish I had not, dear lady,' he replied gravely, his weathered cheeks paling.

'Someone had placed the toxin in his socks,' I repeated. 'His feet may have been damp from his swim, although it's unlikely it would have made a difference. The poison was deadly enough to cause a heart attack, and killed him very quickly.'

'When was it placed in his socks?' Rackham asked.

'Yes, exactly.' St John spoke loudly. 'Be more precise, man.'

I bit back a curse. I couldn't answer the questions because we couldn't be certain when it was done. 'Fine. We know Hackett would go down to the pool in canvas shoes, without his socks. When he returned to his room, he would dress in clothes he'd left out ready to wear. We believe the culprit had poured the powder into his socks while he was swimming.' I stopped to look about. 'Does that answer your question?'

'Why didn't it harm the culprit if it were so deadly?' Baroness Ginny asked.

Damn it, we hadn't thought of that either. 'I assume they used a spoon and gloves.'

They all stared for a moment, minds presumably mulling over the actions I'd just described.

'Freya.' I turned to her.

She had been stroking one of the cats but straightened up when I called her name. 'Yes, are you wanting something?' she questioned in her singsong accent.

'You purchased some carbolic soap from the chemists in Bath,' I replied, picking up the bar I'd purchased and raising it before replacing it again.

'Why would I not?' she replied. 'We use it for to clean and there was not any.'

'Where did you use it to clean?' I asked.

'In the Chamber,' she said. Everyone now turned to look at her, standing near the door. 'It was all used up by the ladies when they made a spill.'

'Did you clean these jars?' I indicated all three on the table.

She hesitated.

'Freya?' Cicely questioned.

'Yes, madam.' The girl took a breath. 'Each had been left on the countertop in the Chamber. This is not the way to have things done. We must be orderly, madam is always saying so. Jiggens should have done this, but he does not like to go into the Chamber, but I do. I like to learn what is kept in there.'

Swift was frowning; he'd apparently just realised what I had: Freya may not have known about the poisons used in the murders.

'Did you tell anyone that you'd cleaned the jars?' Swift's voice was harsh.

Freya was unabashed. She shrugged. 'Why should I do so?'

'You should have told me, Freya,' Cicely spoke up.

'I said I had buyed more soap, madam. You did not ask why,' Freya replied.

'I assumed it was for my house in Bath,' Cicely replied.

'It was not, madam,' Freya replied. 'I used soap here, I had taken it from the cupboard by the Christmas tree and so there was need of more. I have bringed it with me yesterday and now put it in place in the cupboard.'

'You've destroyed any fingerprint evidence there may have been,' Swift said and let out a sharp breath of irritation.

Freya's cheeks flushed at his tone.

'I'm sure it wasn't intentional,' Wilfred Rackham spoke up. 'I'd encouraged her to learn about the herbs in the Chamber, she always cleaned up after we'd been working in there.'

'Did you teach her how poisonous these herbs were?' I turned to him.

'I taught her that some could be dangerous, and told her always to wear rubber gloves,' Rackham replied evenly, one eye on me, the other fixed and unseeing in the puckered side of his face.

'Captain Lockhart.' I swivelled on my heel in his direction. 'Your wife was Norwegian.'

'What of it?' Lockhart replied.

'Does Freya have the same accent?' I continued.

He momentarily closed his eyes, then admitted, 'No.'

'I am not from the town's peoples.' Freya came to confront me, her blue eyes flashing. 'We are not the same.'

'Then which people are you from?' I asked, looking down at her.

She didn't hesitate. 'I am Sami.'

'Are you?' Balthazar's eyes widened. 'But I thought you were Freya?'

'Not *Sammy*,' Norman told him as though the man were deaf. '*Sa-mi*. They herd reindeer and live in tents.'

'Sami?' Rackham leaned forward in his chair, reaching to grasp his walking stick. 'You're a Laplander?'

Freya's chin went up, a fierce gleam in her eyes. 'The land was ours, all the North. The peoples of the towns wanted to remove us, they drove us away. Persecuted by politiet. We were not like them, we did not live their ways; they say we are inferior. They forbid our teaching, our faiths, our language also. We moved always further away, to our old Sápmi lands. We take our herds, the reindeer. And the Russ come then, and we move again to escape them. The Russ are evil, cruel men, more bad than the others. Now we are in Sápmi, but there, we are not left alone, we always move.'

'But were you in Lapland when my team was lost?' Rackham struggled to stand but then gave up and stayed seated.

'It was one of our hunters. He found you. I was helping care for you,' Freya said, causing gasps throughout the room.

'Why didn't you tell me?' Cicely asked, the shock clear in her voice.

'Politiet,' Freya replied. 'They would send me away, just as always.'

'We would not allow it,' St John suddenly boomed. 'This is a civilised country. We do not persecute foreigners here.'

'But why did you come here?' Olivia asked.

'You fell in love with Wilfred,' Lady Matilda declared. 'Oh, what a lovely story, to come all this way–'

'This is not so,' Freya cut her off. 'It is not a story for children. I tried to help make Wilfred better with our herbs and our ways, but he was too hurt for us to make whole again. The peoples of the towns can heal where we cannot.' Her cheeks flushed again. 'We accept this, but it does not make us inferior.' She raised her chin again. 'I went with him when he was given to the peoples in their town.'

'What of the other boys?' Peabody stood up, a hand outstretched. 'What of our sons?'

Baroness Ginny was on her feet too. 'Do you know what happened to them? Please, please tell us of their last days? Did they suffer?'

There was an unspoken question that I imagined to have eaten away in the minds of everyone involved: did Rackham live at their expense? The room became very still as we awaited her answer.

'They had died in the cold. All were frozen,' Freya said, her voice softening. 'After the hunter returned with news of the lost strangers, we went to bring them to our shelter. It was not too far, some of your miles only. We took reindeer and sleds. Only Wilfred was living. All were together in a tight group, trying to keep alive. Wilfred was on the outside, not inside, this is the reason for his leg to be killed by cold.' The room was tight with tension, not a breath of noise to disturb her story. 'But one inside had died first and his cold had made the others colder. They were not damaged, but they were not living. It made us sad. We gathered Wilfred first, wrapped him in fur, then the others, and took them to our camp in the forest. We knew we must return the dead, but Wilfred was near dead also. We treated him, feeded him, so he could be taken alive to the town and mended. This is what we did.'

'Thank you, thank you…' Baroness Ginny murmured then took her handkerchief and wiped tears from her eyes.

Peabody did the same, murmuring something that I think was a prayer under his breath.

Rackham looked bereft. 'You were there…'

'Why does it matter?' Freya said in her direct way. 'You were made alive, and you have come here to be warm and in comfort for all your days.'

He gazed at her, his damaged face taut. I guessed he could not tell her the question mark that must have always hung over his head, the guilt that somehow he survived where the others had not. 'I would like to send thanks to your people, Freya,' he said softly.

'They are good people,' she replied. 'It is their way, and my way, to help those that are in need.'

'How did you come to Bath?' Cicely asked her. 'You never explained properly.'

'By a long way.' Freya began an explanation, how she had remained to work at the hospital in Finland after Wilfred was returned to England, and then once the Great War ended, her decision to come and find somewhere safe to reside and learn the ways of western medicine. While she was talking I went over to Greggs.

'There's something I need, old chap.'

'A drink, sir?' His eyes brightened.

'No, well yes, it wouldn't go amiss, but it's from one of the Saints' rooms. Would you fetch it for me, please?'

'Erm...indeed, sir.' He sounded dubious. 'May I ask why?'

'No,' I replied. 'Would you just go, while they're occupied...although there's something I'd like you to examine, before you bring it here,' I told him and explained what I wanted.

That raised his brows. 'Certainly, sir,' he said and went off as unobtrusively as a chap of his girth was able.

'Did you know I was in Bath?' Rackham was asking Freya.

'I did not, I had come from a train. My English is now excellent after I was working in a hospital in a place called Bournemouth,' she pronounced it born-moth, 'with many old peoples. Bath is same, all like madam.'

'What?' Cicely said, her brows raised.

'Yes, I am happy with old peoples. I can learn, and take this caring back to my people.'

'You are returning to the Sami?' Rackham asked, a quaver in his voice.

'I go for to teach them,' Freya replied. 'As I have done so already, before I find madam. And this I will do more. It is most important. But I will remain with madam, as I have said.'

'This is all very fascinating,' St John spoke up. 'But I expect you to name the culprit, gentlemen.'

Swift looked to me, worry in his eyes. I'd said I'd force it out of them one way or another.

'You are losing your sight Rackham,' I said.

'What of it?' he replied warily.

'Did you want Freya to come and live here before blindness set in? Before it was too late?'

His mouth fell open, then he snapped. 'Don't be ridiculous.'

'If Miss Sissinghurst came to live here, Freya would come with her. All that was required was for one Saint to die.'

'Your insinuations are insulting, Major.' Anger rippled through his voice.

'Are they?' I left that thought to hang as curious looks turned again to Rackham.

I crossed the hearthrug, swung about and came back to stand in front of the table of evidence. 'Ghosts…' I reached for the blackened bauble. 'Lord Balthazar has seen two ghosts, haven't you?'

He looked startled. 'Have I? Ah… yes. The ghosts of Christmas past, and present. They came, then vanished. I went to look for them, but they were gone. I think they were seeking Jasper…he was in need, you see. Not I.'

'They weren't ghosts,' I replied. 'It was a simple trick. Old-fashioned fire lighters made of cotton wool stuffed with vaseline and pushed into a bauble.'

'Major Lennox.' Pastor Peabody held a hand up. 'Please could you enunciate more clearly? I'm afraid I can't quite understand everything you are saying.'

'Yes, sorry–' I began.

'You must project, Major,' Lady Matilda called out. 'Throw the voice to the Gods and then we can hear you.'

I bit back a curse and explained again, at greater volume and in more detail. They all looked blank when I'd finished, so I carried on. 'Freya, where did you find this?' I showed her the golden horse.

They all leaned over to squint at it.

'It was left on my pillow, in my room,' she replied. 'It is nice. A gift for Christmas.'

I put it back on the table.

'Lennox,' Swift said quietly. 'It's evidence, you must question them.'

'No-one's going to admit leaving it there,' I retorted.

'Freya,' Cicely interrupted. 'Is that the truth? You honestly just found it in your room?'

'I have said so, madam,' she replied without batting an eyelid.

Cicely frowned and gave the faintest of shrugs.

I turned back to the girl. 'You understand how important it is to tell the truth, don't you?'

'That is a silly question,' she replied. 'I understand very well.'

'You cleaned the empty jars and told no-one what you'd done.' I walked over to tower above her. 'You're an intelligent young woman, you must have had some idea what was happening. Deadly poisons disappearing in a house where two men had died suddenly. Tell the truth, Freya, who are you covering up for?'

CHAPTER 26

All eyes fixed on her face.

'I did not cover up,' she replied calmly. 'I cleaned only.'

'Did you poison Sir Jasper and the General?' I continued.

'This is utter nonsense,' Rackham said angrily. 'What possible reason could Freya have for harming anyone?'

'Perhaps she'd like to tell us,' I said.

'I have never killed a person,' Freya replied.

'You must tell the truth,' St John demanded. 'I can have you arrested and put in jail until you do.'

'Pah. Always the politiet! I have said the truth and it will not change in jail,' Freya spoke defiantly.

'Intended or not, you've probably destroyed vital evidence,' Swift said, the anger clear in his voice.

'The killer would have worn gloves,' Rackham shouted. 'She didn't destroy anything.'

'Quiet,' Swift snapped.

'Did you think Rackham had done it?' I asked her.

'No,' she said, but the expression on her face betrayed her.

'Yes, you did,' I retorted and walked toward the window,

now framing an overcast sky where large snowflakes fell in slow swirls. Secrets and lies…and love. I bit back a sigh and returned to stand in front of the blazing fire.

Greggs returned; he gave me a thumbs up. I nodded dourly then indicated he stay by the door.

Now I had proof.

I raised my eyes, raking two rows of worried faces watching my every move.

'Lord Balthazar was in the passage when Sir Jasper was discovered in his room, weren't you, your lordship?'

'I…erm, was I?' he flustered, looking surprised that I'd addressed him.

'You were. You told us all about it here, in the library, the day we arrived.' I stood close to where he sat. 'Do you recall what happened when Jiggens senior found Sir Jasper?'

'No, I'm afraid I…are you sure I was, erm…?' He blinked in confusion.

'Perhaps Mr Jiggens senior could remind us?' I looked over everyone's heads to where the old butler was standing huddled and unhappy.

'Oh, please don't ask him, sir,' Essie objected, her face deeply lined and clearly upset. 'The doings in the house have fair floundered him.'

'He told me, sir.' Young Jiggens came forward from the side of the room. 'I can explain what happened.'

'Please do so,' I ordered, then stepped aside.

'He raised his arms and waved them in the air. "Sir Jasper? Are you indisposed, sir?" And then he put a hand on his shoulder, but Sir Jasper was all bent over, and didn't seem to be breathing,' he explained. His face had flushed but he looked determined.

'Thank you,' I said. 'Mr Jiggens,' I called out to the butler. 'Has your grandson demonstrated this correctly?'

The poor butler nodded and then spoke in a trembling voice. 'He has, sir.'

I turned back to Balthazar. 'It was quite amusing, the way you demonstrated old Mr Jiggens' discovery of Sir Jasper. How did you know Mr Jiggens had raised his arms if you were in the passageway?'

'I…well, it was merely my imagining.' He smiled genially.

'Really? It was remarkably insightful,' I said. 'And you said he was smiling, how could you see he was smiling when he was bent over?'

'Someone mentioned it, I don't know who,' he replied.

'Someone who'd seen him earlier?' I raised my voice. 'When the book was placed in his lap? Before he'd been pushed forward until his nose was almost touching the page?'

Swift's eyes narrowed. He took a step forward, but I moved to intercede. 'Lennox,' he rasped.

'Let me finish, Swift,' I warned him.

He nodded, but remained watchful, his lean face hawk-like.

I strode to the table and plucked up the needle. 'The culprit intended to use a needle like this to kill General Hackett. The point was smeared in honey mixed with ricin. Ricin is another deadly poison; there was enough on the needle to kill a man.' I didn't actually know that for certain but it sounded good. 'How was it meant to be used?' I continued with a rhetorical question. 'Not in a blowpipe, it would fall out without some form of fletch.'

'You are lacking precision, Major,' St John reprimanded. 'Make it clear where the evidence pertained.'

I frowned. 'I found it in the bottom of the pool, along with some footprints on the surrounding floor–'

'What sort of prints?' Roger asked.

'From slippers, such as the ones you're wearing,' I replied.

He stared at his feet then quickly drew them back as though to hide them.

'Roger, don't say a word,' Norman hissed at him. 'They will use it against you.'

'I was merely–' Roger quibbled.

'Silence in court,' St John bellowed, then addressed me. 'Continue, Major. How was the needle to be used?'

'One moment.' I handed the needle to Swift and went over to Rackham. 'Could I borrow your cane please?' I swiped it before he could stop me. 'Right,' I said, feeling like a magician about to produce a rabbit from the hat. I took the needle back from Swift, then stopped to examine the rubber fixed to the end of the stick.

'We are waiting, Major,' Cicely said loudly.

'I think you have added sufficient suspense,' Lady Matilda called out.

'Yes, please do stop tormenting us,' Olivia added.

'The needle was placed in the rubber end of a walking stick,' I stated, and held both up, then turned the stick to demonstrate. I fiddled about with cane and needle, then stopped as everyone held their breath. 'Except it wasn't this cane.' I placed it on the table. I raised my hand to Greggs who walked in dignified manner to hand over the stick he had fetched for me. It was an ebony cane, refined and glossy, quite common among gentlemen of means. I turned it over to the rubber end, which had a hole in it, and stuck the needle in it. 'This is how it was done.'

A gasp of astonishment ran around the room, and then they all stared as Lord Balthazar stood up and came over to me. He snatched it from my hands.

'Jasper was going to kill me!' He raised the stick aloft; the needle fell to the floor. 'He had already tried once, I was ill for three days. It was him or me and he didn't deserve to live.'

'What?' Pastor Peabody's brows almost reached his thick white hair. 'This cannot be true–'

'No!' Baroness Ginny cried out. 'No, Balthazar, you couldn't have...please, you couldn't have done this.'

'You opened my eyes! I could see what he was doing,' Balthazar shouted. 'Once I understood Jasper's intentions, I was forced to do it to save my own life. The medicine made it all clear.'

'The medicine...you mean the galantamine?' Lady Matilda was utterly shaken.

'Yes! I fooled you all didn't I!' Balthazar was almost euphoric. Even I was surprised. 'I wasn't going to let him win, not when my life depended on it.' He wielded the cane as he backed towards the bookcase. 'I went to see Gregory in the pool, I told him Jasper must have killed himself. He didn't believe me, he laughed at me. I thought he might, so I went prepared, but the stupid needle fell off, just like that one.' He stamped his slippered foot on the needle on the floor, breaking it into pieces. 'He didn't even notice. I knew he'd guess sooner or later, he was clever, though he thought I was a fool. Just as you all did, well now you see your mistake.'

'You put the powder in his socks?' Cicely said, her voice shaking with fury. 'And killed him?'

'I had to. I had no choice. It was Jasper. Jasper was behind it all,' he shouted, then looked momentarily confused.

'And the ghosts? You fabricated the story of the ghosts?' Olivia was aghast.

'It was in Dickens.' He giggled, glee on his face, his eyes glittering. 'And I made one, and put it in their room.' He pointed at Swift and I. 'So they could see it too.'

We stepped forward, he rushed back, into the corner next to the bookcase. Suddenly he reached up to a shelf and threw aside some books, then pushed on something hidden behind them. The whole bookcase swung ajar. He slipped through the hidden doorway as we moved to stop him. We were too late, the bookcase swung back into place behind him followed by the loud clang of a bar closing into a metal housing.

'Don't just stand there,' St John bellowed. 'Arrest him!'

Shouting broke out and Lockhart raced to the bookcase to heave on it with Swift and I. It was completely immovable.

'Jiggens,' I yelled.

He rushed over, eyes like saucers. 'I never knew it was there, sir.'

'Does your grandfather?' Swift demanded.

He ran back to the poor old butler who had slumped in the nearest chair where Essie was trying to soothe him.

Swift stared at the place where Balthazar had pulled the books away. 'There's something… a knot in the wood.' He pressed it in rapid succession, we could hear the mechanism clicking behind the bookcase, but it wouldn't open.

'It's been locked from the other side,' Lockhart stated, although we'd all realised that.

Rackham hobbled over, Freya had fetched his stick and helped him to his feet. 'The house should be searched, there's nowhere he can go.'

Jiggens came over. 'Grandpa doesn't know about that passage. None of us ever heard there was one there.'

Swift was already getting organised. 'Pastor Peabody, go with Rackham and search the ground floor.' He turned to St John. 'Your Honour, please go to the first floor with Captain Lockhart and search there. Major Lennox will come with me to the top floor.'

'No, Swift,' I said. 'I'll go down to the pool.'

'I will attend with you, Inspector,' Cicely stated, a steely look on her face.

He frowned but didn't object. 'Freya, please stay with the ladies in case he returns here.'

'But we can search too,' Baroness Ginny said.

'And I am strong, I can be of help in an arrest,' Freya said.

'We will go to the kitchens.' Norman stepped forward. 'Roger is an expert in jiu jitsu.' They marched off as I tried to assimilate that.

The other men had already left, talking loudly among themselves. 'Sir, I will stand guard!' Greggs stepped forward and pulled his pocket pistol from the inside pocket of his tailcoat.

'Mr Greggs!' Lady Matilda exclaimed, then gave a tremulous smile. 'How manly.'

He raised the gun and formed a pose, paunch in, chest out.

'Major Lennox, I'm coming with you, do hurry,' Olivia called to me, already halfway out of the door.

'Fine,' I muttered and followed her out.

CHAPTER 27

He wasn't in the house, we searched everywhere numerous times. There could have been more secret passages we didn't know about, but in the end it was young Jiggens who suggested we look outside.

We found him in the chapel, lying on the floor in front of the altar. His death had been quick. A paper bag lay next to him. He'd ripped the bottom corner away and apparently gulped some of the powdered Chironex fleckeri. I doubt it was as easy a death as he'd expected, but he looked peaceful enough.

There was a hidden door near the vestry, it led back to the library by way of the underground passage he'd used to escape. Norman had said Balthazar had been an avid reader, and of course he'd been in the house the longest. I still thought it strange that he'd never thought to share the secret though, and realised there was far more to Lord Balthazar Cholmondeley than anyone had ever recognised.

* * *

‘Why? I simply do not understand it.’ Justice St John was as confounded as everyone else. We were all gathered in the drawing room, waiting for the police and ambulance to arrive. Greggs and Jiggens had served coffee and cream with a shot of brandy for those who wanted it. Which was everyone.

‘He thought Jasper genuinely meant to murder him,’ I answered the question.

‘Was it the medication?’ Baroness Ginny was horrified and still dabbing tears from her crumpled face.

‘It may have been a contributing factor,’ Swift said, then hastily retracted when she broke into sobs again. ‘But his condition must have affected his reasoning. It could have led him to overreact.’

‘Really? You genuinely think it was his condition?’ Lady Matilda sat next to Ginny on the sofa, Olivia the other side of her.

‘No,’ Rackham said. ‘It was within his character, the disease may have exacerbated some latent paranoia.’

‘It wasn’t only paranoia, was it?’ Paster Peabody spoke. ‘Jasper had described Balthazar as a dead weight.’

‘When he became ill earlier this month,’ Swift turned to Lady Matilda, ‘could it have been a form of poisoning?’

‘No, he was stuffed up, it was merely a very bad cold. He took to his bed,’ she replied.

‘And he was given hot lemon and honey,’ Cicely said. ‘Wasn’t he Freya?’

‘He was madam, but reindeer milk and sorrel would have been better,’ Freya said. ‘My peoples use this. It is very good.’

'Rather a lack of reindeer in the vicinity,' Captain Lockhart said dryly.

'Gregory was a good man' Olivia said sadly. 'He'd never done Balthazar a harsh turn.'

'He was clever,' St John said loudly. 'Balthazar himself said he'd have guessed who it was.'

'I'm surprised he didn't notice when Balthazar tried to stab him with the needle,' Peabody said.

'He probably would have made the attempt when Hackett had his back to him,' I said.

'Swimming away from him, you mean?' Rackham asked.

'Most likely,' Swift agreed. 'But the fact of Balthazar coming all the way down to the pool would have raised Hackett's suspicions sooner or later.'

There were a few sighs and a lot of sad faces.

'May we invite our wives to the recital this evening?' I asked, thinking to distract them. 'They are currently staying at The George.'

Lady Matilda's face instantly brightened. 'Oh, of course you may! What a delightful thought.'

'Surely the circumstances dictate that we postpone such frivolity?' Baroness Ginny didn't agree.

'Nonsense,' St John boomed. 'Life is to be lived! Death is a reminder—don't waste a day.' He turned to us. 'Fetch your wives, they will bring cheer to all!' He was effusive; I think the brandy was having an effect.

'Our little boy, Angus, will be with them,' Swift added.

'Oh, a child.' Baroness Ginny's cheeks suddenly glowed pink. 'Yes, yes, please do bring him.'

'A child in the house?' Peabody beamed too. 'What a delight. We must welcome him, and the young ladies too.'

Everybody brightened at the news and the conversation turned to the recital and the songs, which caused another bout of bickering between Roger and Norman making everyone laugh. I'd come to realise that their arguments were largely an act to draw attention and amusement.

Swift and I couldn't leave to collect the girls until the awful aftermath of Balthazar's death had been formally dealt with. The police, doctor and ambulance attended. Questions were asked, which weren't answered. Justice St John declared the case to be under the purview of Scotland Yard and therefore outside of the local coppers' jurisdiction.

Billings was called on the telephone and told by St John that this must go no further. The Judge's word on the matter was enough to satisfy the highest authority and Billing seemed to accept this without quibbling. The Establishment, when it did deign to move, could be very effective indeed.

The grandfather clock in the hall was striking four by the time we were free to leave. I cranked up the Bentley and drove Swift and I to gather our loved ones and then return in drifting snow to Temple House for the festivities.

EPILOGUE

The evening was a celebration of life, and exactly what we all needed. Lady Matilda was in charge, but she had to contend with Cicely Sissinghurst directing from the wings. They had set a "stage" up in the drawing room in front of the curtains, closed against the night. Two large pot plants formed the "set" and the audience were seated in a semicircle in front.

Roger opened the show dressed as a fallen angel – actually I think he was supposed to have come down from heaven, but it's a matter of interpretation. He told the story of the nativity, with the supporting cast of Olivia and Norman playing Mary and Joseph, and Justice St John as the innkeeper.

Jiggens lay straw about the "stage" and the odd couple cooed over a makeshift baby – one of the cats – while the three wise men arrived – Greggs, St John (again) and Pastor Peabody – dressed in cloaks and cardboard crowns. There were all sorts of sumptuous dressing-up gear, they'd clearly been doing this for years.

Old Jiggens and Essie the housekeeper were encouraged

to sit down and watch with us while Freya kept everyone topped up with drinks and tasty snacks. Angus sat in mesmerised awe, and we all clapped appreciatively at the end of each turn. Once they'd finished the traditional Christmas scenes, there was a short interval while we ate and drank, and commented on the excellence of the acting and all the rest. The cast made a quick change into white smocks for the carol service.

Greggs proved himself an excellent tenor, as did Swift, who sang the lead on "The First Noel" and "God Rest Ye Merry Gentlemen."

After that it was modern renditions, and we had everything from duets to solos and everyone joining in together for "Jingle Bells" and the like.

At the very end we had the star turn: Angus singing "Twinkle Twinkle Little Star", with Florence playing for him on the piano.

Dinner followed as a noisy and jolly affair and we finally escaped with our wives, and a very sleepy Angus, to spend the night at The George.

* * *

It was early in the New Year when we heard again from the Saints. Justice St John demanded we attend him in Bath. This was damned inconvenient for Swift who had to travel all the way from the Highlands.

'Be seated,' St John commanded as we walked into the Regent's Office – now officially his domain.

Persi, Florence and Angus had come with us, we'd left them with the ladies in the drawing room taking tea, and the inevitable cake.

'Your Honour,' Swift said. He was in his standard city suit, St John was wearing the black cloak with blue silk lining over a dark grey three-piece and I was in thick country tweeds because it was freezing outside.

'You wanted to see us, sir,' I said, without asking why on earth he couldn't have simply written.

'Peace has settled upon the Order,' he rumbled. 'A sad and sorry business, but it's done. Jasper and the General are interred in the chapel grounds.' He paused to gaze at the pristine blotter on the desk for a moment, his face heavy with sorrow. 'It has affected us all, although death is no stranger here.' He sighed loudly. 'Balthazar's deeds have not been marked in the registers. Jasper's and Gregory Hackett's deaths are recorded as natural, Balthazar's as misadventure. There was no murder, gentlemen, and you will remember this for all your days. There will be no mention in memoirs, or reports, or among your acquaintances.'

'Understood, sir,' Swift said politely, 'but you made this clear when we left just before Christmas.'

'Well, I'm saying it again,' St John replied tetchily, then added, 'and we've decided upon a reward.'

I pricked my ears up at that. 'Really?'

'I'm afraid we cannot accept, Your Honour,' Swift said before I could stop him. 'We are official consultants to Scotland Yard and, as such, any reward must go to the official police charity.'

'What?' I frowned at him. 'Since when?'

'Since we signed the contract, Lennox,' he reminded me through gritted teeth.

I opened my mouth then closed it again to fume silently.

'Actually we thought to offer something more personal.' St John became almost genial. 'A trifle from the Chamber of Curiosities. Not poison, naturally, but I'm sure there will be something in there that would take your fancy.'

That sounded more like it. 'What sort of trifle?'

'Perhaps you'd like to choose,' he replied.

'There's a fossilised egg with tiny bones inside,' I said, having been rather taken with it.

'I think your lovely wives should help you choose.' St John frowned.

'Yes, yes, they should.' Swift suddenly grinned. 'And that's extremely generous, sir.'

'I'll find the girls.' I made to stand.

St John held up a hand to stay me. 'Wilfred Rackham will be attending.'

'Right, fine.' I sat back in my chair. 'How is he?'

'As happy as I've known him. He is very fond of Freya and she is fond of him.'

'No wedding bells?' I raised a brow.

He shook his head. 'Rackham's not equipped and Freya seems quite content as she is. Neither wants to leave here.'

'Has she ever spoken about what happened at Christmas?' Swift asked, ever the policeman.

'About cleaning the jars?' St John replied. 'No, but I'm convinced she was trying to protect Rackham.'

'Good thing it wasn't him,' I said. 'What about the golden horse?'

'I questioned them, nobody has admitted to leaving it in her room.' He shook his head. 'It must have been Balthazar trying to cause confusion.'

'Or part of his confusion,' Swift said.

'Or it was Rackham,' I said. 'Their feelings run deeper than either wants to admit.'

'You may be right.' St John let out a loud sigh. 'I've been racking my brains over the whole incident. What made you realise it was Balthazar?'

'It was him or Rackham.'

'Including Freya?' St John asked.

'She couldn't be the killer,' Swift said. 'I've been considering it too. She wouldn't understand the connotations of *A Christmas Carol*.'

Which we should have thought about at the time, I thought but didn't say.

'So Balthazar?' St John looked at me.

'Everything pointed to him, right from the beginning,' I said. 'But we were all dismissive because he appeared to be nothing more than a bumbling old man. We allowed it to cloud our judgement.' I'd been thinking about it too; one way or the other everyone had said it couldn't be him, and we'd all continued to reinforce it. The strong were more convinced of themselves and therefore more convincing. I now believed Baroness Ginny may have hit upon something in her theory after all.

'Well, it is done, and we have Freya here now, as well as

Miss Sissinghurst,' St John said. 'We need young blood, however disruptive it can be. And she's keen to learn. She's taking a trip back to Lapland in the summer and Cicely, Olivia and Matilda are going with her. They intend teaching the Sami whatever they care to learn, though I'm certain they'll have plenty to teach them in turn.' He broke off as a rap sounded at the door.

Freya walked in. 'Am I to bring tea? I have done so down stairs with the ladies, and young Jiggens has biscuits ready.'

'No, thank you,' St John replied. 'We'll have a proper drink after they've been up to the Chamber of Curiosities.'

'This is not of benefit, as I remind you when your goot is hurt.' She crossed her arms.

'It's not goot, it's gout, and it's my gout, so I'll decide for myself,' St John replied loftily.

'Pah! Men are silly, I have said it too much.' Her blue eyes flashed with something like amusement.

'Where's Wilfred?' St John demanded.

'He is gone to the top,' she replied. 'Where the politiet must go when they are ready.'

'We're not politiet,' I objected.

'We're detectives,' Swift said. 'Officially of Scotland Yard.'

A fact that I found extremely hard to believe.

Author's note

How much is lost and how much is yet to be found?

Mankind has discovered many wondrous things, and then lost them again.

Moly, as mentioned in Homer, is known to us as the snowdrop. It is now one of the medicines, Galantamine, used to treat Alzheimers, among other disorders. Plaitakis A, & Duvoisin RC, rediscovered this at a time much later than I have supposed. The drug helps to stimulate the brain, something the Greeks discovered over 3000 years ago.

Yopo has indeed been used in South America and the Caribbean in Shamanic and healing rituals for many thousands of years. It is usually inhaled, and contains one of the strongest hallucinogenic compounds on earth.

Box Jellyfish, or Chironex fleckeri, is as deadly as described and is considered the most venomous creature in the world. An untreated victim may die within 2 to 5 minutes of being stung. The venom in one jellyfish is sufficient to kill 60 adults.

However, it is not ground to powder and used by the Torres Island people to kill their prey – or not as far as I know. Jellyfish can be dried, and their toxins will, in many cases, remain active. However, the way in which I have described its use is a fiction on my part.

Vaseline in cotton wool really does work and is a handy fire lighter should you need one.

St John's Wort has been recorded as a herbal medicine since Roman times and likely before. Its more modern use is as a herbal product used to treat mild depression and mood disorders.

The Sami were indeed persecuted as described.

I do hope you have enjoyed this book and if you'd like to leave a review, I will be eternally grateful!

Would you like to take a look at the Heathcliff Lennox website? As a member of the Readers Club, you'll receive the FREE audio short story, including the ebook itself, 'Heathcliff Lennox – France 1918' and access to the 'World of Lennox' page, where you can view portraits of Lennox, Swift, Greggs, Foggy, Tubbs, Persi and Tommy Jenkins. There are also 'inspirations' for the books, plus occasional newsletters with updates and free giveaways.

You can find the Heathcliff Lennox Readers Club, and more, at karenmenuhin.com

You can also follow me on Amazon for immediate updates on new releases, plus special deals, sales and free giveaways.

* * *

Here's the full Heathcliff Lennox series list. All the ebooks are on Amazon. Print books can be found on Amazon and online through your favourite book stores.

Book 1: Murder at Melrose Court
Book 2: The Black Cat Murders
Book 3: The Curse of Braeburn Castle
Book 4: Death in Damascus
Book 5: The Monks Hood Murders

Book 6: The Tomb of the Chatelaine
Book 7: The Mystery of Montague Morgan
Book 8: The Birdcage Murders
Book 9: A Wreath of Red Roses
Book 10: Murder at Ashton Steeple
Book 11: The Belvedere Murders
Book 12: The Twelve Saints of Christmas
Book 13: Valentine's Day Murder – ready for pre-order now

There are Audio versions of the Heathcliff Lennox series read by Sam Dewhurst-Phillips, who is superb. He 'acts' all the voices – it's just as if listening to a radio play.

The audio versions of Miss Busby Investigates are narrated by the amazing Corrie James and extremely popular.

These can be found on Amazon, Audible and Apple Books.

Here's the list so far of the Miss Busby series.

Book 1: Murder at Little Minton
Book 2: Death of a Penniless Poet
Book 3: The Lord of Cold Compton – ready for pre-order now

A little about Karen Baugh Menuhin

1920s, Cozy crime, Traditional Detectives, Downton Abbey – I love them! Along with my family, my dog and my cat.

At 60 I decided to write, I don't know why but suddenly the stories came pouring out, along with the characters. Eccentric Uncles, stalwart butlers, idiosyncratic servants, machinating Countesses, and the hapless Major Heathcliff Lennox. A whole world built itself upon the page and I just followed along.

Now, some years later I have reached number 1 in USA and sold over a million books. It's been a huge surprise, and goes to show that it's never too late to try something new.

I grew up in the military, often on RAF bases but preferring to be in the countryside when we could. I adore whodunnits, art and history of any description.

I have two amazing sons – Jonathan and Sam Baugh, and his wife, Wendy, and five grandchildren, Charlie, Joshua, Isabella-Rose, Scarlett and Hugo.

My wonderful husband is Krov Menuhin, a retired film maker, US special forces veteran and eldest son of the violinist, Yehudi Menuhin. We live in the Cotswolds.

For more information you can contact me via my email address, karenmenuhinauthor@littledogpublishing.com

Karen Baugh Menuhin is a member of The Crime Writers Association, The Author's Guild, The Alliance of Independent Authors and The Society of Authors.

Printed in the USA
CPSIA information can be obtained
at www.ICGtesting.com
LVHW020713080924
790457LV00039B/992